Searching
FOR
HARMONY

NEW YORK TIMES & *USA TODAY* BESTSELLING AUTHOR
KELLY ELLIOT

Searching
FOR
HARMONY

NEW YORK TIMES & *USA TODAY* BESTSELLING AUTHOR
KELLY ELLIOT

OTHER BOOKS BY KELLY ELLIOTT

Love in Montana (Meet Me in Montana Spin Off)
Fearless Enough
Cherished Enough — June 6, 2023
Brave Enough — August 29, 2023
Daring Enough — November 21, 2023
Loved Enough — February 6, 2024
Forever Enough — April 30, 2024
Enchanted Enough — July 23, 2024
Perfect Enough — October 15, 2024
Devoted Enough — January 7, 2025

Holidaze in Salem
A Bit of Hocus Pocus | *A Bit of Holly Jolly* | *A Bit of Wee Luck*
A Bit of Razzle Dazzle — Summer 2023

The Seaside Chronicles
Returning Home | *Part of Me* | *Lost to You* | *Someone to Love*
*Series available on audiobook

Stand Alones
*The Journey Home** | *Who We Were** | *The Playbook** | *Made for You**
*Available on audiobook

Boggy Creek Valley Series
*The Butterfly Effect** | *Playing with Words** | *She's the One**
*Surrender to Me** | *Hearts in Motion** | *Looking for You**
Surprise Novella TBD
*Available on audiobook

Meet Me in Montana Series
Never Enough | *Always Enough* | *Good Enough* | *Strong Enough*
*Series available on audiobook

Southern Bride Series
Love at First Sight | *Delicate Promises* | *Divided Interests*
Lucky in Love | *Feels Like Home* | *Take Me Away*
Fool for You | *Fated Hearts*
*Series available on audiobook

Austin Singles Series
Seduce Me | *Entice Me* | *Adore Me*
*Series available on audiobook

"Happiness is when what you *think*,
what you *say*, and what you *do*
are in *harmony*."

−MOHATMA GANDHI

Prologue

TREY REACHED FOR MY HAND as we stood in my living room. My mother and father stared at both of us as I inhaled a deep breath. My brother Jake sat to the side of my parents as he gave me a reassuring smile. "Mom, Dad, we have something we need to tell you."

Glancing at his watch, my father drew in a sharp breath. "Well, Harmony, don't just stand there; go on and tell us. We have a dinner at eight that I cannot be late for."

My heart dropped as I felt Trey squeeze my hand. Two days ago Trey and I had broken up. We were about to graduate from high school and were heading to two different colleges. It wasn't that I didn't love Trey, I did. I simply wasn't in love with Trey, and I knew he felt the same way.

This morning everything changed. Both of our worlds came to a complete stop.

Closing my eyes, I spoke the words in almost a whisper. "I'm pregnant."

Trey dropped my hand and snaked his arm around my waist. I knew it was only a show of support for me. He hated my parents. Hated the way they treated me like I was an asset instead of a daughter. I was used to it since it was all I ever knew.

Standing, my father cracked his neck and nodded. "I'll take care of everything first thing tomorrow morning."

Pulling my head back in surprise, I asked, "Take care of what?"

My mother stood and faced my father. "We'll need to do it swiftly and keep the utmost privacy. Maybe we need to look into Harrison County."

Glancing at Trey, he raised his shoulders and shook his head. Turning back to my parents, I stepped forward. "What are you both talking about?"

Giving me a weak smile, my mother said, "An abortion. It will be done within a week."

Bringing my hands up to my mouth, I stood there stunned. Surely they were not serious. My parents were religious and did not believe in abortion.

Trey laughed as he said, "You're both crazy."

Jake stood up and looked between my parents. "You can't be serious."

Shaking my head, I said, "No. I'm not having an abortion. What are you even talking about?"

Daddy turned to Jake and said, "Stay out of this. It doesn't concern you." Looking at Trey and then me, his eyes turned to sadness. "You have two options, Harmony. Abortion and continue on to Harvard or leave and be disowned by your parents. It's your choice."

Chapter
ONE

IT'S JUST A DREAM

Harmony

Two years later

LOOKING OUT THE WINDOW, I fought to keep my anger down. I didn't want to be angry with Trey. I knew it wasn't his fault he had to go to another business meeting tonight. He had started working for his father's marketing firm as soon as we graduated from high school while he still tried to go to school full time. When I was pregnant with TJ, I began taking classes at the University of Massachusetts to become a nurse. It was hard on both of us, but we managed, considering neither of us had college degrees yet, and we had an almost eighteen-month-old baby.

Glancing into the back seat, I smiled when I saw TJ sleeping. Looking straight ahead I closed my eyes and thought back to this morning.

"We're going to find you, Daddy!" I said as I took TJ's hand as we searched for Trey. Laughing, TJ yelled out, "Daddy! We coming!"

"Oh no!" Trey called out.

Dropping to the floor in front of TJ, I covered my mouth and then whispered, "TJ! I heard Daddy. Did you hear Daddy?"

Slowly nodding his head, his little blue eyes gazed back at mine as they danced with excitement. "Want to go sneak up on him and yell out boo!"

Laughing, TJ wrapped his arms around my neck. "Yes, Mommy! Boo!"

Picking him up, I inhaled a deep breath as I took in his smell. Smiling, I held him tighter as we snuck into the living room and climbed up on the sofa. Putting my finger to my lips I pointed behind the sofa. TJ jumped on the cushion and quickly looked behind the sofa and yelled out, "Boo, Daddy!"

Trey flew up with his hands on his heart as he fell back and said, "You scared me!"

Laughing, TJ reached his arms up for Trey. Reaching for him, Trey scooped up TJ and smiled at me. "It's Mommy's turn to hide."

Pointing at me, TJ smiled and then buried his face into Trey's chest while Trey counted.

With a warm smile in my direction I realized it was the first time in weeks Trey seemed happy.

Turning to Trey, I took in a deep breath and slowly blew it out. "I'm sorry, Trey. I'm sorry I got angry. I know you have to do whatever your dad tells you to do."

He gripped the steering wheel tighter and took in a deep breath before he slowly exhaled. "You know I hate this as much as you do. There's nothing I can do about it though. My dad was nice enough to open up a position for me and let me basically train on the job. I... no... we owe my parents a lot."

The sting of his words was painful. "Yes, I know we owe them a lot. You remind me all the time."

Letting out a sigh, Trey pushed his hand through his hair. "Don't you ever get tired of fighting, Harmony? That's all we do."

I nodded my head as I chewed on my bottom lip. The only reason Trey and I got married was because I was pregnant. We both came into this marriage thinking we could make each other happy enough, but I knew that wasn't the case. I could see it in Trey's eyes. He was far from happy.

"Harmony, there's something I've been needing to talk to you about."

My cell phone began ringing as I glanced down at it. "It's the hospital. I better answer it."

"Can you for once not be at their every beck and call, Harmony?"

"What?" I asked in disbelief. "Trey, this is my job. If I ever want to get my nursing degree, I need to work. If that means picking up a few extra shifts here and there, then that's what I'm going to do."

Letting out a gruff laugh, he whispered, "Of course you are."

I glanced down at my phone, then sent the call to voicemail. "I won't go in, but you need to do the same with your business meeting tonight."

He tossed his head back and laughed. "Jesus. Harmony, are you serious? What in the fuck do you think pays for everything? My job does. I can't tell my father I'm not coming simply because you don't want me to."

Feeling the tears building in my eyes, I turned and looked back out my window as Trey drove down Boylston St. "I miss you, Trey. Spending an evening together was something I thought you would enjoy. It's been over a month since you've even kissed me."

The feel of his hand nearly caused me to let out a sob as he gave it a gentle squeeze. That's when I realized it was gone. That feeling I used to get when he touched me was gone. Who was I kidding? It was gone before I even found out I was pregnant.

"Harmony, there's something I need to tell you — Oh my God. Shit!"

Quickly turning to look at him, I saw the truck. The sound of tires squealing across the hot Boston pavement caused me to let out a scream. Trey slammed on the brakes, but it was too late. The truck was going to hit us. Hard. Turning to look at TJ, my stomach clenched when I saw he was awake. Smiling at me he reached out his hand as he said, "Mommy."

"Trey," I whispered as I closed my eyes and waited. Waited for a miracle.

Opening my eyes, I instantly felt the pain as I tried to move. "Trey?" I screamed out. "Trey, where are you?"

Holding my hands up, I let out a gasp. They were covered in blood.

Oh my God. Is this my blood? Trey? The truck hit on Trey's side. No, dear God what's
happening?

Quickly looking around, I realized I was on my back. Pain shot from my head down to my toes.

A friendly smile was looking down at me. "Ma'am. I need you to lie perfectly still and try to stay calm, okay? I'm a firefighter and you've just been in a car accident."

Her eyes were the bluest eyes I'd ever seen. Not even my eyes were that color blue.

"Is my husband okay? The truck hit on his side. Is he okay?" My world felt as if it was torn in two and I wasn't even sure why. Giving me a smile, she replied, "They are attending to him, ma'am. I need you to lie still."

"My baby?" I asked as I felt my tears fall down the sides of my face and pool in my ears. My heart felt empty.

"Preston is taking care of him, keep looking at me, ma'am."

Preston? Who was Preston?

Turning my head, I saw TJ lying on the ground with a firefighter leaning over him. What was he doing to him? My heart started to pound in my chest. Screaming out his name, I reached my hand out to him. "No! Oh my God. TJ! My baby! What's wrong with my baby?"

The firefighter who was giving TJ mouth-to-mouth looked right at me as he pressed TJ's chest with his hands. Our eyes caught and I saw nothing but fear in his green eyes. Looking away he continued on with trying to get TJ breathing.

"Don't do this to me. Please, God, don't do this!" I yelled out.

My baby needs me. He needs me! Attempting to get up, I yelled out Trey's name as I looked for him. Where was he? *Why isn't he with TJ?* Turning back to the firefighter, I watched as they lifted TJ onto a stretcher.

"No! Wait, please let me go with him. Please let me hold my baby! Please!" I screamed out as the firefighter turned and looked at me. His eyes were so sad as they captured mine. If I hadn't known any better, I would have sworn I saw a tear roll down his cheek. TJ and the firefighter slowly faded away as a cloud of darkness swept me down a dark tunnel.

"Trey. My baby. God, please don't take my baby."

Numbness swept over my body as I heard voices shouting all around me.

"He's gone… we couldn't get to him in time."

It's a dream. This is all just a dream.

Slowly opening my eyes, I looked around the dark room. Machines beeped all around me, causing the ache in my head to hurt more.

Swallowing, I attempted to talk. Where am I? Where is Trey? Where is TJ! Where is my baby?

The door opened, and I turned my head to see my brother Jake standing there. Finding no energy to talk, I barely whispered, "TJ."

Jake closed his eyes and the last thing I saw before slipping back into sleep was the tear making a path down my brother's cheek.

Chapter
TWO

PRECIOUS MOMENTS

Preston

I STOOD IN THE SHOWER and let the hot water fall over my tired and aching body. I wanted nothing more than to crawl back into bed, but I knew I had to see her. I needed to know that she was okay. I couldn't even begin to understand how she was feeling. I wasn't even sure what I was going to say to her. The accident only happened yesterday, and I myself was trying to come to grips with it.

Leaning my head back, I fought to keep this foreign feeling away. This feeling of emptiness, loss, and regret was new to me. Maybe if I had gone to him first I could have saved him. I wasted precious moments.

Precious moments that could have saved his life.

The knock on the bathroom door caused me to jump. "Preston? How long are you going to be in the shower? I'm hungry and tired of waiting for you."

Placing my hand on the wall of the shower, I shook my head. One thing I quickly learned about Sherry after we started dating was she could care less about my job or how it could affect me. "I'll be out in a few minutes. Why don't you go ahead and eat without me? I'm not hungry."

Sherry let out a frustrated moan. "Fine."

The bathroom door slammed, and I rolled my eyes. Sherry and I had been dating for two years now, and I knew she was waiting for me to give her a ring. Every single time I walked into a jewelry store I stood there looking at the rings for about twenty minutes before turning and walking out of the store. I wanted to love her the way she wanted to be loved, but I couldn't seem to do it. When I closed my eyes, I dreamed of a future. Kids running around laughing as my wife and I looked on. No matter how hard I tried, I hadn't seen Sherry in that future. I needed to end things. It wasn't fair to either of us.

Letting out a sigh, I turned the water off and stepped out of the shower. Reaching for the towel, I dried off as the bathroom door opened again. Sherry smiled as she gazed at my body. One thing Sherry was good at was fucking. She knew when I needed to forget things and was more than happy to help out. Licking her lips, she dropped to the floor and took my dick in her mouth. Pushing her away, I took a step back.

"I'm sorry. Not now."

Sherry looked at me with anger in her eyes as she stood. "What do you mean, not now? I know how to make it all go away."

Shaking my head, I wrapped my towel around my waist and pushed past her. "Not this time, Sherry."

I headed into the bedroom, dropped my towel, and pulled my jeans on. Sherry walked up and wrapped her arms around my waist. Closing my eyes, I took in the moment. I willed myself to love Sherry. I cared about her; I just didn't think I was in love with her.

What a bastard I was. I knew she was only trying to help. I turned around and pulled her to me. Placing my lips against hers, I gently kissed her. She returned the kiss but it felt void of something. "Tonight, dinner. You and me here in the apartment."

For a moment she looked panicked, then smiled. "Sounds amazing, Preston. I may just buy a new dress."

Raising my eyebrows, I asked, "Oh yeah?"

Biting on her lip, she nodded her head as she let out a purr. "Maybe one with easy access for you."

I grinned. "Seven sharp. Don't wear panties with that new dress."

Kissing me again, she whispered against my lips. "Deal, Mr. Ward."

Walking up to the nurses' station, I waited patiently as one of the nurses talked to a guy who looked to be a few years older than me. His blond hair was a mess and he looked like he hadn't slept in days.

"Mr. Harris, I assure you, your sister is getting the utmost care."

Nodding his head, he pushed both hands through his hair and let out a long breath. "Please just make sure no one talks to her first before me. Please."

The nurse's eyes softened, and I instantly knew whom they were talking about. It was her, the woman from yesterday's car wreck.

Clearing my throat, I spoke. "Excuse me, are you speaking about the young woman in yesterday's car accident on Boylston Street?"

The guy turned and looked at me. "Yes. Who are you?"

Swallowing the knot in my throat, I said, "I'm one of the responding firefighters. I am... I tried... um—" The words wouldn't form in my mouth as I fought like hell to tell him I was the one who worked on his nephew.

Reaching his hand out for me, he said, "Jake Harris. I'm Harmony's brother."

Harmony. What a beautiful name.

The way she looked at me yesterday flashed across my memory and I squeezed my eyes shut to block it out.

She had counted on me. Begged me and I let her down. Those blue eyes would haunt me for the rest of my life.

"Preston Ward. Have you eaten anything, Jake?"

Jake's voice cracked. "No, I haven't had anything to eat since yesterday morning."

Walking closer, I asked the nurse for a piece of paper and reached for a pen. I wrote down my cell phone number on the paper she handed me and smiled. "If Harmony wakes up, please call or text me."

She nodded. "When Mrs. Banks wakes up, I'll let you know."

I gave Jake a slight pat on the arm as I said, "Come on. Lunch is on me. I hear the food here is amazing."

Jake managed to give me a weak smile.

By the time we got our food and found a table, I discovered that Jake was finishing up medical school at Boston University School of Medicine. His parents no longer talked to Harmony and Jake was all she had left.

Sitting at the table, I decided to go ahead and ask the question. "Why do your parents not speak to Harmony? If you don't mind me asking."

Jake took a bite of his club sandwich, then a sip of Coke. "About two weeks before Harmony and her husband Trey were set to graduate high school, she found out she was two months pregnant. She was set to go to Harvard and Trey was going to the University of Massachusetts. Needless to say, their plans were changed. Trey's parents bought Harmony and Trey a house, and his father brought him into his business with the agreement that he would still go to school. Harmony was also expected to continue with college after the baby was born." Jake let out a small laugh and shook his head. "My sister took classes that fall and right up until she gave birth to TJ at the end of December." Jake smiled as he closed his eyes as if lost in a memory. "Harmony wants to be a nurse. Has since she was little. I remember when I left for college, she cried her eyes out and begged me to take her with me."

Smiling, I said, "She must be pretty smart to have gotten into Harvard."

Jake's smile faded some as he took another bite. After a few minutes, he continued talking. "When Harmony and Trey told my parents she was pregnant, they gave her two options. Abortion or be disowned."

About choking on my sandwich, I gasped for air as I asked, "Are you kidding me?"

"I wish I was, but no. My parents are real assholes. The only reason I stay on their good side is because I'm dating the daughter of a Massachusetts senator. They put up with my behavior because they know it will help me advance. I call bullshit. Daddy likes to hobnob with the senator and I'm pretty sure he's helped my father with a few business deals."

Looking away, I noticed tears beginning to fill Jake's eyes. "It's me and Harmony. It's always been just the two of us." Turning to me, I watched as a tear rolled down Jake's cheek before he quickly swept it away.

"How do I do it, Preston? How do I tell my sister she's lost everything… again?"

I closed my eyes and dropped my head. My heart pounded and I felt my hands start to shake. Taking in a deep breath, I looked back at Jake and whispered, "I'm so sorry I couldn't save him for her. I tried like hell and I can't… I can't get the look in her eyes to leave my mind. They were pleading with me. She was —" My voice cracked and it was my turn to look away while I fought to hold back tears.

"Oh no. You were the firefighter working on TJ?" Jake asked.

I nodded my head quickly. "I'm so sorry. I keep replaying everything over and over in my head. If I hadn't gone to the driver first, would those few split seconds have been enough to bring the baby back? Those few precious moments when I made the wrong decision."

"Trey Jr."

My head snapped to Jake. Tears slid down his cheeks. "The baby, his name was Trey Jr, but we called him TJ."

Smiling weakly, I nodded my head while an ache grew in my chest.

Clearing his throat, Jake spoke. "May I ask you something, Preston?"

"Yes, of course you can."

"How long have you been a firefighter?"

Leaning back in my chair, I took in a deep breath. "I started working at the volunteer fire department that my father ran in our small hometown when I was sixteen. He used to be a captain in the Boston Fire Department. My mother hated the city and wanted to live in the country." Smiling, I shook my head. "So my father moved her out of the city. Anyway, I took the civil service test and started with the Boston Fire Department right out of high school. I've been working at Firehouse 37 the last four years."

Jake searched my face for a few seconds before asking, "Do you like it?"

For a few moments, I attempted to find my answer. "If you had asked me two days ago, I would have told you my job is my life. Right now, I feel a bit lost. Trying to deal with feelings I've never had to deal with before."

Leaning over the table more, Jake said, "It wasn't your fault. Fate played its hand, Preston. Regardless of if you had gone to Trey or TJ first, you would have doubted it either way. There is no right or wrong in this."

"I'm sorry. You've just lost your family and here I am feeling sorry for myself."

Letting out a gruff laugh, I said, "I'm totally acting like a douche."

Jake shook his head. "No man, I can't imagine what you're feeling. Was this your first… loss?"

A shiver ran over my body as the words seeped into my brain. I whispered, "First child."

My phone buzzed and Jake and I both looked down at it. "It's my girlfriend."

I could see Jake's body relax as he sat back in his seat.

Sherry: Don't be late. I have a spa appointment early tomorrow morning and I need a good night's sleep. I'm picking up takeout for dinner.

Setting my phone back down, I pushed my sandwich away from me. "You're probably wondering why I'm here."

Jake smiled. "Now that you mention it."

I stared into his eyes and could see the hurt and confusion. Wondering if my eyes mirrored his, I glanced around the room. "I had to know if she was okay. My mind won't stop thinking about her eyes as she pleaded with me to save her child."

Jake covered his face with his hands and let out a frustrated groan. "Damn it. Preston, how in the hell am I going to tell her? I can't even understand this myself. She's going to be destroyed. I'm about to start my residency and I'm afraid she's going to be alone in her... grief." Jake looked away and closed his eyes as tears fell once again.

"Jake, when the time comes and you need to tell her, you'll find the strength. I'm sure of it."

My phone buzzed again but this time it was from an unknown number.

Unknown: Mrs. Banks is awake.

Swallowing hard, I took in a deep breath. "Jake, your sister is awake."

Jake jumped up, nearly knocking the chair out from behind him. Without so much as a word, he turned and jogged to the elevator. My limbs felt like they had a hundred pounds on each one as I cleared off the table. Slowly making my way to the elevator, I hit the floor for ICU and silently said a prayer that Jake would indeed find the strength he needed to get through this and to be there for his sister.

Chapter
THREE

THE HERO

Harmony

MY BODY ACHED. MY HEAD hurt the worst of all. Opening my eyes, I looked up at someone who was smiling back at me. "Welcome back, Harmony." Smiling, she said, "Let me go get your brother."

Turning before I had a chance to even ask about Trey and the baby, she vanished through the door. I closed my eyes and then snapped them back open. All I saw were *his* green eyes looking into mine. The fear in them had scared me, yet there was something in those eyes that captured me as well. It was as if I'd seen those eyes before in my dreams.

The door slowly opened and Jake walked in. He smiled but it didn't reach his eyes. It was probably the fakest smile I'd ever seen my brother wear. Before the door closed all the way, I looked out and saw those green eyes staring back at me. Again.

"Harmony, sweetheart, how are you feeling?" Jake asked as he approached the side of my bed.

My mouth was so dry I couldn't talk. Pointing to my mouth, I looked into Jake's eyes.

"Water? You need water?"

Nodding my head, Jake leaned down and kissed my forehead. "Shit. Let me go grab some."

Watching Jake open the door, I strained to see if he was still there. He was. This time he walked up to Jake and spoke to him. Nodding his head, he took the water pitcher from Jake and walked away. The door almost closed but Jake pushed it open.

"Just one second, sweetheart, Preston's going to get you some water."

Preston.

Preston is taking care of him.

Opening my mouth, I attempted to talk but Jake shook his head. "Shh, Harmony, let's wet your whistle, okay? Don't try to talk just yet."

The door opened and Preston walked in. Pushing his hand through his brown hair, Preston set the pitcher down, but not before looking into my eyes. Something happened between us. Words couldn't describe it, but I knew he felt it too because his mouth dropped open and his eyes pinched together as he poured a glass of water and handed it to my brother.

Jake reached behind me and lifted my head as I took a drink.

"Small sips, Harmony. We don't want you getting sick from drinking too much."

I couldn't pull my eyes off of Preston as I took a few small sips.

"Um… I'll just wait outside."

Jake turned to him and said, "Thanks, Preston. You're not leaving, right?"

Pulling my lips from the plastic cup, I spoke. "Wait." My voice sounded strained. As if it had been months since I last spoke a word.

Preston froze, as did Jake. He stood with his back to me. "Please tell me. TJ, is he okay? Is my baby okay?"

Jake's lower lip trembled as he pulled back and set the water on the table. My heartbeat raced, nearly exploding in my chest. I began to gulp in breaths… the feeling of not getting enough air was beginning to scare me.

Jake's expression turned slack as his eyes began to wet. "Jake… where's TJ? What about Trey? Is he okay?" Tears fell freely from my eyes as I watched my brother's face turn white as a ghost.

My eyes darted to Preston's back. "Preston. You… you saved him, right? It was you? I remember… you saved him, right?" My body shook as sobs took over. I didn't even care that everything on me hurt.

Preston slowly turned around; his movements lacking the energy to even move his body.

The moment his eyes captured mine, I knew. "Please tell me you saved him. *Please.*"

Jake's head dropped as he cried. Preston looked at Jake and then back to me. Taking a step forward, his eyes never left mine.

"Harmony, I tried with everything I had… but… I couldn't… I'm so sorry. I'm so sorry I wasn't able to save him."

Shaking my head, my lower lip trembled as I whispered, "No."

Closing his eyes and dragging in a deep breath, Preston whispered, "I wasn't able to save your son, and I'm sorry."

Covering my mouth with my hand, I let out a scream as Jake quickly wrapped me up in his arms. Pushing him away, I began getting out of the bed. "No! I don't believe you. Please take me to him!"

Preston grabbed me before I fell to the floor. "Harmony, please get back into bed. You can't be getting out of bed." Looking into Preston's eyes, I saw his pain, and it about destroyed what little hope I had left. "I'm so sorry, Harmony. I'd give anything to take this away for you."

Falling into Preston's arms, I cried into his chest. "Please, please God no."

Preston held me tighter to him as he whispered, "I'm so sorry, Harmony." I lost all control. The door to my room opened and two nurses came rushing in.

"No! My baby! Not my baby! Why? Dear God, why?" I screamed out as one of the nurses attempted to place me back in the bed.

"Go get a doctor, quickly. We're going to need to sedate her," the nurse called out to the other nurse.

Turning to look at Preston, I noticed he was crying, and my heart broke even more knowing he was in pain as well. I heard it in his voice. I saw it in his eyes.

Jake stood back, tears streaming down his cheeks.

Shaking my head, I closed my eyes and went limp, as I called out one last time, "Not my baby, please not my baby."

The room was dark. The only light that could be seen was coming from the flashlight on his phone that he must have turned on to read. Staring at him, I took everything in. His light brown hair was a mess. His body looked cramped as he slept in the chair. Preston held a book in one hand and his phone in another. Both looking like they would slip from his grip at any moment. Turning away, I stared up at the ceiling as the realization hit me again. I lost them both. After getting over the shock of losing my son, Jake told me Trey had died on impact. My heart ached more than I could have ever imagined. Shaking my head, I slipped into a memory.

"I will forever protect you, my sweet baby boy."

Trey walked up and kissed TJ on the forehead as I walked around the living room.

"The only way to keep him from crying is to carry him around in my arms."

Trey smiled and shook his head. "You don't seem too bothered by that."

Laughing, I replied. "Nope, not at all. I'd do anything for him. I'd give up my own life for him."

Walking back up to us, Trey looked down at our three-week-old son and whispered, "As would I."

The sound of Preston's phone buzzing pulled me from my memory. He jumped up. Closing my eyes, I pretended I was still asleep.

"H-hello?"

I could hear someone talking. Rather, yelling through the phone.

Opening my eyes, I turned to look at him. Just as I expected, he was standing with his back to me as he looked out into the darkness on the other side of the window.

"Sherry, I'm so sorry. Things got really crazy and I didn't want to leave Jake and — "

More shouting. His body tightened and his hand went up to his hair where he grabbed a fistful of it before pushing it all the way through. That explained his hair. Now I just needed to figure out why the firefighter who'd attempted to save my son's life was sleeping in my hospital room.

"I understand I haven't been back home. It means something to me, Sherry. I can't leave her. She only has her brother. ... Well, I'm sorry you don't understand that."

Biting on my lower lip, I felt tears well in my eyes.

I can't leave her. She only has her brother.

Turning away from him, I squeezed my eyes shut and forced the tears to stay at bay. When I opened them again, I saw the water and my mouth went instantly dry. Reaching for the tray, I attempted to move it closer, but all I did was hit the bed and make a loud noise.

"Listen, we'll talk when I get home. I've got to run."

The next thing I knew, Preston was pouring water into the cup and reaching down to help me drink it.

After a few sips, I whispered, "Thank you." Preston slowly let my head rest back on the pillow.

Smiling, he whispered, "Sure."

I wasn't sure what to say to him. I wanted to know why he was here, but I had overheard his reason. Maybe that wasn't the truth though. My guess was he felt guilty and was now trying to play the hero by taking care of me. The thought made me angry.

"Why are you here, Preston?" I asked in a cold voice. "If you're here because you feel guilty, you might as well just leave."

The hurt in his eyes caused my stomach to drop. He slowly took a step back and nodded his head. "Right, um... I can leave if you're not comfortable with me being here."

I wanted to take the words back the moment they left my lips. Preston's voice was laced with sadness, and I knew the words I had spoken were the reason why. I hated myself in that moment. I was projecting my hurt onto him.

"I promised Jake I'd stay with you while he went to his hotel to take a shower and eat, but I'm sure he'll be back soon."

He gave me a weak smile and turned to leave. Turning and looking out the dark window, I softly spoke. "Preston, wait."

His footsteps stopped, but I knew he hadn't turned back around. "Harmony, I'm not here because I'm trying to be a hero. I'm here because I'm genuinely concerned about you and your brother Jake. He hasn't slept at all and barely eats."

A tear slowly moved down my cheek as I looked at him and asked, "Why?"

Turning around and walking up to the side of my bed, he asked, "Why?"

Our eyes met and once again, that feeling I knew we both shared moved throughout my body. A small sob escaped past my lips as I tried to keep my crazy emotions at bay.

"Why are you concerned about me?"

Shrugging his shoulders, he looked away briefly before glancing back at me. "I guess maybe it's because we share a loss. I've never... I've never had..." Turning, he spoke under his breath.

"You've never what?" I asked as my stomach felt sick.

Chewing on his bottom lip, he drew in a breath then said, "I've never lost a child;" His voice cracked and his words broke off as he looked away. "I'm sorry. My loss is nothing compared to yours. It's just, I don't even know how to explain without sounding crazy."

I smiled. "Try."

He nodded. "I felt a connection with you." Rolling his eyes, he dropped his head back. "Jesus, I'm making myself sound like a real idiot here."

I reached for his hand. "I don't think you are." His thumb moved across my skin, and it instantly made me think of Trey. He would do the same thing with his thumb. My heart felt like it might not ever be able to heal. I would forever be broken from losing not only my son, but my husband as well.

"I feel the connection too, Preston, and I appreciate everything you're doing for both Jake and me. But it sounds like your girlfriend might be upset."

Preston chuckled. "When is she not upset? I'm sorry. Things aren't so great there either."

The door opened and Jake walked in. He looked refreshed and wore a smile on his face.

"Hey, sleeping beauty. How are you feeling?"

Giving Jake a fake smile, I tried to give him peace of mind that I was somewhat okay. Once I had calmed down after learning about TJ, I knew almost immediately that Trey had also died in the wreck, only to have Jake confirm it to me. My crying gave way to exhaustion, which gave way to sleeping. I'd woken up off and on and at one point heard Preston telling Jake to go get a few hours of sleep.

"What time is it?" I asked as I glanced back to Preston.

Pulling out his phone, Preston said, "It's five thirty in the morning."

Squeezing his hand, I smiled bigger. "Preston, go home to your girlfriend. I promise you, I'm all right."

His eyes searched mine. He knew I was lying, but he nodded his head and said, "Okay. But I'll be back later to check on you and Jake." Preston looked over at Jake, who gave a wide grin and a thumbs-up to Preston.

Oh yeah. My brother was trying his best to put up a front. I didn't have the energy to even think about that right now.

"Sounds good," I said as I closed my eyes and let sleep take over again.

I was soon lost in the most amazing dream. I was running after TJ in the backyard as we played chase.

My baby. I miss my baby.

Chapter FOUR

FALLING APART

Preston

WALKING IN THROUGH THE FRONT door, I dropped my keys on the small table. The kitchen and living room lights were on. I overheard Sherry on the phone.

"I know. I know. It was a wasted night. I'm sorry, I'll make it up to you."

I frowned. Who was she talking to?

Walking around the corner, she said, "I need to go." She was wearing nothing but a long T-shirt of mine that she liked sleeping in.

"It's about damn time, Preston. What in the hell? You have never gone and stayed at the hospital like this. I mean, what does this family think of you hanging around? That is creepy as fuck!" Rolling her eyes, she walked up to me and scrunched up her nose. "You stink. Go take a shower and we'll talk."

Pushing out a breath, I walked past her. "Nice to see you too, Sherry."

"Oh, don't even lay a guilt trip on me, buddy. I took the time to go pick up dinner, set it all up, get dressed in a skimpy new dress, and—hell, I even lit candles for Christ's sake. And for what? Nothing! You decided you wanted to play pity party with some chick who got in a car wreck. What, were you fucking her before the accident or something, you asshole?"

Gripping my hands into fists, I turned and walked up to her so fast she began walking backward until she hit the wall.

"I couldn't save her eighteen-month-old baby. Her husband died and all she has is a brother who is so fucking freaked out he couldn't even tell her that her son died. I had to be the one who told her. *Me!* The fucking firefighter she begged to save her son's life had to be the one to tell her I failed. I failed to save her baby. Failed!"

Sherry jumped when I screamed out the last *failed*. "So don't stand here and give me some goddamn sob story about what a fucked-up night you had. And no, Sherry, I wasn't fucking her. I didn't even know her name until yesterday."

I turned and stormed into the bedroom and to our bathroom. Slamming the door shut, I stripped out of my cloths and walked into the shower. The water was hot and felt good on my aching body.

Closing my eyes, I stood there and tried to block out her screams. Block out the look in her eyes when she found out her son and husband had died.

Sherry's arms snaked around my waist. "If you need to forget, I'm here."

I needed to forget. Even if it was just for a few moments, I needed it all to go away. Lifting Sherry up, she let me do what I needed to do.

Forget.

Walking into the firehouse, I looked around. Everyone was moving about their business like normal. I made my way to the bunkhouse and tossed my bag onto my bed and dropped down as I let out a sigh.

Sharp, another firefighter and one of my best friends, stuck his head around the corner and shouted, "Ward, Cap wants to see you right away."

Nodding, I stood and said, "Thanks. I'll be right there."

He gave me quick nod before he turned to leave but stopped. "Preston?"

"Yeah, what's up?" I asked as I looked over at him.

I knew what he was about to say, and I would bet he had been struggling all day wondering how to say it. Mitchel Sharp and I had started here at Firehouse 37 together. Same day, same scared look in our eyes.

"It's okay you know, to not to be okay. You know that, right?"

With a small head pop, I replied, "I know, Mitch. I'll be all right."

He flashed a smile. "Hey, if that ball and chain will let you, let's hit the club this weekend."

Laughing, I picked up my pillow and threw it at him. "Shut the fuck up, asshole."

He pointed to me and said, "Truth hurts!"

Before I could say anything else, he disappeared around the corner. I shook my head and headed to the bathroom where I splashed my face with cold water, did a few jumping jacks in place then made my way to the captain's office.

I sat back and waited anxiously at Captain Ryan. He cleared his throat, and then finally started to talk. "Ward, I've been in your shoes, and I know how you're feeling. So wipe that fake-ass confident smile off your face and let me see your true feelings."

My heart dropped and I adjusted some in the chair. One thing my father always said was you hold it in. Don't let your cap see the fear. Fear makes you weak, and there is no room for weakness.

"I'm not going to lie, sir, and tell you that I'm not bothered by the events of the other day. He was a child, and his mother pleaded with me to save his life and I couldn't."

Cap leaned forward. "No, you couldn't. And even if that had been Sharp, Wister, me — hell, any of these guys — no one would have been able to save that little boy. His father died on impact, and how the mother didn't die, I have no idea. I guess God has plans for her. There was *nothing* any of us could have done differently, Ward. You need to get that into your head right now and don't forget it. Do you hear me?"

Nodding my head, I whispered, "Yes sir."

He stood and reached his hand out for me. I followed his lead and reached my hand out. "I mean it, Preston.

Do not dwell on this. Do not go up and see her again at the hospital, because I know damn well you did because I'd have done the same thing. You cannot get emotionally attached. Move on."

Everything in me wanted to argue with him. To tell him Jake and Harmony needed me… or was it the other way around? I forced a smile.

"Now, go eat. Wister made lasagna."

As I turned to leave the room, I tried to let his words sink in. There was nothing any one of us could have done to save TJ.

Fate was in control, and as much as I wanted to believe that, I couldn't.

Almost a week after Harmony's accident, I found myself standing outside the door to her house. Jake had called to tell me Harmony had left the hospital two days ago and was home. I'd only gone back up one other time to see Harmony and prayed Cap wouldn't find out. I needed to make sure she was okay.

Not sure why I was even here, I turned and headed back down to my car until I heard my name. "Preston?"

Closing my eyes, I tried to push away the drop in my stomach when she said my name. I turned and faced her with a smile. The bruises on her face were slowly fading but the bright pink cast was a clear reminder of what had brought us together in the first place.

"Hey!" I said as I walked toward her.

With a weak smile, she tilted her head. "Did you ring the bell?"

I stopped at the bottom of the stairs and let out a nervous chuckle. "What? No, I thought I had left my phone in the car." I began patting all around until I felt my phone. "Nope, there it is. Just in case the station calls or something."

"Oh, okay. Jake just left."

Shit. I didn't really want to be alone with Harmony, and I wasn't sure why I didn't want to be alone with her.

"Are you going to come in or stand out here?" she asked.

Coming to my senses, I started up the stairs. "Right, sorry, I just got off shift so I'm a bit tired."

Harmony's face fell briefly before giving me a weak smile and turning into the house. I followed her into the living room. Her house was nice and decorated in a style that reminded me of something my mother would like. Lots of whites, and nothing out of place.

"Want a cup of coffee?" Harmony asked as she made her way into the kitchen. Looking back at her, I could hear it in her voice. She was putting on a show for me.

"Sure. Black, please," I said as I looked around. The living room and kitchen were all in one open-concept room. Pictures of Harmony, her husband, and TJ covered the walls. Walking over to the mantel above the brick fireplace, I smiled as I picked up a picture of the three of them. TJ couldn't have been more than a few days old.

"Jake will be starting his residency in a few days. I hate that he's missed so much schooling because of me."

I placed the picture back down and headed to the large kitchen. Harmony gestured for me to sit at the kitchen island bar. I did and glanced around the area. Light grey granite covered the counters and the island and black cabinets filled nearly every space on the walls.

"I'm sure it's fine, Harmony. Jake seems like a pretty bright guy."

She turned and looked at me. Her eyes filled with sadness. "Fine?" Harmony shook her head and went back to moving about the kitchen. Reaching into a cabinet she pulled out two mugs. "Oh, Preston, everything is far from fine."

"I didn't mean—"

Dropping her head, Harmony cried. I quickly jumped up and went to her. Turning her, I pulled her into my arms. "I have to bury my son and husband tomorrow, Preston, and I don't think I can do it." Burying her face into my chest, she gripped my shirt and cried harder. Her legs gave out and I dropped down to the tile floor with her and held her while she cried.

She cried until she fell asleep in my arms. I could only guess she was exhausted. When I looked up, I saw Jake.

"She broke down and I didn't know what to do but hold her while she cried."

Jake gave me a sad smile. "Let me show you where to put her."

Standing up as carefully as I could while I held Harmony, I followed Jake to a room down the hall.

He opened the door and stood to the side while I walked into the room. It was fairly bare, with just a bed, dresser, and a small desk in the corner. Jake sighed as he spoke in a hushed tone. "It's the guest room. She won't sleep anywhere else but in this room."

Pulling the covers back, I placed Harmony down and placed the covers back over her. Her blonde hair was pulled back in a ponytail and was spread across the pillow. Before I knew what I was doing, I reached down and pushed a strand of hair back and behind her ear as I stared at her.

Twenty years old and already so much pain and hurt in her life. My heart broke as I watched her sleep for a few minutes more before I made my way out of the room and back into the kitchen.

Jake was leaning against the counter with a somber look on his face. "Trey's parents couldn't even give her a few days to get settled before they had to do the burial. I'd like to bash their fucking heads together."

Dropping his head back he swore under his breath before looking back at me. "Do you know I had to threaten to get a court order to keep them from burying Trey and TJ while Harmony was still in the hospital?"

I drew in a breath and I asked, "Why would they do that?"

He shrugged. "I don't know. Something is so very wrong, and I can't put my finger on it. Trey's dad is acting really weird. It feels as if they are hiding something but I can't figure it out."

Following Jake back to the kitchen, I sat on the bar stool and asked, "Could it be he's just in shock, Jake? I mean, he did lose his son and grandchild."

Nodding his head, he agreed. "You're probably right. I can't even begin to imagine how they both feel. I called my parents."

I sat up straighter, my interest peaked. "And?"

Shaking his head, he said, "They told me the accident was God's way of saying Harmony made the wrong choice."

My mouth dropped open. "Are you fucking kidding me?"

Jake shook his head. "Nope. That's my parents for you. I told them that was the last straw. For them not to even be there for their daughter during a time like this showed the true heart they had. They said they would think about showing up. I told them not to do me any favors. I wouldn't be surprised if I started getting bills for school."

Closing my eyes, I shook my head and said, "Shit. Jake, I'm so sorry."

Jake shrugged his shoulders and let out a heavy sigh. "My sister means more to me than their money. If that happens I'll work something out. I don't have that much longer to go so I'm not too worried about it."

My head tried to wrap itself around all of this. My parents were the total opposite of Jake and Harmony's. There wasn't a damn thing they wouldn't do for me, and I knew that they would always stand by my side no matter what.

Clearing his throat, Jake pushed off the counter. "Listen, I know it would mean a lot to Harmony if you would be there tomorrow."

I felt sick to my stomach and tried to swallow the bile that had gathered in my throat. "Um, I'm not sure I can make it."

Jake's face fell with disappointment as he nodded his head. "Sure, I understand."

Standing, I pushed the stool back in. "Where is it at?"

"Colonial Park Cemetery at one."

I rubbed the back of my neck. "I'll try to make it, but no promises, Jake."

Smiling, Jake held out his hand. "Hey, that's good enough for me. Thanks, Preston, for being here for her.

I know she appreciates it. I'd forgotten something here, and now I'm glad I did. She promised me she was okay for me to leave."

I pushed down the feelings that were slowly growing for Harmony, not really understanding what they were. "Of course. It's the least I can do."

Jake walked me out to my car and shook my hand one more time. As I made my way to the driver's side, I glanced back up at Harmony's house. My heart stopped when I saw Harmony standing in the window looking out. Lifting my hand, I smiled and waved. Harmony barely lifted her hand before she dropped the curtain and walked away.

Once I was in my car and pulled away, I gripped the steering wheel tighter. I turned the opposite way of my apartment and drove for another hour and a half. Pulling down the gravel road, I instantly felt a weight lift off my shoulders.

I put my car in park behind my father's truck and got out. Taking in a deep breath, I let the smells of my parents' country home soak in.

"Preston?"

I spun around to see my mother standing on the front porch. "Mom, damn it's good to see you."

Practically running to her, I took the steps two at a time. When I reached her, I wrapped her in my arms and held her.

She hugged me tighter than normal. "Preston. Talk to me."

Her voice was my undoing. Finally… my tears fell, and it was my turn to be held while I fell apart.

Chapter FIVE

JUST A DREAM

Harmony

I FOCUSED ON THE SOUNDS of the birds singing all around me as my fingers rubbed the charm that Jake had given me this morning. The engraving was taken from a picture frame Trey had given me on TJ's one-month birthday. The photo was of me holding TJ when he was only a few minutes old, as Trey kissed me on the check. My mind drifted back to the day TJ was born.

The moment the nurse placed our baby across my chest I knew my life would never be the same. Tears flowed freely from my eyes as I looked at Trey. Smiling, he wiped his own tears away as he gazed down at our son. Turning to me, he gently kissed my lips before whispering in my ear, "Everything happens for a reason."

Each breath felt as if I was battling for air.

This is just a dream.

Jake took my hand in his and gave it a light squeeze. The preacher talked, but I hadn't heard a word he said.

Birds. Focus on the birds, Harmony.

My memory took me back to the day TJ was born and how happy Trey and I were. The way he looked into my eyes and told me how happy he was. I knew in that moment; we had made the right decision to keep our baby.

Jake leaned in and whispered in my ear. "Harmony, do you want to lay a flower on their caskets?"

My eyes snapped open. Two boxes. That's what they were. One box held the man I loved, the other held my boy, who would never get to be a man.

This wasn't a dream. This was very real. My baby was gone. Forever. My husband… gone… forever.

Swallowing hard, I turned to look at Jake, and that's when I saw him standing about forty yards away. He was dressed in a black suit, and I couldn't help but notice how he wiped his tears away. The heavy feeling on my chest seemed to lift the tiniest bit.

Preston.

It was as if he knew I needed something to help me move my feet and pay my last respects to Trey and TJ. He gave me a weak smile before I looked back at the caskets. I grabbed a hold of Jake's arm.

"I feel sick, Jake," I whispered.

"Harmony, draw from the strength I know you have. You can fall apart later, sweetheart. Just not right now."

Slowly nodding my head, I made my way to Trey's casket first. Placing a single red rose on his casket, I kissed my fingers and laid them over the rose. "Trey," was all I could manage to get out.

Jake wrapped his hand around my waist and led me to TJ's casket. My breathing became labored as I stopped in front of it.

It's so small. My baby is all alone in the dark.

"Jake, he hates the dark," I whispered.

Jake cleared his throat and held me closer. "He's not in the dark, Harmony. He's in a beautiful light that has him wrapped up warm and safe."

"No. Jake, please tell me I'm dreaming." Turning to him, I looked into his blue eyes.

"Harmony, sweetheart," he pleaded.

Nodding my head, I quickly wiped my tears away and took another rose from Jake and placed it on the small casket. Leaning over, I kissed the casket and let a small sob escape from my lips.

Sounds of people crying surrounded me, drowning out the birds.

Focus on the birds, Harmony.

"Mommy loves you, baby boy. I love you so much, and I'm so sorry I couldn't protect you. I'm so sorry."

Tears fell freely from my eyes as I kept myself from falling to the ground and screaming. As much as I wanted to, I knew it wouldn't bring him back. I'd never hold my child in my arms again. Sing to him while he fell asleep. Laugh while he ran from me during chase.

"Harmony," Jake whispered as he pulled me up and turned me around. My eyes scanned all the people. I didn't even know half of them. They were friends of

Trey's from work, or friends of his parents. Everyone looked at me with sad eyes. Trey's mother stood up and walked up to me and pulled me into her arms.

"Harmony, darling we are here for you... please know that."

Dropping my arms loosely at my side, I nodded my head and whispered, "Thank you, Anne. I know you are, and I'm here for you and Dan as well."

Anne pushed a piece of my blonde hair behind my ear and gave me a weak smile. The missing pieces of my heart were so evident it hurt to even exist.

Looking at Jake, Anne said, "She looks like she hasn't slept in days, Jake. Please make sure she rests."

I wasn't sure how I felt about Anne talking about me like I wasn't standing right there. Jake pulled me closer to his side and replied. "Yes ma'am. I intend on making sure she takes care of herself."

Nodding her head, she smiled. "Good. Dan and I are very worried about our sweet Harmony."

Closing my eyes, my body swayed. Jake took the hint and began leading me away from Anne and all the prying eyes. As we neared the last row of chairs a young woman caught my eye. She had dark hair and was dressed in black. Her body shook as she cried. Stopping, I looked at her and she looked at me. Standing, she wiped her tears from her eyes and made her way over to me.

"Harmony?"

Nodding my head, I barely said, "Yes."

Swallowing, she continued to speak. "My name is Margie, I... um... I worked with Trey. We actually all went to high school together, but I'm not sure if you remember me."

Staring at her I swore I had seen her before, but I just couldn't place her.

"You said we went to high school together?"

Nodding her head, she smiled. "Yes. I was a year younger. Big into cheerleading," she said with a nervous laugh.

My head began to spin and all I wanted to do was run. Run away from everything and anyone who reminded me of Trey or TJ.

Giving Margie a weak smile, I said. "Thank you for coming, Margie. I'm sure Trey would have appreciated it."

She broke down sobbing again as Jake quickly led me away. Looking back over my shoulder I watched as Margie made her way over to Trey's casket as Anne wrapped her arms around her. I didn't want to be anywhere near here when they lowered my husband and child into the cold, dark ground.

Margie turned and looked over her shoulder at me before turning back. She just stood there with Anne and Dan as they looked down at Trey's casket.

I turned and stared straight ahead while my brother guided me to his car. The sooner I got out of here, the better.

One month after the accident I found myself in an unmoving stance at the intersection where the accident happened. My eyes traveled to the road and where TJ had been laying on the ground. My chest ached even more than it did the day I found out I had lost Trey and TJ. Pulling the charm out of my pocket, I inhaled a deep breath as I looked at.

I was tired of everyone telling me I would be okay. Tired of how people looked at me as if I would break at any moment. In my desire to escape the memory of losing Trey and TJ, I found myself staying in a hotel in downtown Boston. It was the only thing I asked of my parents when they called to tell me how sorry they were to hear about Trey and TJ. They offered to help in any way they could, and I knew it was just to stay on Jake's good side. I didn't care though; if asking them to put me up in a hotel kept me out of the house and away from the memories, I'd ask. The thought of going home made me sick.

My phone beeped in my pocket. Pulling my eyes off the road, I turned and blew out a breath as I placed the charm back in my pocket.

"God, please help me," I whispered.

Shaking my head, I pulled my phone from my pocket.

> **Jake:** When was the last time you went home?

Pulling my head back in surprise, I responded.

> **Me:** How did you know I wasn't home?

> **Jake:** Preston has stopped by a few times and left a few things at your front door. He stopped by today and they were still there. He was worried.

Letting out a deep breath, I walked away and headed to Trey's office. Anne had called and said there were a few personal items of Trey's that they thought I might like.

Glancing down at the text again, his name stood out. *Preston.*

I wasn't sure why I was so afraid to see him. He was a reminder of that day. His eyes haunted my dreams, yet something powerful pulled me to him. I just couldn't figure out what it was and that scared me.

Me:	I needed to be alone and away from memories. I'm headed back home today. I've decided to sell the house.
Jake:	Damn, Harmony. I'm here for you sweetheart. Just let me know what you need.
Me:	Maybe you could help with packing up and sorting through things.
Jake:	Just let me know when and I'm there.
Me:	Thanks, Jake. I need to run. Love you.
Jake:	Love you too, Harmony.

I pushed my phone back into my pocket. Sometimes I wondered how I lucked out with Jake. He was by far more than just my brother. He was my best friend. I talked to him about everything.

Pulling the door open, I walked into the modern glass building. My heart pounded in my chest as I made my way to the elevator. The security guard, Tom, tipped his hat and gave me a sweet smile.

"Harmony, how are you, darling?"

Nodding my head, I decided to stop acting like everything was okay and just be honest with how I felt. "I'm hanging in there day-to-day, Tom."

"That's my girl."

As I stepped into the elevator, I smiled at Tom. When the doors shut I closed my eyes and prayed for strength. With how busy we both were, I hadn't been by Trey's office in over six months before he died. The last time I was here I showed up in nothing but a sexy teddy, trying desperately to rekindle some sort of spark between us. The memory of Trey screwing me up against the wall that was shared with his father flooded my mind. It had been the last time we had really been together where it hadn't seemed forced.

The last four months of Trey's life he had pulled away more and more. Our sex life was almost nonexistent. The hugs stopped, soon followed by his kisses.

Shaking the memories out of my head, I took in a deep breath and concentrated on slowing my heartbeat down.

The elevator door opened as I squeezed my fists into balls and reached deep down inside for the strength to get through this. I had already decided I would just tell Dan to pack everything up and donate it. The last thing I needed was more items of Trey's for me to go through when I sold the house.

Walking past Kim, the main receptionist, she smiled kindly. "I'll let Dan know you're here, Harmony."

Nodding, for fear my voice would crack if I tried to talk, I kept walking toward Trey's office.

When I walked up, I was stunned to see who sat outside his office.

"Harmony, w-what are you doing here?"

My mouth opened slightly at the sight of Margie sitting at the desk.

"I um… came to go through Trey's personal effects."

Looking away, Margie nodded. "I haven't let anyone but Dan into the office. Per Dan's request."

"Dan?" I asked, shocked that she would refer to the CEO of the company on a first-name basis.

"Mr. Banks, excuse me."

Raising an eyebrow, my eyes traveled over Margie. "How long have you worked here, Margie?"

Attempting to give me a smile, it came across fake as hell. "A little over six months."

My stomach fell and I felt sick. "As Trey's receptionist?"

Smiling bigger, she nodded. "Not at first, but yes, most of the time as his receptionist."

That's when it hit me, and I remembered where I had seen Margie before.

"Margie McDaniels," Trey said as he pointed to the cheerleader out on the football field.

Looking back at her, I smiled. "She's cute. I guess."

Trey laughed. "You're not jealous are you, Harmony? It was your idea to date other people."

Pushing Trey lightly on the chest, I chuckled. "No, I'm not jealous. I'm glad you're going to ask her out. Trey, you know I'll always love you."

He pulled me into his chest then rested his chin on the top of my head and whispered, "I'll always love you too, pumpkin."

Four days later I found out I was pregnant, and Trey never got to go out with Margie McDaniels. A few short months after that, we were married and had both made a promise to each other that we would really make an effort at this marriage for the baby. The love we had for our child was strong enough to hold our little family together.

Snapping out of the memory, it all hit me. Anger rushed through my veins, and I started to feel sick. "Tell Dan I'll be in Trey's office."

Margie jumped up, "Do you want me to go in with you? I can help you… um… pack up things if you need help. I pretty much know where Trey kept everything in that office."

Feeling a lump form in the back of my throat, I whispered, "I'm sure you did, Margie."

Her smile dropped as I spun on my heels and stormed into the office. Shutting the door, I locked it and I placed my hand on my chest while I fought to drag in air.

Oh my God. He was having an affair. Trey was cheating on me.

My mind spun as everything fell into place. The late dinners at work Trey supposedly had with his father. Trey avoiding me when I asked who his new receptionist was. The way he stopped touching me… even kissing me… around the same time Margie came to work for him.

Sliding down the door, I buried my face into my hands and cried.

The memory of Trey talking to me right before the accident popped into my head.

"Harmony, there's something I've been needing to talk to you about."

Lifting my face from my hands, I looked through the glass window. "He was about to tell me. He was about to tell me he was sleeping with her."

I stood and unlocked the door as I got a grip on my emotions. Walking forward, I stopped and looked at the pictures he had on his desk. One was of all of us in Florida. Picking up the picture frame, I ran my finger over Trey's face as my heart broke a little bit more. Setting the picture down, I sat in his chair. I pulled out drawers, searching through them as if I knew what I was looking for. When I got to the bottom right drawer it was locked.

Chewing on my lower lip, I tried to think where Trey would keep the key. Opening the middle drawer, I reached under the drawer and felt a key taped to the underside of it.

Pulling it off, I looked at it. My heart raced as my hands shook. Squatting, I placed the key in the drawer and unlocked it. Slowly opening it, I let out a gasp as my hand slammed to my mouth and I fell backward.

"Dear God, Trey. Why?"

Turning my eyes away from the contents of the drawer, I fought like hell not to cry. I would never shed another tear over him. Not. One. Tear.

The door to the office opened. Staying on the floor, I waited to hear who it was.

"Um… Harmony? Are you okay?"

The sound of her voice made my skin crawl instantly. Inhaling a deep breath, I rose slowly. Margie stood in the doorway. Dan was walking up behind her and smiled when he saw me.

"How long were you sleeping with my husband, Margie?"

Dan immediately stopped behind Margie.

Margie let out a nervous giggle. "W-what are you talking about, Harmony? Trey and I were not having an affair."

Narrowing my eyes, I tilted my head. "Are you sure you want to stick with that answer?"

Dan cleared his throat. "Margie, Harmony's been under a lot of stress, it's probably best if you leave."

Tossing my head back, I laughed. "I wonder, Margie. Did he fuck you on the desk? Maybe up against the wall like he did me."

Dan stepped around Margie. "Harmony, now honey, I know you've been—"

Margie glared at me. Oh. Guess she didn't like me bringing up how I let my own husband fuck me in his office.

"Margie? You want to change your answer?"

Swallowing hard, she looked away.

Bending over, I grabbed a handful of shit out of the drawer and threw it onto the desk.

"Answer me! Were you having an affair with my husband because I know for a fact we didn't use condoms, and he has never used a vibrator on me here in his office. Nor do my panties have your fucking initials on them."

Margie kept looking in the other direction. Glancing down, I saw our wedding picture and my mouth dropped open. Picking it up, I looked at how happy we were. Taking a closer look, however, I noticed Trey's eyes didn't look happy at all. They looked sad. His smile forced.

A small sob passed through my lips, and I pressed them together harder.

"Harmony, let's you and I go through Trey's belongings and we can talk."

Looking directly at Margie my voice cracked as I talked. "The least you could do is tell me the truth. You owe me that."

Margie turned and when her eyes caught mine, I knew she didn't have to utter a word. They had been having an affair.

Letting out a gruff laugh, I threw the picture as hard as I could at her. I never was good at throwing things, because it hit the door and nowhere near Margie. It did scare the hell out of her, and she let out a scream.

"I hope you enjoyed yourself while you fucked my husband with pictures of his wife and son surrounding you. Did that make you feel good, Margie?"

Grabbing the picture of the three of us, I threw it onto the floor and stepped on it as Dan rushed over to me.

"Harmony, please stop this. Let's go into my office."

I held my hand up and shouted. "Stop! I'm finished here. Whatever that bastard had in this office, let his mistress take it all home with her."

Walking around the desk I made my way over to the door, not before stopping and looking into Margie's tear-filled eyes.

I leaned in closer to her. "I hope karma comes back around on you someday. He was married with a small child. But then again, I guess whores don't care about that, do they?"

Pushing past her, I made my way through the office as everyone stared at me. Keeping my eyes directly on the elevator, I counted my steps.

I jabbed my finger on the down button and stood there as I concentrated on breathing in and out. I needed to get out of the building before I broke down.

When the doors opened I rushed in and leaned against the back wall as I looked at Dan rushing to the elevator.

"Harmony! Please don't do this!"

The doors shut and I pressed my hands to my mouth tightly.

Do not cry. He isn't worth the tears. Find your inner strength, Harmony.

He isn't worth the tears.

Chapter SIX

HIDDEN FEELINGS

Preston

"PRESTON? EARTH TO PRESTON?"

Fingers snapped in front of my face as I was torn from my memory. "Sorry, Sherry. I was lost in thought."

Rolling her eyes, she let out a frustrated sigh and leaned against the elevator doors that led to Sandy and Jake's condo. "Have you gone and talked to the counselor like I said?"

Pinching my brows in, I glared at her. "I don't need to talk to a shrink, Sherry."

Sherry mumbled under her breath, "Yeah you do."

I ignored her.

"Listen, Preston," she continued, "I've needed a fun night out, and when Sandy said she was having a party with a few friends I jumped all over it. With how important her dad is, the tighter we get with her, the better for you and for me."

I pulled my head back in surprise. When Jake had asked if Sherry and I wanted to meet him and his girlfriend, Sandy, for dinner three months ago, I wasn't sure. Now I knew why I wasn't sure. Sherry and her obsession with Sandy's father. Shaking my head, I asked, "How is getting in tight with Sandy going to be better for me?"

Giving me her naughty smile, Sherry winked at me. "Don't you want to do something else with your life besides be a firefighter? I mean, look at Jake. He's going to be a doctor for Christ's sake, Preston. *A doctor*."

My mouth dropped open, and I was about to tell Sherry it was over with us. I couldn't keep going on like this. I felt nothing for her, and we hadn't slept together in nearly two months. The elevators opened straight into Sandy and Jake's condo. The first time Jake introduced us to Sandy, I saw Sherry's eyes light up and knew I was in trouble. Ever since then, Sherry has tried like hell to become Sandy's BFF.

I looked around for Jake as we stepped into the room. We had been hanging out more and more and met for lunch when Jake had the extra time. I wanted to ask him about Harmony, but I didn't want to seem desperate for information. It had been almost four months since I saw her at the funeral. I'd casually asked a few times about her, and when Jake suggested I give her a call, I panicked at the thought of talking to her.

Catching a glimpse of Jake across the room, I made my way over to him. He was my saving grace at these parties, and he knew it. His smile from across the room told me he knew Sherry had dragged me here. I had already confessed to him I was going to be breaking up with her. I needed to stop dragging my damn feet and just do it.

"Dude, what a surprise seeing you here tonight. I thought you were on shift."

I kicked my foot at nothing as I glanced down to the floor and said, "Nah, I took a couple days off."

Slapping his hand on my back, he laughed. "Jesus, it's about time. You've been working too hard. Let's go out onto the balcony; I need some air."

I quickly glanced around the room. Something felt… different. The hairs on my arms stood, and I swore someone was watching me.

Stepping out into the cool fall night air, I inhaled a deep breath. The view of downtown Boston from Sandy and Jake's condo was amazing. I could spend hours out here just thinking.

"How's the residency going?" I asked as I took a sip of the beer I'd grabbed on the way out.

"Busy as hell, but it's going. I can't complain."

Jake took a sip of his beer. "Hey, at least you got to do your residency here at Mass General."

Laughing, he shook his head. "Yeah, with the help of someone."

Surprised, I asked, "No shit? Sandy's dad?"

Pointing at me he said, "Ding! Ding! Ding! You got it. Sandy worked her daddy some and managed to get me on at Mass General."

"Damn, dude, I'm sorry. I know you didn't want to use your parents or Sandy's dad to pull strings."

He shrugged his shoulders and looked out over the city. I took this as my opportunity to ask about Harmony.

"At least it kept you close to your sister. Speaking of, how's Harmony? The last you told me she was selling the house and looking for something downtown, close to school and the hospital."

Jake cracked his neck. "She sold the house over a month ago. Moved into her new condo about three weeks ago."

"Wow."

Jake laughed. "Yeah." Jake's smile faded as he said, "I'm worried about her."

Before I could ask any more questions, someone cleared their throat. "Are you guys going to hide out here all night, or are you going to come in and play a few games?"

Glancing over my shoulder, I frowned when I saw Sherry. She held her hand out and motioned for me to take it. "Preston, come on, you're making a bad impression."

I simply stared at her outreached hand. "We'll be there in a second."

She huffed before she spun on her heels.

"I figured you would have called things off by now," Jake said.

My hand scrubbed down my face. "I need to. Sooner rather than later."

He motioned with his head. "Come on, let's go inside."

Sandy slapped her hands together and said, "First game for the night is Sixes!" Dropping the dice onto the coffee table, Sandy let out a small squeal. Sitting down, I glanced across the giant coffee table and was met with blue eyes. My breath caught, and I was stunned with how my heart tripped at the sight of her.

"Harmony?"

Flashing me a smile that would for sure knock any guy off his feet, Harmony held up her wine glass, winked, and said, "Preston."

Jake sat down next to me and whispered. "Dude, I've never seen my sister drink, so this should be fun."

Sandy cleared her throat and began talking. I couldn't pull my eyes off of Harmony as I watched her taking in everything Sandy was saying.

"Okay, listen up. Each person will roll the dice. If you roll a six, or two numbers that add up to a six, you have to take a shot."

Harmony smiled bigger, and I had a feeling she didn't get to have too many good times with getting pregnant at eighteen.

"Harmony, you're up first." Sandy said as she handed the dice to Harmony. Looking back at me, her face lit up with excitement, and I couldn't help but laugh. Jake did the same next to me.

"I fear my little sister has led a very sheltered life."

Harmony nodded her head and said, "Very sheltered."

Rolling the dice, everyone let out a cheer. Double sixes. "Drink up, Harmony," Jake said as he poured two shots for her. After she downed them both, she made a gagging sound that had everyone laughing again. Everyone but Sherry.

Sandy and Harmony were giggling like crazy as Sandy whispered something into Harmony's ear. Sherry glared at Harmony like she was an interruption in the grand plan to win Sandy over as her BFF. A status I was pretty sure Harmony held without even trying.

Four rounds later and it was clear Harmony was not one to bring to Vegas. Every time she rolled the dice she ended up taking a shot.

Standing, Sherry clapped her hands. "I think it's time to move on from Sixes. Let's play 'I've Never.'"

Harmony tittered. "I've never played that."

Laughter exploded throughout the room, and Sherry frowned at Harmony. "Then it looks like you'll be good at this game, too."

Harmony's smile faded some as she looked down.

Looking away from Harmony, Sherry went over the rules. "Okay, so for Harmony's sake, I'll explain the game. I'll say something I've never done. If anyone else around the table has never done it, they have to drink up. If you think I'm not telling the truth you can call me out, and if you're right, I have to take a drink. If you're wrong, you have to take a drink." Turning to face Harmony, Sherry dryly asked, "Do you get it?"

Nodding her head, Harmony quickly looked at me. I gave her a reassuring wink, and I saw her body immediately relax.

Someone called out, "I'll go first. I've never been to Canada."

Everyone took a drink. Well, everyone but Sandy and Jake, who spent a week in Canada last year. Jake just happened to have told me about the trip a few weeks ago.

Next was Harmony. Chewing on her lower lip, she said, "I've never had a one-night stand."

No one picked up their drinks. Harmony's mouth dropped open. "Are you kidding me? All of you have?"

Jake laughed and pointed to the next person. By the time we got to me, Harmony had taken another three drinks. After her one-night stand comment, folks caught on to how naïve and inexperienced Harmony was.

"Preston!" Sherry shouted as I pulled my eyes off Harmony. "Will you pay attention. It's your turn."

The way Sherry glared at me told me she was pissed about something. Smiling, I said, "I've never had a dog."

Harmony tilted her head and gave me the sweetest grin and said, "That's kind of sad."

Shrugging my shoulders, I pouted and pretended like I wiped a tear away. Harmony laughed, and I glanced over to Sherry again. If looks could kill I'd have been laid out on the floor. I shrugged again, causing Sherry to look away and whisper something into the ear of the guy sitting next to her. It wasn't lost on me how Sherry had been flirting with the guy the entire time we had been playing these stupid games. The thing that struck me as odd was that I wasn't bothered by it. At all. The last month we had grown so far apart it was unreal. I was actually almost positive she was cheating.

The game came back around to Harmony. Lifting her eyes up as if she was thinking hard, she said, "I've never had sex in—"

Jake jumped up and shouted, "Okay! I think we've had enough fun with the drinking games."

Sherry stood up and nodded her head. "I agree, it's become rather boring." Turning she made her way over to the bar and made a drink. The guy she had been sitting next to followed her. Harmony stayed sitting where she was as I sat across from her.

Not knowing what to say, I grinned and said, "Hey."

Her eyes still held the same sadness they held that first day in the hospital. "Hey," she whispered back.

"How are you doing, Harmony?"

Falling back in the sofa, she let out a frustrated sigh. "Considering I have discovered that not even drinking numbs my pain, I'd say I'm doing pretty shitty."

My heart felt as if it was physically aching. Her eyes caught mine, and I wasn't sure how long we sat there and stared at each other.

"I heard you moved."

Nodding her head, she bit down on her lower lip and my body reacted in a way that surprised the hell out of me. For the first time since I'd known Harmony, I was physically attracted to her.

"Yep. You'll have to come see my new place. I bought a condo on Comm Ave."

Swallowing hard, I could barely speak. "I'd like that." My heart began pounding as I pictured kissing Harmony's soft lips.

Tonight. I was breaking up with Sherry tonight for sure. When I glanced over to where she stood, she was running her finger down the chest of the guy she'd been talking to. I looked back at Harmony.

Leaning forward, Harmony's eyes searched my face as she smiled slightly. "You're looking at me differently than you ever have before, Preston."

Feeling my face flush, I looked away as I stood up. "Um… excuse me, Harmony. I need some fresh air."

Quickly making my way out onto the patio, I dragged in a few deep breaths as I pushed my hands through my hair.

What the fuck is happening? For one brief second, I wanted to take Harmony in my arms. I wanted her. Seriously wanted her.

Jesus, Preston. Get a grip on yourself, you douche.

Staring out over the lights of the city, I closed my eyes and all I could see was Harmony's smile. *You cannot be falling for Harmony Banks. Jesus, get it together, Ward.*

"P-Preston?"

Her voice moved through my body like a warm sensation. For the first time in months, it was the only thing that made me forget everything.

Glancing over my shoulder, I smiled. "Yeah?"

Harmony stood at the door. Beyond her I saw Sherry hanging all over the guy she had been talking to most of the night. "I think I'm going to get sick."

My eyes snapped back to Harmony. "What?"

She swallowed and I saw it on her face. She was about to throw up. "I'm trying really hard to hold it down."

Rushing over to her, I picked her up in my arms and made my way through Sandy and Jake's condo to the guest bathroom. "It's okay, just hang on."

Burying her head into my neck, I prayed like hell she wouldn't throw up on me. I can handle anything. But puke on me? That was a hard pass.

Pushing the bathroom door open, I brought Harmony over to the toilet and gently set her down and lifted the lid.

"Oh God!" She moaned as she leaned over and threw up. Spinning around in the bathroom, I looked for a washcloth. I pulled one out of a drawer and ran it under hot water.

Kicking the door shut, I got down next to Harmony and held her blonde hair back as she continued to get sick.

When nothing else would come out she leaned back into me and cried. "I'm so embarrassed. I can't believe I got drunk at my brother's party and then threw up."

I ran my hand softly down her back as I attempted to get her to settle down. "Shh, it's okay. Every single one of those people out there has prayed to the porcelain god at some point in their life."

Laughing, Harmony pulled back and looked at me. "Thanks for taking care of me."

"Anytime," I whispered as I brushed a piece of hair from her face.

Harmony's mouth parted open slightly, as if she was about to say something but stopped herself. Looking away she said, "I better call a cab."

"No. No way am I letting you take a cab home. I'll give you a ride."

Giving me a knee-knocking smile, she asked, "Are you sure? What about... Sherry?"

"She might not be ready to go, and I have a feeling she wants to leave with someone else."

Harmony's eyes went wide. "Oh."

Standing, I reached down and helped her up.

Once Harmony rinsed out her mouth again, we headed back out to the living room. Harmony was definitely drunk. She could hardly walk as she made her way over to Jake and Sandy. Following her, I stood there while she said I was taking her home.

Jake reached for my hand to shake it. "Do you work tomorrow?"

Shaking my head, I said, "No. I never drink before I've got a shift."

He gave me an appreciative smile. "Thanks for taking her home, dude. I appreciate it."

Sandy helped Harmony gather up her things while I made my way over to Sherry.

Stepping between her and her new friend, I smiled at her. "Harmony is sick, and we have to take her home."

Sherry's smile faded as she narrowed her eyes at me. "Jake will have to take her home. I'm not ready to leave."

Anger washed over me as Sherry looked back at the guy and chuckled. "Besides, I'm working a *business* deal. Isn't that right, Jerry?"

The guy smiled and nodded his head. That's when I remembered hearing her say that name before. The night I stayed at the hospital; she was on the phone with someone. She had called him Jerry.

Taking Sherry by the arm I excused us and walked her to a corner. "I'm taking Harmony home. You're either coming with me or finding another way home."

Sherry poked me in the chest. "You don't owe her anything. Stop acting like you owe her something. So her kid and husband died. It wasn't your fault. Jesus Christ, Preston, it's time to move on. Let her hook up with some guy here tonight. Lord knows she needs to get laid. It's pathetic how innocent she acts."

I lowered my voice. "Don't talk about her like that."

Sherry's mouth pulled into a twisted smile. "I knew it. You're attracted to her. What do you want to do, Preston?

Give her a courtesy fuck. Maybe if you can fuck her, it will help with the fact that you couldn't save her son."

I dropped her arm and took a step back. The pain that shot through my chest about brought me to my knees. Shaking her head, Sherry laughed. "I'm done wasting my time with you tonight. Just leave and I'll see you tomorrow."

Looking into Sherry's eyes everything was clearer than ever. This relationship was a joke.

"This isn't working." Motioning between us, I kept talking. "This thing between us, it hasn't been working for months."

Letting out a gruff laugh, Sherry placed her hands on her hips. "What in the hell do you think you're doing?"

"I think it's probably best if you moved out." I glanced over to Jerry who was watching the whole thing play out.

Dropping her mouth open, Sherry stared at me. "You're breaking up with me, Preston? I don't think so. I've invested my time into this damn relationship, patiently waiting for you to give me a ring while I kissed ass with your new-found friends. You are not breaking things off between us."

"Sherry, that's just it. I should want to walk into a store, buy you a ring, and place it on your finger, but I don't. I haven't truly felt anything for you in months, and I know you feel the same way. This is all a sham."

Anger filled her eyes. "This is because of her. You feel guilty, so you're pushing me away to be with her."

Shaking my head, I let out a sigh. "This has nothing to do with Harmony and everything to do with the fact that you want things I don't want, Sherry. Things I'm never going to want with you."

Laughing, she placed her hands on my chest and gave me a push. "You are a complete douchebag. Do you know that? My mother told me I was crazy for dating a lowlife like you. You'll never get anywhere, Preston. You're content in your mediocre life and your job that makes you feel like a hero. Well fuck you, Preston Ward. I found someone better."

Pushing past me she stormed off, but not before turning around. "By the way, six months into our relationship, I slept with one of the guys at the firehouse. He stopped by and took care of things while you were in Seattle. Best fuck I've ever had."

I couldn't lie and say I was surprised. I'd had a feeling Sherry and Richards had hooked up. I saw it in their faces every time they were near each other.

Walking up to her, I looked into her eyes. "You just made this so much easier. Thank you."

Harmony had passed out almost immediately after she sat down in my car. I prayed silently she didn't throw up in my new Subaru. Glancing over at Harmony sleeping, I let out a chuckle. Luckily, I had asked Jake where Harmony's new place was. Before we left, Sandy made sure to let me know she was happy I had broken things off with Sherry.

"She's a user, Preston. You were the only person who didn't see it."

The problem was, I had seen and hadn't wanted to admit it.

Harmony let out a snore that caused me to jump. Chuckling, I pulled up to a giant Victorian house that was marked with her address.

"Holy shit," I whispered as I remembered Jake telling me to pull down the alley behind the house. There was a parking spot that was Harmony's even though she'd sold her car. I was impressed that she had been able to find a place that had parking on Comm Ave. Cars, parking, and downtown Boston didn't go hand in hand at all.

Putting my car in park, I peeked over at Harmony. She was sleeping so peacefully; I almost didn't want to wake her up. For some reason, I was scared to death to carry her into her house.

Chill the hell out, Ward. You're just bringing her home. That's it. Nothing more can ever come from this.

Opening the passenger side door, I smiled as I looked down at her. She opened her eyes and smiled up at me, and that was the moment I knew I was screwed.

Yep. I'm totally fucked.

Chapter SEVEN

I'VE NEVER

Harmony

MY HEAD THROBBED AND I felt like I was going to throw up, but something about the way Preston was looking at me made my insides warm. I hadn't had that feeling in a very, very, long time. He reached in and scooped me up into his arms. He frowned as he kicked his door shut.

"You're not eating, Harmony," he whispered as I buried my face into his broad chest. I'd never had anyone take care of me like this, and I didn't want to think for one minute that Preston was only doing this because he felt guilty. I honestly couldn't bear it.

As he walked up to the door, I managed to say, "Preston, I can stand up, honestly. I'm not that drunk."

"Just open the door, Harmony, and let's get you inside. It's cold out."

It was October and it was unseasonably warm out, so why he said it was cold was beyond me. Giggling, I reached over and attempted three times to put in the code.

"What's the code?" he asked as he carefully set me down.

I whispered the code while trying not to laugh. I wasn't even sure what was so funny.

Preston typed it in then walked into the foyer. He shook his head as he looked up the stairs.

"Fuck," he whispered. "Of course it would be a walk up."

After climbing the stairs, he stopped at the top and looked for a light. That's when I realized he had me in his arms yet again.

"I'm in your arms again, Preston."

Letting out a chuckle, he said, "I know. This is becoming a habit, Ms. Banks."

I was about to say something when Preston took a few steps forward and tripped. "Shit! Harmony!"

Spinning around, Preston twisted so that he landed first. I ended up on top of him, laughing hysterically. Then I realized my body was up against his, and I liked how it felt. Oh boy, did I like how it felt.

I attempted to stand up. "Oh my goodness! Are you okay?"

Lying on the ground, Preston moaned out in pain. "What in the hell did I land on?"

Deciding I wanted to have a bit of fun, I let out a gasp and shouted, "My cat! Are you on my cat?"

Flying up, Preston's head hit something, and he yelled out again. "Shit!"

Managing to get over to the lights, I flipped them on. I was laughing so hard, I had tears streaming down my face. This feeling of being tipsy was something new, and I wasn't sure I liked how being drunk made me feel. But I was laughing, and I hadn't really laughed in months.

Oh my. Look how cute he looks spinning around as he looks for a nonexistent cat.

"Did I land on it?"

"On what?" I asked as I fell onto the sofa and kept laughing as Preston kept looking around my place.

Oh man. The room is spinning.

"Harmony, have you even unpacked?"

Wiping my tears away, I pointed at him. "You should have seen your face when I said you landed on my cat. I don't even have a cat!" Wrapping my arms around my waist, I attempted to stop laughing.

He sat down in the chair opposite the sofa and laughed. "I'm glad I amuse you."

Pulling my knees up, I rested my chin and looked at Preston. "I haven't laughed like that in a long time. It felt good."

Giving me a sexy-as-hell wink, Preston spoke softly. "Good. I'm glad my clumsiness, or your lack of unpacking rather, caused you to laugh."

Brushing him off with my hand, I giggled, "Oh it has nothing to do with my lack of unpacking."

He pointed to the row of shoeboxes that were lined up at the front door. and asked, "How many damn pairs of shoes do you own?"

My heart began to get that familiar ache as I shrugged my shoulders. "I went on a shoe-shopping spree. Trey said he never liked seeing me in heels. Said it made other guys want to look at my legs. Once I found out he had been cheating on me... I kind of went shoe crazy."

Preston's face moved from happy to sad in an instant. "What? Trey cheated on you?"

Tears filled my eyes as I looked away. "I think he was about to tell me right before the accident. He said he had to tell me something and then my phone rang. We argued, and... well... anyway. After the accident I went up to his office to get some of his personal things, and I found the play drawer he used with his secretary."

"Holy shit," Preston whispered.

Letting out a gruff laugh, I nodded my head. "Yeah. That was my reaction too. The best part of all this, she was a girl we went to high school with." Throwing my hands up in the air and letting out a frustrated moan, I stood up. Well, I stood up and then stumbled forward. "Ugh, it's a long story and one I don't feel like talking about. I've had too much fun tonight."

Preston jumped up and caught me before I fell over. I didn't want to admit to myself how much I liked being in his arms. My blue eyes met his green, and I found myself wanting to know more about Preston Ward.

"Preston," I whispered and then hiccupped rather loudly.

His smile melted my heart, and I pushed away from him. "I don't want to be alone tonight."

Swallowing hard, Preston took a few steps away from me. Ha! I must have some damn aura around me that tells guys to keep away. My own husband didn't even want me.

Pushing his hand through his hair, Preston tried to talk. "Um... Harmony, I should probably —"

Narrowing my eyes at him I pushed him hard on the chest. "I don't want to sleep with you, asshole. I just don't want to be alone. When I'm alone I think about my son. Even my husband Trey, the dick that cheated on me."

Preston's body relaxed and a small part of me was disappointed in knowing that he didn't desire me. Turning, I stumbled to the sofa and fell face forward on it while letting out a long, drawn-out moan.

"Where's your room, Harmony?" he asked as he scooped me up into his arms once again.

Placing my hand on the side of his face as he lifted me, I licked my lips and said, "You're cute, Preston."

Laughing, he winked at me and said, "You're kind of cute too, Harmony."

Smiling, I felt my eyes closing. "You're more than cute. You're very, very cute."

Preston chuckled as he whispered. "And you're beautiful. Now where is your room, princess."

Smiling at the sweet endearment, I said, "It's on the second floor. Last door on the left."

Snuggling my face into his neck, I took in a deep breath while I felt Preston's chest vibrate when he muttered, "More damn stairs."

"Mommy? Mommy, it's dark and I'm all alone. Please come get me."

Standing in the dark hallway I felt along the wall. "TJ! Baby, Mommy is coming for you!"

"Mommy! It hurts. It hurts, Mommy!"

"Trey!" I screamed as I ran in the dark until I came to a door.

"Mommy! Help me! Please."

Throwing the door open, I sucked in a breath of air as I saw Trey's body lying on the ground. Looking away I saw TJ.

"No!" I screamed as I ran over to him and pulled him into my arms. "Please God, don't take him. Please!"

Darkness swept over the room and I couldn't see a thing. The pain. The pain was so strong.

"Harmony!"

TJ slipped from my arms as I screamed out his name. "TJ, no, please don't leave me!"

"Harmony, please wake up. Harmony."

Snapping my eyes open, I saw his eyes. The eyes that should cause pain, yet they did just the opposite. They calmed me almost instantly. Sitting up, I threw myself into Preston's arms.

"You... you were dreaming, and you screamed," Preston said as he held me tightly.

Inhaling a deep breath, I fought like hell to keep my tears at bay.

"Nightmare," I whispered.

Pulling back, Preston searched my face. "Do you have them often?"

Shaking my head, I pulled my eyes from his. "No. At first I had the same dream every night. Now it's about once a week."

Preston closed his eyes and then scrubbed his hands down his face.

"You stayed?" I asked as I took him in. Holy moly. He didn't have a shirt on.

Look away, Harmony. Look away and count to twenty.

I attempted to focus on anything other than this chest and amazingly fit abs.

Jesus, Harmony. Get a grip on yourself.

Risking another peek, I turned slightly and moved my eyes over Preston's fit body.

Preston slowly stood up, and I forced my betraying body to keep my feelings deep inside.

"Do you want me to leave, Harmony? I will if you'd rather be alone. It's just... you asked me to stay last night, and I didn't want you to be upset if you woke up and I was gone. Of course, you could be upset that I stayed."

When I didn't respond, he shook his head and turned around as he headed out the door.

Pursing my lips, I kept my giggle suppressed. "Preston, please don't leave. It's five in the morning."

He must have noticed he wasn't wearing a shirt, probably from the cold draft that blew through this old house. Or it was because I was eyeing him up and down... again.

"Shit, let me go get a shirt on." Spinning on his heels, he disappeared.

Pushing the covers off, I noticed I was in a T-shirt and sweats. I wonder if I changed into these clothes or if Preston had changed me? God I hope I changed myself. I'm pretty sure I haven't shaved under my arms in two weeks.

Rolling my eyes, I walked out of my bedroom and leaned over the railing. Closing my eyes briefly I let out a sigh. *Oh lord do I feel like crap.* My head was pounding and my mouth tasted like a bar. *I think my drinking days might be over before they even get started.*

"Preston? I'm going to jump in the shower. I feel like shit, and my mouth tastes worse."

He appeared before my eyes as he looked up at me. "How about I make you some breakfast?"

Laughing, I brushed him off and said, "Ha! If you can find food in this house and make a meal out of it, I'll spend the entire day doing whatever you want to do."

Winking at me, Preston said, "Deal."

Smiling weakly, I headed back into my bedroom and to the master bathroom. I turned on the hot water and stripped out of my clothes and walked into the shower. Letting the water move across my body, I let out the breath I hadn't even realized I had been holding in. Moving my face into the water, I made a decision. These feelings that I was experiencing — these confusing feelings. I was going to push them away and lock them somewhere deep down inside. My husband and child died four months ago and I'm drooling over another man.

Placing my hands over my face, I leaned against the shower wall and slowly slid down as I cried. What was wrong with me? Why should it be wrong to desire another man? My own husband hadn't even wanted me.

After a few minutes of sitting there, I looked up. "I've never done this before. I've never experienced these feelings about anyone other than Trey. I'm so confused and scared, and I feel guilty. What is happening? Please… please help me."

Please, God. Please.

Chapter
EIGHT

JUST FRIENDS

Preston

Opening up Harmony's refrigerator, I attempted to find some sort of food to work with. I was met with pretty much an empty refrigerator. "Jesus, no wonder she looks like she's lost weight. Pushing a bag of lettuce out of the way I saw some eggs.

I grabbed the eggs and said, "Perfect." Taking another look around, I saw a purple onion and a green pepper. Picking up the pepper, it felt a bit soft but it was workable.

Setting the eggs down next to the onion and bell pepper, I searched for a bowl and a frying pan.

Once I got the eggs beaten and poured over the sautéed onion and peppers, I put a dash of salt on it and some black pepper. Taking a look around, I took in Harmony's place. I wasn't sure how I should be feeling. Harmony's nightmare did a number on me when I heard her screaming out TJ's name. I almost dropped to my knees on the stairs when I heard it.

Then the way she was looking at me like she wanted me had me even more confused. The look was gone as fast as it came. I was crazy for even thinking about having any sort of relationship with Harmony. She was a friend. That was it.

Bullshit, Ward. She is more than a friend.

Closing my eyes, I thought back to last night when I helped her get undressed. The moment she unclasped her bra and let it fall to the ground I wanted to take her right then and there. Especially when she began flirting. Luckily, she passed out and I finished getting her dressed while I thought of every scary movie I could think of. And the puke in her hair. The puke in her hair gagged me every time I looked at it. Every time my dick started to come up, I'd look at the puke.

"Daydreaming?"

I practically jumped out of my skin as my eyes opened and I saw Harmony standing in front of me. Her blonde hair was pulled up into a sloppy bun that sat on top of her head. She had on a New York Yankees pinstripe baseball jersey and sweatpants that read Yankees on the side of them.

She looked so damn cute I didn't even care that she was wearing the enemies' clothing. Well, I didn't care for all of five seconds. She sat down on the bar stool and looked around me to see what was cooking.

Chuckling, she asked, "Did you find food?"

"What. In. The. Hell. Are. You. Wearing?" I asked slowly.

Looking down at her shirt, Harmony smiled an evil smile. "My favorite baseball team: the Yankees."

Dropping my mouth open, I let the spatula fall from my hand as I took a few steps back while I covered my heart.

"That's blasphemy. What... why... how?" I couldn't even form a sentence.

Tilting her head, Harmony rolled her eyes. "Oh please. Don't tell me you're one of *those* guys."

Remembering our breakfast, I picked up the spatula and cleaned it off before I got to work on the eggs.

"What exactly is one of *those* guys?" I asked as I looked over my shoulder.

Scrunching her nose in the most adorable way, she shrugged her shoulders. "You know. The 'gung-ho crazy for the Boston Red Sox, doesn't change his socks for fear the team will lose' guy." Shaking her head, she laughed. I didn't dare tell her my lucky socks had not been washed or changed since the beginning of the season.

Letting out a nervous laugh, I rolled my eyes. "No. I'm not one of those guys."

Harmony grinned and I loved that it reached her eyes. "Good. 'Cause I can't stand those guys. Especially the Irish ones. Oh. My. God. They're the worst. With the way they take their sports so seriously. Good lord."

I made a mental note to myself not to tell Harmony I was fifty percent Irish, even though my mother insists it was more like sixty percent. I also made a note not to tell her that my dream was to own an Irish pub someday. Sherry hated when I talked about owning a pub. She made sure to let me know it was beneath her to be married to someone who owned a bar.

"Preston? Are you okay? You're lost in thought."

Giving her a quick smile, I nodded my head. "Yep. Totally fine. Now, if you would please get out two plates and two glasses, I have our breakfast."

Standing, Harmony laughed as she made her way over and took out two plates. "No way you found enough food to feed us both!"

Once she set the plates down, I halved the eggs on her plate, and the other half on mine. After setting the frying pan back on the stove, I grabbed the two small boxes of orange juice and poured them into the glass. My heart stopped beating for a few seconds when Harmony looked at me. For the first time since I'd known her, I saw happiness there.

Sliding her plate in front of her, along with the orange juice, I smiled. "Looks like I won, Ms. Banks. I know exactly what we'll do today. Dress casual, it will be a long day."

Stopping her fork before it went into her mouth, Harmony frowned. "What?"

"Your bet. You said if I found food, you'd spend the entire day doing what I wanted to do."

"Are you sure I said that?" Harmony asked with a wink.

Taking a bite of my eggs, I chewed as I looked up and thought hard about what the bet was. "Yep. It was a challenge and I won."

Smiling a smile that left me breathless, Harmony shook her head. "Is that so? And if I refuse?"

I took another bite and swallowed it before I pouted. "Would you really refuse me after I cleaned puke out of your hair last night?"

Harmony's mouth dropped open and a beautiful shade of red swept across her cheeks. "How embarrassing."

"Then it's a date."

Narrowing her left eye at me, she shook her head. "Not a date. Two friends just hanging out."

Lifting my hands up in surrender, I said, "That's what I said. Two friends. Hanging out."

Chewing on her lower lip, I saw the mask coming back up.

"Harmony, please. Just spend the day with me. I can't bear the idea of going back to my place and seeing Sherry packing up."

"Why is she packing?"

Shit. That piece of information I hadn't wanted to talk about just yet. "Well, um… I kind of broke up with Sherry. Last night. After you puked."

Slapping her hands over her mouth, Harmony's eyes widened. "I wasn't even thinking of Sherry last night when I asked you to stay. Oh, Preston, if I somehow —"

I held up my hands to get her to stop. "Harmony, stop. Please let me talk."

Closing her mouth abruptly, she nodded her head and remained quiet.

"Sherry and I have been over for months now. It was a long time coming and had nothing to do with you. Besides, I'm pretty sure she was cheating on me. Last night she admitted to sleeping with one of the firefighters at the station where I work."

Harmony looked horrified. "She cheated on you?"

I nodded.

"Do you promise, Preston, that it had nothing to do with me? And please don't lie to me... I don't think I could take it if you lied to me."

My heart dropped to the floor and my stomach instantly formed into a knot.

Setting down my fork, I walked over to Harmony and picked up her hand. Lacing my pinky around hers, I whispered, "I pinky swear to you, Sherry and I were not meant to be, and you didn't have anything to do with me breaking up with her. Before we even met, I was wanting to break things off. I'm not sure why I hadn't."

Glancing down at our pinkies, Harmony's eyes filled with tears. She quickly drew her emotions back in, burying them like she always does and managed to smile. It didn't touch her eyes though. My goal was to see a smile and the happiness that had been in her eyes last night. I'd do whatever it took to make it happen.

Dropping her hand down from mine, she slowly stood. "Do you mind if I take a nap? I don't want to be tired when you show me the town today."

Throwing my head back, I let out a laugh. "I think I'll crash for a bit longer too on your couch, if you don't mind."

She walked her plate over to the sink and downed the last of her OJ. "The sofa is all yours, Mr. Ward. Leave the dishes. They can wait until later."

Standing, I walked over and placed my dish in the sink but waited for Harmony to walk out of the kitchen. Leaning against the sink, I attempted to calm my beating heart down.

Just friends. We're just friends.

Walking back in from the balcony, I stopped dead in my tracks. Harmony was standing in front of me with a huge smile on her face. Closing my eyes, I shook my head as I said, "You have to change, Harmony."

"Nope. This is my most favorite sweatshirt. Plus it keeps me warm and makes me feel better since I feel like I've been hit by a Mack truck."

My mouth dropped open. "You don't play fair."

Giving me a crooked grin, she slowly walked up to me and placed her hand on my chest. I was praying like hell she wouldn't feel my heart pounding. "If you admit to me that you are not wearing any article of clothing that you've had on since the Sox started their season, I'll go change."

Harmony's eyes danced with excitement and for one brief moment I wondered what kind of an asshole her husband was for cheating on her.

Raising her eyebrow she purred, "I'm waiting."

Ah shit. She sure as hell doesn't play fair.

Shrugging my shoulders, I let out a gruff laugh. "It doesn't bother me that you're wearing a Yankees sweatshirt. I'm not the one who will be getting all the dirty looks."

"So you don't mind if I wear it?"

Swallowing hard, I shook my head. "Nope."

Smiling even bigger, she pulled out a Yankees baseball cap and placed it on her head. My mouth dropped open and my knees went weak. She looked adorable in it. Damn it all to hell. She looked fucking adorable in the damn Yankees cap.

I drew in a deep breath and slowly exhaled. I prayed like hell Harmony made it through this day with all the

Yankees garbage on. And I made a bet with myself I would be able to get her to take it all off by lunch.

"Are you ready for our day, Harmony?" I asked as I put my arm out for her.

Biting down gently on her lower lip, Harmony looked everywhere but at me as she spoke. "Preston, I just wanted you to know that... well..." Landing her eyes on my face, she slowly looked up until our eyes met. "I want you to know how much I appreciate this. It's nice to spend some time where my thoughts aren't flooded by memories or nightmares."

My heart broke in two. "Thank you for allowing me this day, Harmony."

Smiling, she nodded her head as she laced her arm around mine. "Are we walking or driving in your fancy sports car, Mr. Ward?"

Letting out a chortle, I replied, "I think the fresh air will do your hangover wonders."

Making a face, Harmony cursed under her breath. "Damn it. I was hoping it didn't show."

As we made our way down the steps, I found myself actually looking forward to something for once in a very long time. I was excited and terrified to share my world with Harmony, but if it meant she got to spend a day laughing and having fun instead of sitting in an empty house alone, then so be it.

Now if my brain could just tell my heart to pull back some, everything would be perfect.

Just friends, Ward. You're just friends.

Chapter
NINE

LAUGHTER IS MEDICINE FOR THE SOUL

Harmony

P RESTON AND I WALKED ALONG Comm Ave., then turned and made our way down Dartmouth Street. The cool, crisp fall air actually felt amazing and seemed to ease my dull headache. Checking my pocket, I rubbed my fingers against the charm.

Preston had seen it in my hand and asked what it was. When I told him, he gave me the sweetest smile I'd ever seen.

Clearing my thoughts, I asked Preston, "So are you going to tell me where we're going?"

His strong jawline was set as he stared straight ahead. Something was weighing on his mind, and I wanted to ask what it was but decided best not to.

"Preston?"

Snapping his head over to me, he let out a chuckle. "Sorry, Harmony. I was lost in thought. What did you ask?"

Grinning, I asked again. "Are you going to tell me where we're going?"

He shook his head. "Nope."

Throwing my head back, I laughed and gave him a push. It felt good to laugh. The guilt slowly crept in, but I quickly pushed it aside. I'd give myself one day. That's all I needed.

I peeked over at Preston and took in his features. He was tall, probably about six feet. He was for sure taller than Trey. Preston's brown hair was messy, like he washed it and just ran his hand through it and let it dry that way. It was sexy as hell and worked very well for him. His eyes were a light green, and they held so many emotions. I found myself lying in bed this morning thinking about those eyes.

Preston reached down and took my hand. A small part of me wanted to let the butterflies in my stomach take off, but I pushed the feeling away. As we walked, Preston turned down Huntington Avenue and he led me into the Westin Hotel.

Coming to a dead stop in the lobby, I dropped Preston's hand. "What are we doing in a hotel, Preston?" My heart was beating at a crazy pace and I was shocked by the confusing emotions running through my head. For one brief moment I was hoping Preston had brought me here to make love to me.

Where in the hell did that thought come from?

Jesus, Harmony. Stow away the hormones.

Preston looked at me with his head slightly tilted. Taking a step closer, he leaned in close to me as my chest heaved up and down. "Why Harmony, you don't think I brought you to a hotel to have sex with you, do you?"

Letting out a nervous chuckle, I shook my head. "Of course not." My betraying voice cracked.

Then it happened. Preston smiled the most gorgeous smile ever, and I knew I was going to have to fight like hell to keep my feelings for him from growing. "'Cause if I wanted to make love to you, I sure as hell would give you more than a midmorning roll in the sack at a local hotel."

Swallowing hard, I gave him a smile and forced my eyes to roll, even though my mind was racing with what Preston would do if he wanted to make love to me.

"Okay, so what are we doing here?" I asked, trying to sound normal. Like the way he just spoke to me didn't have my insides completely melting.

Reaching for my hand again, Preston led me to the elevator. "I want to show you something." Hitting the button marked for meeting rooms, the elevator took us up the short distance.

When the door opened, I couldn't help but notice Preston's smile. He was giddy about something and that made me smile. The feeling was foreign but nice. As we approached the America Ballroom I saw the display sign but couldn't read it. Preston walked too quickly and kept the sign blocked.

Walking through the door I drew in a gasp. The room was filled with paintings. Not just any paintings, but

Geoffrey Chatten paintings. "Preston," I whispered as I walked further into the room. The first thing that popped into my head was that I was walking around an art exhibit dressed in New York Yankees stuff. Then I noticed we were the only people in the room.

Spinning around, I let out a giggle. "Chatten is one of my favorite painters." Glancing over to Preston, my smile faded. "How did you know?"

His face beamed with pride as he looked around. "Jake mentioned it to me a while back. One of my best friends is a manager here and he happened to mention the art show and I called in a favor. Asked him if we could preview it before it opened to the public."

I didn't know what to say. No one had ever done anything like this for me before. My lower lip trembled and Preston's smile faded. "Harmony? If you want to leave we can. I just thought — "

Lifting my hand to stop him from talking, I shook my head. "No! This is just so… amazing. I didn't even know that Jake knew Chatten was a favorite of mine."

Smiling, Preston took my hand and I had to fight double time now to keep the feelings away. "Do you have any of his paintings?"

"I have one." I whispered. "My mother brought it back from the UK on one of their trips abroad. I fell in love with his impressionist painting right away."

"Impressionist painting. What does that mean?" Preston asked.

"It's a style where the artist captures the object like someone is catching a glimpse of it. They are usually landscapes, and the artist will use bright, vibrant colors."

Nodding his head, Preston walked up to a painting. "I like the seascape paintings."

My stomach fluttered deep in my belly. "Me too. They're my favorite. I think it's because the ocean is my favorite place to be. Being near the sea allows me to think better. Clears my mind." My voice drifted off as I gazed at one of the paintings.

Preston walked off and looked at the paintings. "I like this one too. I love the color blue."

Turning, I made my way over to the painting. *Iris in Blue Vase* was the title. The colors were amazing as I stood and looked at all the details. "It's beautiful," I whispered.

"Yeah, it really is," Preston said as he stood next to me. Sneaking a look at him, I smiled when I saw how the painting had him captivated.

We spent the next hour walking from piece to piece. While Preston chatted with his friend, I made arrangements to buy two paintings. They were expensive but I could afford it. My mother and father's way of reaching out to me after Trey and TJ died was to send me a large sum of money. Little did they know I knew it came from my grandparents. Jake had inherited his when he turned twenty-one, and I was to inherit mine at twenty-one as well. Of course, my parents made it look like it was from them and had made special arrangements for me to get it early.

Preston walked up to me and placed his hand on the small of my back as he spoke.

Ignore how your heart is tripping over itself, Harmony. It means nothing. You're just lonely.

"Ready for lunch?"

Right on cue, my stomach growled and Preston chuckled. "I'll take that as a yes."

Nodding my head, I giggled. "At least my hangover is slowly fading."

Preston kept his hand on my lower back, and I wasn't surprised by how much I enjoyed him leading me like he was. "Have you ever eaten at Temptations Café?"

"Nope. Is it casual?" Pointing to my clothing, I smiled.

Throwing his head back, Preston laughed. "Yes ma'am it is. Soups, sandwiches, wraps, and my favorite dessert ever."

"Hmm, I'm intrigued now by this dessert."

He winked. "It's pretty awesome."

Less than five minutes later we were walking into Temptations Café. "How did you find this place?" I asked.

Walking up to order, Preston turned to me. "It's right down the road from my station."

My interest was immediately peaked once again. "The fire station?"

Nodding, he looked at me with a puzzled look on his face. "Yeah."

"Can we stop by?"

I wasn't sure how to read him. His eyes turned from happiness to something else I wasn't able to read.

Preston's eyes searched my face. "You want to stop by the station? That won't... be hard for you?"

Shrugging my shoulders, I made a face. "I don't think so, I'm really curious to see where you work. See what you do."

A slight smile moved across his face. "Really?"

Letting out a small laugh, I nodded my head. "Really. Really."

The girl behind the counter called out next and Preston stepped up.

She looked to be about my age. "Hey, Preston. Are you off today?"

Giving her a polite smile he took a quick look at me before turning back and talking. "Hey, Lori. Yeah, I have today off. I'll have the usual, garden wrap with a bottled water."

Glancing up at the menu I read what Preston ordered. "That sounds good, I'll have the same," I said as I smiled at the girl behind the counter. Her eyes snapped between Preston and me before she looked at me with a death stare.

Whoa. Someone has a crush on the handsome firefighter. Biting down on my lower lip, I attempted to hold back my chuckle.

"We'll also take two Nutella and bananas." Preston snuck a peak at me and wiggled his eyebrows. I couldn't hold back my laughter that time.

"That's your amazing dessert?" I asked as Preston handed Lori money.

His face looked horrified. "Yes! Nutella and banana on a brioche. It's heaven, Harmony. Pure heaven."

Rolling my eyes, I looked around the restaurant. The place was cute. Small white tables with black chairs were sprinkled throughout the place. It gave a very modern, yet classic feel. And it smelled good in there. The baked items looked to die for, and I was shocked Preston liked something so simple as Nutella and bananas. I'll admit, I'd never tasted Nutella. so for all I knew, I was missing out on something good.

Preston pulled my chair out for me as we sat down. We talked the entire time we ate. Preston told me about growing up in Boston before his father retired to the country. He had two brothers and a sister. His favorite place to be was at his parents' country house or on the ocean sailing.

I decided to keep the conversation on Preston, and he didn't seem to mind.

Lori walked over and placed the Nutella and banana dessert down in front of us.

"Dig in," Preston said with a smile.

Chewing on my bottom lip, I asked, "Um… is Nutella good?"

His head snapped up as he stared at me.

"You've never had Nutella? Like *ever*?"

Pressing my lips together so I didn't giggle, I shook my head.

Preston leaned back in his chair and put his hand over his heart. "I've so much to teach you. So much."

Swallowing hard, I felt my face flush.

Oh, the things I wanted Preston to teach me.

Chapter
TEN

NUTELLA AND BASEBALL

Preston

SITTING BACK IN THE CHAIR, I stared at Harmony in disbelief. That was until her eyes turned dark and she licked her lips.

I cleared my throat. "I can't believe you've never had the pleasure of eating Nutella. This is a landmark occasion. You're gonna wanna put this down on your calendar as the day I changed your life."

Harmony laughed and picked up the brioche and took a bite. Her eyes lit up before she closed them and let out a moan that moved through my entire body and settled between my legs.

Friends. Just friends.

"Holy crap. This is amazing. It's like… chocolate!"

Laughing, I picked up my brioche and gestured to her. "I told you, it's the most amazing dessert ever."

After finishing up our dessert, we headed over to the station. I wasn't sure why Harmony wanted to see where I worked, but a part of me liked that she wanted to see it. Sherry never once asked to see where I worked. Of course, she did see where I worked, but she couldn't have cared less. She hated what I did, but for me, I loved it. I was proud of my job. At least I used to be. Now all I had were mixed emotions, and I felt like I wasn't sure about anything anymore.

Stopping in front of the station, I gestured to the firehouse. "This is it. Engine 37 and Ladder 26."

Smiling back at me, she asked the one question I was hoping she wouldn't.

"Can we go inside?"

Tightening my hands into fists, I quickly loosened them. "Um, sure, if you want to."

The bay doors were open so we walked in. Directly in front of us was Sharp. Cursing under my breath, I slowly inhaled and let it back out.

Turning, Sharp gave me a smile that went from ear to ear. "Ward, you don't know what it means to take a day off."

Letting out a nervous laugh, I tilted my head and raised my eyebrow. Stopping directly in front of Sharp and a few other guys, I said a silent prayer they wouldn't put two and two together. Sharp walked away from the other guys who were all playing a card game.

"Mitchel Sharp, this is Harmony Banks, a friend of mine. She wanted to see where I worked."

Reaching his hand out for Harmony's, Sharp gave her a polite smile. "Harmony, huh? That's a beautiful name."

Harmony blushed and changed her posture just a bit. "I can't take the credit on that one. My mother came up with it."

I watched as Sharp's eyes moved across Harmony's body. Glancing back at me he said, "So you guys are just friends, huh?"

Before I even had a chance to respond, Harmony laughed. "Yes! Very much just friends. Preston is being a gentleman of a guy and spending the day with me to cure my hangover."

I wasn't sure why Harmony's words hurt more than I thought they should. Sharp smiled bigger. "I see. So, Harmony, how about I show you around."

Smiling, Harmony went to speak but looked at me. Her smile faded briefly before she turned and looked around. That's when I noticed the pain in my jaw from clenching my teeth together.

"I've always wondered what a firehouse looked like on the inside. So this it, huh?"

"This is it," I said as I glared at Sharp. The way he was looking at Harmony turned my stomach.

Walking up to her, he placed his hand on her lower back and I looked away, not being able to take the sight of it.

Fucking hell. What is the matter with me? I want to pound my best friend's face in just for touching her.

"How about that tour now, darling," Sharp said as he stood a little too close to Harmony.

She cleared her throat, and I forced myself to turn and look at them.

"Um… Actually… Mitchel, was it?"

"Mitchel, Mitch, I'll answer to anything you call me."

Rolling my eyes, I glanced over to the other guys as they attempted to hold their laughter back.

Harmony let out a small chuckle and said, "I was kind of wanting *Preston* to show me where he worked and give me the tour."

Pressing my lips together to hide my smile, Sharp placed his hand over his chest and said, "Ouch. Shot down before I was even out of the gate."

Walking over to me I was shocked that Harmony reached for my hand and said, "Shall we?"

Glancing back over to Sharp, I gave him a small grin. "Um… Yeah sure."

After introducing Harmony to the rest of the guys, I showed her where we slept, ate, and hung out between calls. I attempted to avoid Captain Ryan's office but he had glanced up and saw me showing Harmony around. I knew it wouldn't be long before he came out here. Sharp had told me that the captain had gone and visited Harmony in the hospital. I was sure he would remember her.

"Wow, Preston. Your family must be pretty proud of you."

Pulling my head back, I looked at her. "For what?"

She looked around as she pointed. "For this. Your job. I mean, you risk your life to save others. I can't even begin to wonder how your poor mother did it with her husband and now you."

"My other brother Finn is a firefighter as well. So she not only has to worry about me, she has to worry about him as well."

Harmony's eyes widened in horror. "And your other brother? What does he do? Nothing dangerous I hope, for your mother's sake."

Scrunching up my face, I said, "Wes is a banker in New York City. Dresses in suits every day and expensive shoes. I'm positive one of his suits cost more than what I make in a year."

Laughing, Harmony gave me a gentle push. "What about your sister? You mentioned she was younger. What does she do?"

"Angie's a senior in high school."

"Oh wow. Do you mind if I ask how old you are, Preston?" The way Harmony was chewing on her lower lip had my stomach going all kinds of crazy.

"He's twenty-three. One of the best firefighters I've had the pleasure of working alongside of me. Well, since his daddy, that is."

Closing my eyes, I held my breath and turned to see my captain standing in front of me. "Hey there, Cap. This is a friend of mine, Harmony Banks. She wanted to see where I worked."

Reaching her hand out, Harmony spoke first. "Captain Ryan, it's a pleasure seeing you again."

My eyes snapped to Harmony and then to the floor. Harmony and the cap talked for a few minutes while I stood there and tried to calm the pounding of my heart. The cap had warned me to stay away from Harmony, and here I was, not only with her but showing her where I worked.

"Harmony, do you mind if I speak with Ward—I mean Preston—for a moment?"

My mouth went dry and I had an overwhelming urge to flee.

"No, not at all. Should I just wait here?"

"Yes!" I said almost in a panicked state. If she stayed here I could keep my eye on her and would know if Sharp tried to talk to her. "Um, just have a seat, and I'll be right back."

Reaching for the cap's hand again, Harmony shook it and said, "It was nice seeing you again."

"It was my pleasure, Harmony." Cap turned and walked toward his office as I followed. Glancing over my shoulder, I smiled when I saw Harmony watching us walk away.

"Shut the door Ward and have a seat."

Fuck.

Doing as he asked, I sat down and held my breath, waiting for the unexpected.

Cap sat and leaned back in his chair. He rested his elbows on the arms of the chair and tented his fingers under his chin. "Want to tell me what you're doing, son?"

Sitting up straight, I gave him a confused look. "What do you mean, Cap?"

Glancing over my shoulder to Harmony, he looked back at me and straight into my eyes.

"Preston, you'll never be able to ease her pain. The loss of her child was not your fault and by becoming her friend you're not making it easier on either one of you."

Anger built up in my veins as I gripped the armrests. "I'm not being her friend out of sympathy. I enjoy her company and it has nothing to do with her son. I know Cap, it wasn't my fault. I've moved on from it."

Raising his eyebrow, he said, "Have you? Why are you always taking off, Preston? You're damn near out of vacation time and you never took vacation time before that accident. Ever."

Shrugging my shoulders, I looked into his eyes. "I'm over it, sir. I'm fine."

Nodding, he looked at his desk and said, "I'm going to ask you one question. And this is not me being your boss asking it. It's me, a long-time family friend asking. Do you have feelings for her?"

There was one thing I would never do, and that was lie to the man sitting across from me. "Honestly sir, I'm not sure. I've been having some confusing thoughts going through my mind. I keep telling myself we're just friends. That's all we are... friends... just friends. I enjoy her company, and I think she enjoys mine. I mean, is that so bad?"

Smiling slightly, he shook his head. "No, that's not bad at all. Just remember what she's been through, Preston. I don't want to see you getting hurt. What about Sherry?"

Moving nervously in my seat, I looked away as I said, "We broke up."

"Really? Why?"

Looking back at him, I caught his eyes. "Cap, I've told you my feelings for Sherry weren't what I first thought they were. It was a long time coming."

Standing up, he pushed his hands through his hair and said, "Preston, I want you to take things slow. Whether this is a friendship or something more... Take it slow."

Cap's eyes moved to the window, and he frowned for just a brief second. It was long enough to cause me to look over my shoulder back at Harmony.

That fucking bastard. Sharp was sitting next to Harmony with his arm draped on the sofa behind her.

Standing up, I looked back at the Cap. "Okay, well I guess we ought to be going."

He grabbed my arm, stopping me. I closed my eyes and waited for what was coming.

"I see the way you look at her, Preston. And the way you just reacted when you saw Sharp sitting next to her."

Smiling, I turned around and said, "Cap, it's nothing. If anything I'm probably just being protective, like a big brother kind of thing."

"Uh-huh. I don't ever remember you looking at Sherry like that once in the two years you dated her, son."

My smile dropped and I quickly spun around and headed to the door. Opening it up, I stepped outside the office and inhaled a deep breath as I tried to compose myself before walking over to Harmony and Sharp.

After leaving the fire station, Harmony asked if we could stop in a few stores. She was still trying to decorate her new place and needed some things to add life to the condo. I'd never had so much fun shopping in my life. The best part was, Harmony couldn't make a decision to save her life, so we only had two bags to carry.

"Are you getting hungry?" I asked as we walked out of a store.

Stopping and looking at me she laughed. "Yes! I've been having so much fun I didn't even realize it was so late. Dinner sounds amazing. What did you have in mind?"

"How about we go to my uncle's place? He owns a beer joint with some of the best food in Boston."

Harmony grinned and said, "Sounds like we found our place for dinner. I can't wait to see it."

Laughing, I remembered Harmony's comment about Irish guys. "Oh I can't wait for them to see you."

Grabbing her hand, I called for a taxi. Taking a quick look at her Yankees gear, I cursed myself for not being able to get it off her by lunchtime. I'd tried a few times to get her to buy another shirt. I even bet her once or twice on something, and if I won, she had to change. Nothing worked. I silently said a prayer everyone would take it easy on her.

Glancing at Harmony, I couldn't help but let out a laugh. "John's Place on Broad Street," I said after we climbed into the taxi.

Chapter ELEVEN

IRISH MEN AND THE YANKEES

Harmony

THE TAXI DROVE TO THE financial district as Preston and the taxi driver talked about baseball. Rolling my eyes, I let out a sigh. I never understood why everyone was so crazy about the Red Sox. I think that was the main reason I became a Yankees fan. Because Jake drove me mad with all the Red Sox crap.

The taxi pulled up and parked as Preston paid him and grabbed the two shopping bags. Reaching his hand into the cab, he helped me out.

I wonder if Preston was always such a gentleman, or is it just because he was trying to give me a nice day?

My eyes traveled down his well-toned body. Twenty-three. He sure seemed more mature for just being twenty-three. Licking my lips, I wondered how good of a kisser he was.

Oh holy hell. I needed to stop this and stop it now.

Taking a few steps down the street, Preston turned and said, "We're here."

Glancing to my right I saw an Irish pub and that was it. "Where is it?"

Pointing to the pub, Preston smiled bigger.

Oh no. Is Ward an Irish name? One more look at the door caused me to let out a groan. I was in for a serious shit storm.

Walking closer to the door, I read the sign out loud. "Red Sox fans only." Jerking my head back to Preston, he threw his head back and laughed.

"Ah hell, this should be interesting. Come on Harmony, this Irish boy wants to introduce you to some friends."

No. No. No. No.

Grabbing his arm, I glared at Preston with what I was hoping was a horrified look on my face. "Preston! I'm wearing Yankees stuff."

Tapping my nose with his finger, he chuckled as he said, "I think you're *just* pretty enough for them to let it slide."

My mouth dropped open as Preston pulled the door open. Standing my ground, I refused to move. One quick push by Preston and I was stumbling into the pub. Everyone turned and looked at me. Smiles instantly turned to frowns.

Oh shit. Please let me be pretty enough. Please let me be pretty enough.

There was a tall man standing behind the bar. His blue eyes pierced mine, and I immediately saw the resemblance to Preston. "Preston, what have you brought us this evening? I'm guessing she didn't see the sign on the door."

I could see the papers now. Young girl thrown out of pub for wearing Yankees shirt and cap. The Irish are supposed to be friendly. Aren't they?

Grabbing Preston's arm, I pulled him down to me. "Ward is not *Irish*."

Laughing, he said, "No, it's not. It's British. This is my mother's brother. Last name is Flanagan. Actually, her parents changed it to Flanagan when they came to America. It was originally O'Flannagan."

Shaking my head and letting out a faint whimper, I said, "Oh lord. I'm never going to forgive you for this, Preston."

Wrapping his arm around my waist he pulled me closer to him, he whispered, "Harmony Banks, by eight o'clock this evening I promise I will have converted you to a Sox fan."

My breathing began to pick up as Preston held me close to his body. I didn't like the way my body reacted to Preston. Okay, that was a lie. I liked it way more than I should have.

"What if you fail, Mr. Ward?" I asked with a bit of a teasing edge to my voice.

Giving me a wicked smile, he moved his lips to my ear and whispered, "Then I'm totally at your mercy, Ms. Banks."

Closing my eyes, I took in the feel of his hot breath on my neck. I found myself clutching onto his shirt as I whispered back, "You have to be a Yankees fan for a whole season."

Preston's lips grazed my neck as he whispered, "Deal."

And just like that, he let me go and walked up to the bar as I stood there trying to understand what had just happened to me. I drew in a deep breath and blew it out. I was about to turn around when Preston said, "Take it easy on my girl, she's been misled."

My girl. God how I like the sound of that.

Shaking it off, I pushed the feelings away and spun around as I plastered on my best smile. The one I had to wear when I attended all the stupid business parties with Trey or my parents.

Walking toward the bar, Preston introduced me to everyone. Of course he saved the best for last.

"Uncle John, this is my friend, Harmony Banks. Harmony, this is my favorite uncle ever, John."

Reaching his hand across the bar he gave me the sweetest smile, "Don't let this little bastard fool ya. I'm his only uncle. Your brother is Jake?"

My mouth dropped open as I looked at Preston. Shrugging, he winked. "I take it my big brother has graced your pub before?"

"Yes he has, pretty lady. I might add when he comes in he has his lucky Sox T-shirt on."

Rolling my eyes, I moaned. Then it hit me. Turning to Preston I gasped. "Please tell me you're not..." Watching the smile spread across Preston's face I knew my answer before he even said it.

"It's my socks."

My whole body slumped. "Preston, why? I was really starting to think we had a good BFF thing going."

Preston's smile faded but just for a brief second before he smiled bigger and lifted up his jeans to reveal the nasty socks he hadn't changed since the Sox started their season.

Sitting on the bar stool, I mumbled to myself, "And to think I let you stay in my house."

John and Preston both laughed. Pointing at me John said, "You're lucky you're so pretty, and that my boy Preston is friends with you. Otherwise, your little ass would be sitting out on the street right now."

Biting on my lower lip, I held up my hands and innocently asked, "Who are the Yankees?"

Those sitting around us erupted into laughter as Preston gave me a smile that caused my stupid heart to trip over itself.

Preston took the liberty of ordering our food. We started with Irish spring rolls that were to die for. He also ordered me the Irish sampler that consisted of Guinness beef stew, shepherd's pie, and country cottage pie. Preston ordered bangers and mash, which was Irish sausage with mashed potatoes topped with the most amazing brown gravy I'd ever had. Then of course there were the Irish baked beans. I'd never eaten such amazing food in my life.

By the time I was finished eating, I could barely move. My stomach muscles were also sore from laughing so hard. Preston was truly in his environment in this pub. I could see it not only in his face, but I could hear it in his laughter. This was home to him. When one of the patrons asked Preston to hop up and play the fiddle I was stunned to hear how good he was.

"His mum and dad are truly proud of that boy," John said with a smile.

Watching Preston I realized it was the first time I'd seen such a gleam in his eyes. It wasn't there when we were at the firehouse. I couldn't help but smile as I watched him on the fiddle with a bunch of crazy Red Sox-loving Irish men singing along to something he was playing.

"He seems to be at home here," I said as I turned back to look at John.

John was looking at Preston with such a loving look. "He wants this place. Always has."

Pulling my head back in shock, I asked, "What do you mean he wants this place?"

John shook his head and laughed. "Preston must have been about ten years old when he stood on this bar — almost in the exact location you're sitting — and he proclaimed that he was going to run the pub someday."

Letting out a chuckle, I looked over to Preston. My smile faded some. "I thought he loved being a firefighter." Preston looked up at me right then and smiled the biggest smile I think I've ever seen. My smile back to him came so naturally. We hadn't really known each other all that long but it was important for me to know Preston was happy. I saw the sadness in his eyes, and I knew from talking to Jake that Preston was having a very hard time dealing with TJ's death and the confusion about where he saw his future going.

John's voice pulled me from my thoughts and I jumped slightly. "That boy loves firefighting. It's in his blood. Firefighting goes back four generations on his daddy's side of the family."

"But his dream is to own a pub?" I asked, glancing back at John.

"Not just any pub, darlin'. *This* pub."

Tilting my head, I looked into John's eyes. "Why doesn't he work here?"

Shrugging his shoulders he made a face. "That's something you'd have to ask him. He used to work here, but then stopped when he started dating that Sherry girl."

Leaning in closer, he used his finger to motion me in closer. "According to his momma, Sherry thought it was beneath Preston to work here. Even more so, she thought he should be working like his older brother, Weston, doing banking and shit." Shaking his head, John looked back at Preston who was now standing there talking to a few people. "Nah, not my Preston. Out of all my sister's kids, Preston I think has the strongest flow of Irish blood moving through those veins of his."

Preston walked back over and sat down. "Man oh man, that was some fun shit."

"Language, Preston James Ward."

Giggling, I looked at Preston. "You're in trouble now. The middle name was used."

Preston rolled his eyes as he downed his beer. The way his lips wrapped around the bottle was almost sinful. Chewing on my bottom lip, I fought the pull in my lower stomach. I wasn't sure why Preston looked extra hot, but he did and I needed to look away.

My eyes moved down to his lips as I watched him talking to his uncle.

Look away, Harmony.

His jaw clenched and I knew he was agitated. I'd seen him do the same thing earlier today when his friend at the station started flirting with me. At the time, I didn't think anything of it until Preston came storming out of his captain's office. I saw it all over his face. Worry... or maybe it was jealousy. I wasn't sure because he kept making sure he told people I was just his friend. Of course I'd been doing the same.

Preston licked his lips and a small moan slipped from my lips as I quickly looked away.

"You okay, Harmony? Are you feeling okay?"

Glancing back at him, I scrunched up my nose and said, "Yeah, why?"

Preston looked confused as he said, "Nothing, I thought I heard you moan."

My eyes caught Preston's, and we were both lost in our stare.

John slammed his hand down on the bar and we both jumped. "Who wants dessert?"

I tried like hell to look away but Preston's green eyes held mine. Then he smiled that smile I was quickly finding myself longing for. "I've got dessert covered, Uncle John."

Lifting my eyebrow, I narrowed my eye at Preston and said, "Oh really?"

His smile grew bigger and his eyes danced with excitement. It didn't take long for that excitement to pass over to me. All kinds of thoughts entered my mind on what I hoped dessert would be.

Ugh. Stop this Harmony. You're just friends.

John laughed when Preston turned and looked at him. "I'm going to guess you gave your cousin a call."

Slipping off the bar stool, Preston nodded his head. "Yes sir, I did."

Looking between both men, I asked, "Wait. What's dessert going to be that you had to call in a favor? Your last favor was pretty big, Preston."

Preston reached over and pulled my baseball cap down over my eyes as he said, "Don't you worry your pretty little head, Yankees girl. I've got this."

Pushing the cap up, I decided I wanted to be surprised, so I let it drop.

After saying goodbye to John and the rest of the patrons of the pub, Preston and I headed outside where he flagged down a cab.

Once we slipped into the cab, Preston handed the cab driver a note. Turning and looking at Preston, he smiled and nodded his head.

"Really? Note passing?" I chuckled.

Giving me a wink, Preston said, "It's a surprise, Harmony. Now close your eyes and don't open them or I'll put a blindfold on you."

My mouth parted slightly and I tried not to let my imagination go wild, but it was too late. Dropping my head back, I closed my eyes and pictured Preston tying a blindfold on me. I imagined my hands slowly making their way down his strong fit abs, shaking with anticipation at what surprise was beneath his pants.

"Good God, stop this, Harmony," I whispered.

Warm breath hit my neck and goose bumps covered my entire body. "Stop what?"

"What?" I asked as I kept my head back and my eyes closed.

"You told yourself to stop. What are you wanting to stop?"

Shit! Shit! Shit!

I can't tell Preston I was telling myself to stop thinking naughty thoughts of him. "Um… I was going to press you for more information but decided to let it go."

My body jumped when I felt Preston's hand touch the side of my face. Tingles engulfed my entire face as he slowly ran the back of his hand down my face. "That's probably a good idea."

I immediately felt the loss of his warmth when he pulled his hand away. Focus on your breathing, Harmony. Slowly breathe in and slowly breathe out. My body quickly relaxed as I felt myself slipping off into sleep. For once in a long time I felt completely safe just knowing Preston was next to me.

My body was being moved, and I had no desire to open my eyes. I knew Preston was carrying me, and I knew the moment he knew I was awake he'd put me down.

I heard a voice I didn't recognize talking to Preston. "Dude, did you knock her out just to get her in here?"

Preston chuckled and it moved through my entire body. Allowing myself this one time to enjoy the way Preston made me feel, I let the feeling rush through my body.

"No, asshole. She fell asleep. Is it all set up?" Snuggling my face further into his chest, I took a deep breath. Goodness, what does he wear as cologne? It was driving me insane.

"You doubt me, baby cousin? I'm not the one who needs to impress a girl. And may I point out she's wearing Yankees shit. I shouldn't even let you put her down on the sacred ground."

"Fuck you, Kyle."

Smiling, I took notice how Preston was willing to defend me even though I was wearing New York Yankees stuff. Deciding I should probably get out of

Preston's arms before I grew to love it, I lifted my head and looked into his eyes.

Oh dear. Maybe I should have kept pretending to be asleep. The way he was looking at me had my heart dropping to my stomach. I'd never had anyone look at me the way he looked at me. My heart soared as I lost myself in his smile. "Hey," I whispered.

"Hey," he whispered back. "We're here."

Grinning slightly, I looked around. "Where are we?"

Preston laughed as he slowly put me down and Kyle said, "Dude, she doesn't even know where she is!"

Taking my hand, Preston led me out toward the lights. The moment my eyes adjusted; I knew where we were. My brother had dragged me to Fenway Park more times than I could count.

My eyes widened in surprise as I took it all in. "Fenway Park," I whispered. A small blanket was set in the middle of the field... or infield, or whatever they called it. Preston took my hand and led me over to the blanket. Stopping, I looked up and spun around. "Oh my God! I'm on the field... in Fenway Park!" My stomach felt like I was on a rollercoaster I was so excited.

Preston laughed and took a step back to allow me to behave like a three-year-old. Jake was going to be insanely jealous. I had to control the urge to text him and show him where I was.

Facing Preston, I smiled. "Why are you doing all of this, Preston?" My heart ached at the thought that he was doing this because he felt guilty.

Taking a few steps toward me, he took my hands in his. "Because I like to see you smile."

Sucking in a breath I gazed into his eyes.

"Harmony, my only wish is that you enjoyed this day as much as I did."

Grinning, I nodded my head like a small child in a candy store. "This day has been amazing. But you did all of this just to make me smile? Is that the only reason?" I hoped like hell Preston was doing this because he enjoyed my company, because I sure as hell enjoyed his.

Preston swallowed hard and looked down and inhaled a deep breath. "I like being with you. I can't explain it, but I feel a connection with you. I'm not doing this because I feel guilty, Harmony. I *need* you to know that. I'm doing it because I genuinely like being around you."

I slowly let the breath I was holding out. Thank God Preston wasn't spending time with me because he felt guilty about TJ.

"I feel a connection with you too, and I like spending time with you as well."

We stood there and stared at each other. I was positive Preston felt the electricity between us. Taking a step back, I looked down at the blanket and noticed a small cooler. "Is that dessert?"

Preston motioned for me to sit down as he sat down next to me. Opening the cooler, he pulled out two ice cream sandwiches. Falling back onto the blanket, I giggled. "You're killing me!" Lying down next to me he unwrapped the ice cream sandwich and handed it to me.

"Your brother threatened my life if I asked him one more thing about the things you liked."

Taking a bite of the ice cream sandwich, I looked over at Preston and asked, "You never thought to ask him who my favorite baseball team was?"

His head snapped over and he looked at me as he shouted, "No! You live in Boston for Christ's sake. Being a Sox fan should be bred into your blood, woman!"

Laughing, I rolled over onto my side and looked at him. "I think I'm going to like this friendship. A Red Sox diehard fan, who happens to be Irish and is going to have to be a Yankees fan all of next season."

Preston closed his eyes and shook his head. "Harmony, you're on the infield of Fenway Park, how can you still be a Yankees fan?"

Leaning over, I brushed my lips against his neck and smiled when I saw the goosebumps appear on his skin. "You'll have to do more than swoon me on the infield of Fenway Park to get me to become a Sox fan."

Preston leaned up on his elbows and smiled. "I swooned you?"

Pushing him over, I jumped up and finished off my ice cream sandwich. I needed to get this back on track and quickly. I could feel the way Preston was looking at me, and I knew I was most likely looking at him the same way. "I better get back home, Preston. I have an early class tomorrow."

The disappointment spread across his face as he stood, and I wanted to kick myself. "I had a wonderful day today Preston, but —"

"But?"

Placing my hands on his chest I felt his body tremble under my touch. "But I'm just tired. I haven't had this much fun in a long time, and I'm emotionally spent."

Nodding his head, Preston took my hand and led me out of Fenway Park.

As we drove back in a cab to my condo in silence, I stared out the window and second-guessed my decision to end the night. Turning, I peeked over to Preston. He was texting someone and my heart dropped.

What if he was texting another girl? Maybe someone else he had made plans with tonight. Looking back out the window, I fought to hold my tears back. This is why I can't open my heart to anyone... especially Preston Ward. The way I was feeling for him, I couldn't risk being hurt again.

Preston walked me up to my door and stopped. "Thank you for spending the day with me, Harmony. I had a wonderful day."

My eyes landed on Preston's lips. "I did too," I whispered.

Preston took a few steps back. "Okay, well, I guess I'll be heading back home."

"O-okay."

"Sleep good, Harmony."

Trying to smile, I knew that was impossible. I hadn't been sleeping hardly at all since the accident. The feeling of being alone swept over my body. The warm fuzzy happy feeling I'd been experiencing all day was slowly slipping away the further Preston walked away.

"Preston! Wait."

Stopping, he turned and looked back at me. "Yeah?"

"Will you stay and... um... stay and—" Oh shit. What do I want him to stay and do? Think, Harmony. Think!

"Watch a movie with me?" I groaned internally. *Really Harmony?*

Preston's smile grew bigger on his face. "Sure!"

The moment he came bouncing back up the stairs I knew I was in trouble. He couldn't stay away from me anymore than I could stay away from him.

Opening the door and heading up the stairs, I glanced over my shoulder. "I'll have you know I'm breaking all my rules here."

Letting out a chuckle, Preston asked, "How so?"

Walking up to the coffee table, I reached down and turned the TV on. "I'm watching a movie with an Irish, crazy-tradition sock-wearing Red Sox fan."

Preston flopped down on my sofa and laughed. "Bring on the movie."

Dropping my keys on the coffee table, I sat down next to Preston and snuggled into his side as he surfed for a movie. When *Pride and Prejudice* flashed across the TV and Preston kept it on, my heart about stopped. That movie was my all-time favorite movie ever. Of course, a true *Pride and Prejudice* fan would have a worn-out copy of the book always close by, like I did. On my nightstand. I would beg Trey to watch this movie with me and he always said no. "Is this okay, Harmony?"

Nodding my head, I barely got the words out. "Yep. This is perfect." Just like Preston was perfect. Closing my eyes, I settled more into Preston's side.

Why does he have to be a Sox fan?

Chapter

TWELVE

A NIGHT TO REMEMBER

Preston

HARMONY HAD FALLEN ASLEEP ALMOST immediately. By the time the movie was over my arm was also asleep and felt like pins sticking me every time Harmony would move an inch.

Looking at her, I smiled. She was sleeping so peacefully, I hated to move her. Looking around, I saw the blanket lying across the back of the sofa. Reaching for it, I pulled it over Harmony and somewhat adjusted my body to where I was laying on the sofa and had

Harmony wrapped in my arms.

This is not good. So not good.

Moaning internally, I closed my eyes. *Jesus, this is so good. So very good.*

No. No, this is not good. Friends. We're just friends.

Harmony let out a small whimper. Pulling her in closer to me, her body completely relaxed. Fighting to keep my eyes open, I finally gave up the battle and drifted off to sleep. As much as I didn't want to admit it, holding Harmony in my arms felt amazing. I'd never felt so complete in my entire life.

As sleep took over, I whispered, "Just friends."

Harmony moved slightly in my arms as I held her against me. Even though every inch of me was aching, and I was sure my body would cramp the moment I stood up, I prayed like hell it wasn't morning yet. This was for sure going to be a night I would never forget.

Inhaling a deep breath, Harmony's scent filled my senses. That's when I heard her clear her throat.

Wow. Harmony sure has a deep morning voice.

Opening my eyes, I saw Jake sitting on the coffee table wearing a wide grin. Glancing down, Harmony was laying snuggled up against me with my arms wrapped around her.

"You're sure holding on to her for dear life," Jake whispered.

Giving Jake a dirty look, I mouthed, *Screw you.* I was almost positive Jake knew I had feelings for his sister. Hell, I'm holding on to her for dear life as I slept on her sofa with her.

Smiling bigger, he leaned over and looked at Harmony. "She sure is sleeping peacefully."

"My arm is about to fall off," I whispered.

Harmony moved about and then stretched. Opening her eyes she saw Jake smiling at her.

"Hey," Harmony said in a sleepy voice.

"Sleep good, baby sister?"

Nodding her head, she said, "I slept amazingly." Harmony started to move and then stopped. Sitting up quickly, she turned to look at me. "Preston?"

Giving her a slight smile, I replied back. "Harmony?"

Snapping her head back over to Jake she asked, "What time is it? I've got class this morning."

Looking at his watch, he said, "It's almost eight."

Jumping up, I flew off the sofa. "Shit! I've gotta go."

Harmony stood up and watched as I put my shoes back on. "You had your shoes off, Preston? With those socks?"

Laughing, I looked at Jake and shrugged my shoulders as Jake busted out laughing.

"Sorry, Harmony." Reaching out to shake Jake's hand, I said, "Sorry I can't stay and chat, but I'm late."

Turning to Harmony, my heart stopped. Her eyes looked so sad. "Where are you going?" Harmony asked.

"I promised my mom I'd take her and my sister shopping in Boston. Something about a winter formal."

The smile that spread across Harmony's face about dropped me to my knees. "Sounds like fun," Jake said sarcastically. Harmony shot him a dirty look before looking back at me.

"I'll walk you out, Preston."

Nodding my head, I pointed for her to lead the way.

Looking over my shoulder, I lifted my hand, "Talk to you later, Jake."

Narrowing his eyes at me, he said, "Oh you better believe we'll be talking later."

That can't be good.

Harmony walked me out to my car, and I could tell she had something on her mind. "Is everything okay, Harmony?"

Sucking in her upper lip, she bit down on it before giving me a forced smile. "Yeah, sorry. Um… Thank you for staying with me last night, Preston. I'm sure you had somewhere better to be."

Lifting my hand up, I placed it on the side of her face. "There is nowhere else I wanted to be last night than where I was."

Harmony's mouth parted open as she drew in breath. Taking a step away from me, I dropped my hand and smiled weakly.

"I'll see you around, Preston. Thanks again for yesterday and for… ahh… staying again last night."

My heart dropped slightly. It was clear Harmony didn't want anything other than a friendship with me. That's how it should be. At least that's what my head was telling me. My heart on the other hand was quickly falling for Harmony.

"Anytime, Harmony. I enjoyed myself."

Raising her hand and giving me another good-bye, Harmony turned and headed toward her place.

I got into my car and shut the door as I watched her walk into her condo. Closing my eyes, I shook my head.

"What in the hell are you doing, Preston?"

Hitting my sister's number on my cell phone, I

waited for her to answer.

"PJ! Are you on your way?"

Just hearing my sister Angie's voice caused me to smile. She was the only person to call me PJ. When she was a baby, Angie had a hard time saying Preston. My grandmother used to call me PJ, short for Preston James, when I was in trouble. Apparently while Angie was growing up, I was in trouble a lot because she quickly caught on to PJ.

As I headed out on Comm Ave., I felt heaviness in my heart for some reason. "I'm on my way, short stack. I woke up late, but I'm on my way."

Hearing Angie squeal, I imagined her jumping up and down. "Mom said be careful driving but hurry up!"

Laughing, I shook my head. "Yes ma'am. I'll be there shortly."

"Okay, see ya soon. I love you, PJ."

"Love you too, Angie."

Hitting end on the screen in the middle of my car dash, I tried to push back the uneasy feeling I had creeping up on me.

Walking down Newbury Street, I let out a frustrated sigh as I listened to my mother and Angie go on and on about how happy they were to have found a dress for the winter formal dance. Angie's boyfriend attended a private school and had asked Angie to go to the dance with him.

Lacing her arm through mine, Angie looked up at me with those big green eyes of hers. "How about lunch now, big brother?"

Chuckling, I said, "Sounds good. I worked up an

appetite watching you try on all those pretty dresses."

Giving me a wink, Angie said, "So, Mom said you finally broke up with Sherry the snob."

I glanced over to my mother. "Wow, news travels fast."

Shrugging her shoulders, my mother said, "I won't say I'm sad over this."

Shaking my head, I looked ahead. "Did anyone other than me like Sherry at all?"

"Nope," my mother and sister said at once.

"Oh, Preston! There is Papa Razzi, we haven't been there in forever," my mother said as she headed over to the restaurant.

Angie giggled, "Guess Mom wants Italian."

"I guess so," I said as Angie and I followed our mother into the Italian restaurant.

The waitress immediately began flirting with me as I did my best to ignore her. "Table for three?" she asked as she licked her bottom lip and eye fucked the hell out of me. Nodding my head, I smiled politely and said, "Yes, ma'am. Table for three."

Giving me a wink, the hostess said, "Follow me then."

Walking through the restaurant it felt like I was being watched. Setting the menus down on the table, the hostess blocked me from sitting down. Turning to me she said, "You don't remember me, do you, Preston?"

Glancing at my mother and sister before turning back to the hostess I said, "Um, no, I'm sorry I don't."

"Cassie Sharp."

The name didn't ring a bell at all and I was racking my brain trying to think if I had gone on a date with her before I started dating Sherry.

Letting out a nervous chuckle, I shook my head. Tilting her head and letting out a fake laugh, Cassie put her hand on my chest. "Mitchel's sister. We met at his birthday party a few years back."

Holy shit. Sharp's baby sister. Looking her body up and down I was shocked at how much she had… grown up.

"Wow. Cassie Sharp. You certainly have grown up."

My mother cleared her throat as my sister laughed.

Leaning in closer to me, she whispered, "In more ways than one." Taking a step back, I gave her a weak smile.

"Right, well, I'll be sure to let Mitchel know I ran into you."

Picking up my hand she wrote her number on the back and said, "Let's not."

Turning on her heels, Cassie headed back to the hostess station.

Shaking my head, I sat down at the table. My mother and Angie were both staring at me. "What?" I asked as I looked between both of them.

"Seriously? Do women just throw themselves at you like that all the time?" Angie asked. "I mean, yuk. That was gross."

Laughing, I glanced around the restaurant and that was when I saw her.

Harmony.

She was staring at me. Once our eyes met she gave me a small smile. Smiling, I lifted my hand and waved to her. That's when he turned around and I quickly dropped my hand and balled my fists.

Who was that guy? Was Harmony on a date? The guy gave me a good onceover before turning back and talking to Harmony. She smiled and let out a small chuckle as she shook her head.

What the fuck was that all about?

"Preston? Darling, what's wrong?"

"PJ? Earth to PJ!"

Fingers snapped in front of my face as I forced myself to pull my eyes off of Harmony and the mystery man.

"What?" I asked.

"Is everything okay? You look upset," my mother asked as she looked around.

Letting out a gruff laugh, I said, "Yeah, yeah everything is fine. Sorry." Rubbing my hands together, I asked, "So what is everyone getting?"

"Oh, that's easy. I'm totally getting the penne con pollo," Angie said as she folded her menu shut.

"Penne al pomodoro for me," my mother said with a smile and wink.

Shutting my menu, I attempted to keep my eyes off of Harmony. "Guess I'll get the Tuscan chicken salad club."

"That sounds heavenly too," my mother said with a sweet smile.

Our waitress came and got our drink and food orders. My mother and Angie began talking about shoes as I glanced over to Harmony and the guy she was with. Reaching across the table, he placed his hand over Harmony's as she smiled gently at him while drawing her hand away. Harmony glanced over to me and I quickly looked away.

Pulling out my phone, I sent Jake a text. I wasn't sure

if he would be working today or not. He seemed to be working crazy insane hours ever since he started his residency.

Me:	Hey. Sorry I had to leave so quick this morning.

Setting my phone on the table, it pinged back with a text message. My mom and Angie were still deep in shoe talk so I picked up my phone.

Jake:	Hey dude, on a quick break. No worries. Harmony sure seemed to be happy this morning. Said she had a wonderful day yesterday. Thanks, Preston for being such a great friend to Harmony

Ugh. There is that damn word again. *Friend.* Trying like hell not to look over at Harmony, I took a chance and stole a peek.

Fuck. I shouldn't have. Her smile was beautiful. My stomach turned at the thought of some asshole making her smile like that.

Me:	It was a fun day. At lunch with my mom and sister. Speaking of… Harmony is here with some guy.
Jake:	Really? I wonder who she's with? Shit, I've got to go. Give me a call tonight.

Well that got me nowhere.

"Preston? Are you listening to me?"

Pushing my phone back into my pocket, I looked at my mother and gave her my best smile. "Sorry, Mom. What were you saying?"

"Angie and I are thinking we are done for the day. After lunch we're ready to head back if you are. Are you going to stay at the house for dinner tonight?"

The waitress brought over our food as my mother tried to persuade me to stay for dinner tonight.

Going to take a bite of my sandwich, I noticed Harmony and the guy stand up. Harmony walked around the table up to the guy. He placed his hands on her upper arms as they stood there and continued to talk as I just sat there and watched them.

"Preston? Where are you, sweetheart?"

Looking back at my mother, I took a bite of my sandwich. Chewing it, I swallowed and smiled. "Sorry, Mom. I wish I could, but I've got to work tomorrow so I'm planning on hitting bed early tonight. I've had a crazy last two days."

Raising her eyebrow, she nodded. "I'd say. Your uncle told me about your stop by the pub. Said you were with a girl."

Narrowing my eyes at my mother, I said, "Mom, she's just a friend. Besides, I just broke up with Sherry. The last thing I'm looking for is to be in another relationship."

Giving me that look that only your mother could give, she slowly nodded and said, "Uh-huh. So do you want to tell me why you keep staring at the young lady over there?"

Shaking my head, I said, "No. I really don't."

Angie chuckled. "What's wrong, PJ, don't want Mom in your private life?"

Letting out a chuckle, I went to talk when I heard her voice.

"Hey, Preston."

My mother and Angie both turned and looked at Harmony standing next to our table.

Setting my sandwich down, I stood and turned to Harmony and smiled as I glanced around for the mystery man she was on a date with.

"Hey, Harmony." I cursed under my breath when I heard my voice crack. Angie noticed because she giggled.

Harmony smiled as she looked at Mom and Angie. Clearing my throat, I pointed to Angie as she gave me that smile like she knew everything that had to be known. "Harmony, this is my sister Angie. Angie, this is my friend, Harmony."

Angie stood up and instead of acting like a normal human being, she pulled Harmony into her arms and whispered something into Harmony's ear that made her laugh and look at my sister with a confused look. Next came my mother. Standing up, she extended her hand toward Harmony. "Harmony, this is my mother, Jennifer Ward. Mom, this is a friend of mine, Harmony."

Shaking my mother's hand, Harmony smiled. "You must be very proud of Preston, Mrs. Ward."

Beaming with pride, my mother nodded as she looked at me. Looking back at Harmony she said, "Please, call me Jenn."

Grinning, Harmony said, "Jenn it is."

"How did you both meet?" Angie asked as she sat back down and my knees about buckled out from under me. I hadn't even thought for two seconds that anyone would ask how we met.

My head snapped over to Harmony as her smile faltered some before she replaced it with a smile that didn't touch her eyes.

Trying to think of something to say, Harmony began talking. "Preston responded to a wreck I was in." Turning and looking at me, her eyes seemed lost and confused. "He tried to save my son but..."

Harmony's voice faded as my mother quickly took control of the situation. "I'm so sorry for your loss, Harmony."

Turning to my mother, Harmony nodded. "Thank you."

"Harmony is such a beautiful name. Is that your real name?" Angie asked. If I could, I would reach over and kiss my sister.

Letting out a chuckle, Harmony nodded. "Yep. My mother loves the symphony."

Taking a step back, Harmony looked at me. "I didn't mean to interrupt. I saw you and wanted to say hi." Turning to my mother and sister, Harmony held up her hand and said, "It was a pleasure meeting you both."

"The pleasure was all ours, dear," my mother said in such a soothing voice.

Before turning and leaving, Harmony said, "Enjoy your afternoon."

"See ya around, Harmony," I said as I looked back down at my plate as I sat down.

Giving me another kick, I let out a yell. "Ouch, you little brat!"

"Why are you not going after her?"

Looking at my sister like she'd lost her damn mind, I pulled my head back and stared at her. "Huh?"

Rolling her eyes and letting out a frustrated moan, she said, "Clearly she wants you to go after her, PJ."

Looking back toward the door, I asked, "Why?"

"Oh my gosh, Mom! He knows nothing about women."

My mother laughed as she continued to eat. "Angie, eat your lunch and leave your brother alone."

Dropping her mouth open, Angie looked at me, then back to my mother. "Mom, tell me you didn't notice the way that girl's eyes lit up when she talked to PJ."

Letting out a gruff laugh, I shook my head. "Ha! You're dreaming, Angie."

Tilting her head, Angie stared at me as I attempted to eat with her glaring at me.

"Oh. My. Gosh. You like her, Preston, don't you?"

My sandwich stopped at my mouth. "You called me Preston."

Nodding her head she let out a laugh. "Yeah I did. This is serious and calls for using our grown-up names. Preston. Do you have feelings for her?"

Now *that* caught my mother's attention. "Preston?" she asked with concern laced in her voice.

Swallowing hard, I couldn't find my voice. Finally getting some control of the situation, I said, "No. We're friends. I mean, she lost her husband in the wreck also, and… no… Angie, you're crazy." My eyes caught my mother's and I knew she could see right through me.

"Preston." My name off my mother's lips was almost my undoing. I wanted to jump up and shout to the world that I had fallen for Harmony hard and fast. And all it took was spending one day making her laugh and one night holding her in my arms.

"Not now, Mom. Please not now."

Nodding her head, she turned to Angie. "Let's finish up so we can get home."

Angie smiled. "I've gotten a bit of renewed energy!"

Moaning, I rolled my eyes as my mother chuckled.

The rest of the afternoon was spent looking for the perfect pair of shoes for Angie. My mother and Angie talked of designer shoes while I tried not to think of the guy Harmony had been out with.

Walking my mother and sister up to the house, I leaned over and kissed Angie on the cheek. "Behave, Angie."

Winking, she gave me a naughty smile and said, "Always!"

My mother turned and gave me a onceover. "The only way you'll know for sure is to ask her."

"Excuse me, ma'am?"

Narrowing her eyes at me, she shook her head. "Preston, I've seen that look before. I saw it on your father's face the first time he saw me on a date with another man. Talk to her and ask her."

"Nah, Mom, it's not like that with me and Harmony. We're just friends."

Nodding her head she said, "Okay, Preston." Reaching up on her toes, she kissed my cheek. Turning to walk into the house she looked over her shoulder and said, "Life is too short, darling. You of all people should know that."

"What does that mean, Mom?"

Lifting her hand she gave me a wave and walked into the house.

Pushing my hand through my hair, I let out a sigh. I'll never understand women.

Ever.

Chapter THIRTEEN

HOLIDAYS SUCK

Harmony

F LOPPING DOWN ON THE BEAT-UP sofa in the break room, I let out a sigh. The door opened and one of the nurses walked in. Chuck. Just the sight of him made my skin crawl. I closed my eyes and hoped he would just get what he needed and head right back out.

"Harmony! How's it going?"

Ugh. I knew I couldn't get that lucky. Opening one eye, I smiled. "It's going."

Closing my eye again, I prayed he got the hint that I was tired and not in the mood to talk. It had been a little over a week since I'd seen Preston and I was exhausted from lack of sleep. The night he held me in his arms was the best night I'd slept since the accident.

"You look tired," Chuck said as he flopped down next to me.

Go. Away.

"I am, Chuck. School and work have taken their toll on me."

"Yeah, I bet. I'm sure with the holidays coming up it's got to be hard on you too. You know, not having your son and husband."

Jesus, did he really just bring that up?

What a dick and a half. No. No, Chuck was a full-on dick. He didn't think I noticed him brush up against me yesterday as I was bending over. I could feel his nasty hard-on and it made me want to jump out of my skin.

Oh God. I'm going to puke simply thinking about it.

Just as I was about to tell Chuck to get the hell away from me, the door opened again. Opening my eyes, I smiled when I saw the head of nursing walk in. "Joel, did you say you needed to talk to me?"

It only took Joel half a second to notice what was going on. "Yes, if you have a minute, Harmony. I'd like to talk to you in my office."

Closing my eyes and saying a quick prayer, I jumped up and said, "See ya later, Chuck."

"Oh yeah. Um, see ya later, Harmony."

Following Joel into his office, I let out a moan as my eyes went heavenward. "Thank goodness you showed up when you did."

Sitting down in one of his chairs, he gave me a look and asked, "Is everything okay, Harmony?"

Nodding my head, my eyes roamed freely over his body. *Why in the hell do I not find this man attractive?*

Oh wait. It could be because he's my boss. Or maybe it's the fact that he is ten years older than me.

"Yes, I'm just tired. Thank you again for meeting with me for lunch yesterday. It really meant a lot that you would take time out of your schedule to discuss my concerns on where I saw my nursing career going."

Sitting back in his chair, it was Joel's turn to let his eyes roam freely over me. Biting down on my lip, I looked away. I didn't think he meant to look at me the way he did, but it still made me uncomfortable. Ever since he saw Preston staring at us at the restaurant, he seemed to act differently toward me.

I looked back at him, and he smiled. "I know it's been a rough few months, Harmony, and that's what I'm here for. I was thinking though, how does the maternity ward sound?"

Feeling my smile spread across my face, I nodded my head and asked, "How did you know?"

Throwing his head back, Joel laughed. "Harmony, do you know how many times I've caught you on the third floor looking at the babies?"

I didn't want to tell him it was because I was missing my own baby. Shrugging my shoulders, I said, "Labor and delivery has always been my main interest."

His smile faded and he turned back to all business. Just like that day at lunch. "Then consider it done."

I wanted to jump up and down and scream out how happy I was. My heart was pounding and my hands began to sweat. "When can I transfer?"

"I'll put in for it today."

Standing up, I held out my hand. Joel stood and extended his hand to me. "Joel, thank you for understanding. I really enjoyed working for you and I'll miss—"

"Harmony, you'll still be working under me. I manage the nurses and staff on the third floor as well."

Smiling, I said, "Oh. I didn't know that."

Joel kept a hold of my hand and walked around his desk. His eyes turned to something I had never seen before. I couldn't say for sure, but it sure looked like lust. *No. Surely not.*

"Harmony, do you have plans for Thanksgiving?"

My mind spun. God, please don't let my boss be asking me out. *Please.*

"Um... Thanksgiving?"

"Yeah, my wife loves cooking. I'm sure she would love to have you and your brother over for dinner."

His wife? I let out a nervous chuckle. *Oh shit. Did I read into that all wrong.*

"I'll ask my brother, but I think we are going over to his girlfriend's parents' house for dinner."

Nodding his head, Joel dropped my hand. "Well the invite is open, if you should change your mind."

"Thank you so much. I, um, I better get back to work."

Turning, I quickly made my way out of Joel's office. Leaning against his door, I took in a deep breath. Not looking where I was going, I walked right into someone.

The moment his hands grabbed my arms, I knew it was him.

Green eyes caught my blue eyes. "Preston," I whispered.

The office door opened and Joel stepped out. "Harmony, if you do decide, dinner will be served at four." Giving me a polite smile, Joel looked and saw Preston standing there.

I quickly turned back to Preston and noticed his eyes turned from happy to sad in an instant. His hands fell to his sides as he looked between Joel and me.

I went to talk but noticed Preston was in his uniform. My heart began to beat wildly in my chest as my gaze took him in. Dear God, he looked handsome as hell. My voice was lost as I stared at him. *Wow. Just wow.* I thought Preston was hot before but seeing him like this had me wishing for an ice-cold drink to pour over me.

"Excuse me, Harmony." Preston took off and headed down the hallway before I even had a chance to say anything to him. I knew instantly he thought Joel and I were together. I could see it on his face in the restaurant, and I saw it on his face just now. A part of me wanted him to think we were together because it would be easier to guard my own heart.

"That's twice he's looked at me like he wants to kill me, Harmony. Boyfriend?"

Shaking my head, I watched Preston until he went through the double doors at the end of the hallway. "No, he's just a friend."

Leaning in closer, Joel asked, "Does he know that?"

Looking at Joel, I gave him a weak smile and turned to go back to the nurse's station. I only had thirty more minutes before I could leave and head home for the weekend.

Wrapping my coat tighter around me to keep the cold wind out, I found myself standing in front of Station 37.

I had texted Jake earlier to see when he had talked to Preston last. I was shocked to find out that Preston had gone out last night with Jake and Sandy. I had sent him a few text messages but he had only sent back one- to two-word replies. I knew he was busy with his residency and honestly, I'm not sure why I was shocked Preston hung out with him and Sandy. Preston and Jake had quickly become good friends after the accident.

Chewing on my lower lip, I turned to leave when I heard my name being called.

"Hey Harmony! How is it going?"

Spinning around, I plastered a fake smile on my face. I was so exhausted. Even attempting to act happy was a feat in itself.

Mitchel walked up and his smile faded the moment he looked into my eyes.

"Hey, Mitchel. Is… um… is Preston working today?"

Mitchel's face tightened as he looked at me. "Are you okay, Harmony?"

My eyes stung with the threat of tears. Nothing had been okay since three weeks ago when Preston walked out of my condo after holding me all night long. Or the look on his face when he saw me with my boss at that restaurant or outside of Joel's office.

"I just need to talk to—" My voice cracked, and I hated how vulnerable I was feeling. So tired. I'm just so tired.

"Harmony?"

Closing my eyes, I let his voice penetrate my body before opening them again and seeing him.

Preston.

Mitchel stepped out of the way, and Preston stood there in front of me. Pressing my lips together tightly, I fought like hell not to be attracted to him. His brown hair was a mess and I could guess why. He couldn't keep his damn hands out of it. His eyes looked so tired and sad. It was as if I was looking into a mirror.

Without saying a word, I walked up to him and threw myself into his body. Preston's arms quickly wrapped me up, and I felt like I could breathe for the first time in weeks.

"Princess, what's wrong?"

My body sagged as Preston held me up. Hearing him call me the endearment was more than I could take. I wasn't sure how long I could keep fighting the intense pull Preston had on me.

"Preston," I sobbed into his chest.

Pulling back, Preston placed his hands on the sides of my face and brushed his thumbs across my cheeks. "Harmony, what happened?" His look of concern had my heart feeling so full.

"I… need… you. This is crazy… but I need—" My voice cracked, and I buried my face into his chest as I said, "Preston, please take me home. *Please.*"

Not two seconds later Preston was guiding me to his car. Once I got in, I dropped my head back against his seat. I didn't dare look at him for fear I would spill my heart out about my feelings for him.

No. I just need to sleep. Then I can think clearly.

Hot breath touched my neck as I sucked in a breath of air. "Harmony, I need to grab my stuff. I'll be right back."

Nodding my head, I tried to memorize the sound of my name coming off his lips.

A few minutes later, I heard the door to the car open, then the engine start. "Do you want me to take you to Sandy and Jake's?"

Snapping my head over to him, I yelled out, "No!"

Nodding his head, Preston whispered, "Okay. Your house?"

The words were out before I could stop them. "Will you take me to your house?"

Preston's mouth dropped open slightly. He swallowed hard, then licked his lips and looked straightforward. "Ah... sure."

As we drove to Preston's house a thought occurred to me. What if he had gotten back with Sherry or maybe started to date someone?

Oh shit, Harmony. You idiot.

Preston drove a little ways out of town and pulled into a small house and parked in the driveway. Jumping out of the car, he ran around to the other side and opened my door. Before I could even get out, he had me in his arms and was walking up the steps to the door.

"I thought you lived in an apartment," I whispered.

"I moved out. This is my aunt and uncle's place. They're in Ireland visiting family."

Smiling, I asked, "Uncle John?"

Preston smiled, but it didn't reach his eyes. "Yeah, Uncle John and Aunt Sue. I'm staying here until I find a place."

Opening the door, Preston walked into a modest-sized home. Looking around I instantly felt a sense of peace as a calmness moved across my body that I had never experienced before. Family pictures covered the fireplace mantel and the walls that led upstairs.

Walking over to the sofa, Preston set me down on it. "Do you want something to drink? Water? Um... beer?"

Shaking my head, I whispered, "No thank you." I suddenly felt foolish being here. Needing someone near me simply to sleep was a sign of weakness, and I couldn't afford to be weak.

Preston sat down in the chair opposite me and rested his arms on his legs as he looked at me. "Harmony, I need to ask you something."

Nodding my head, I barely spoke. "Anything."

Preston looked to the floor as he rubbed the back of his neck. I felt a churning in my stomach as I waited for what he was going to ask me.

"Are you dating anyone?"

My head pulled back as I looked at him with a shocked expression. I wasn't expecting that.

"No," I whispered. My eyes narrowed as I looked at Preston. I wanted desperately to ask him how that answer made him feel.

"Are you dating anyone?" I asked before thinking.

"No. No, there isn't anyone but—" Preston's voice sounded strained. Clearing his throat, he continued. "The guy at the hospital. I saw you with him twice, and he invited you to dinner, so I just thought, I mean, I just wanted to make sure he hadn't done anything to you."

My chest nearly exploded with the way Preston cared so much about me. I wanted to ask him to finish his sentence but my body was starting to relax just being near him.

"He's my boss. I was having a problem deciding where I wanted to see my nursing career go. I ran into him outside the restaurant and asked if I could speak with him. When I was coming out of his office the day I ran into you, he was asking me if Jake and I wanted to spend Thanksgiving with him and his wife."

Preston's body relaxed and I noticed he was fighting to hide a smile at the corner of his mouth.

"Okay," was all he managed to say.

Shaking my head, I looked away. "I can't sleep."

"What?"

Looking back at Preston, I finally gave up the fight and let my tears fall. Preston quickly dropped to the ground in front of me. "Hey, tell me what's going on."

"I haven't been able to sleep since the night you stayed on the sofa with me. It was the first night I slept without having any nightmares. And now... I can't sleep at all, and I'm so tired I feel like I can't function." Dropping my head into my hands, I sobbed uncontrollably.

Weakness was not an option, Harmony.

Too tired to care.

Preston picked me up in his strong arms and carried me upstairs. Wrapping my arms around his neck, I nestled my face in the crook of his neck. Kicking open a door, Preston walked into a bedroom that was filled with boxes.

Gently setting me down, Preston pulled the covers back from his bed and turned to me. Looking into my eyes, he pushed a piece of my blonde hair behind my ear as he dropped his hands to my pants and unbuttoned them.

My breathing picked up as I grabbed onto him for stability. My legs felt as if they were barely holding my body up.

Preston squatted down but kept his eyes locked on mine as he pushed my pants down. I silently thanked God that I had put on a pair of stupid boy short panties.

Swallowing hard, I moved my hands to his shoulders and stepped out of my pants. Preston stood up and set my pants on a chair, his eyes never leaving mine. I'd never experienced such powerful emotions before. Not even with Trey. The way Preston looked at me was as if I was his entire world.

Moving his hands to my hips, I jumped when he touched my bare skin. Lifting my shirt up, he pulled it over my head and tossed it over onto my pants. Inhaling a deep breath, I tried like hell to calm my breathing down as Preston's eyes fell to my pink and white polka dot bra.

Closing his eyes shut tight, Preston opened them again and gave me the sweetest smile. Reaching down, he picked me up again. His hands on my bare skin caused electricity to rip through my body as he moved and placed me on his bed. Reaching down he went to cover me up when I grabbed his arm. It wasn't lost on me that he sucked in a breath of air when I touched him.

My eyes pleaded with him as I said, "Please, Preston. I don't want to be alone."

His muscles went rigid as he stared at me with an incredulous look. Slowly standing up, Preston reached for his shirt and pulled it over his head. Biting down on my lip, I contained the moan I wanted to let out when I looked at his broad muscular chest. My eyes moved down to a set of perfect six-pack abs. And I mean perfect, like if you looked up six-pack abs in the dictionary, Preston's abs would be there in a picture.

Preston slowly unbuttoned his pants as I felt my whole body flush. Dear God, please let him be commando.

Closing my eyes, I attempted to calm my betraying body down. *Harmony, stop this now*. Commando would be very, very bad. Peaking my eyes open, I watched as

Preston pushed his pants down to reveal a pair of boxer briefs.

Oh. My. God. So much sexier than commando. Moving over, I made room for Preston as he slipped under the covers. Rolling over on my side, I prayed he would spoon me and hold me in his arms. I could hear him taking in a few deep breaths before he finally turned and pulled me into his body, noticeably keeping me away from his lower section.

Tingles raced over my skin as I felt myself melt into his body and relax completely.

"Is that better, princess?" Preston whispered against my hair.

It felt as if I was home in more than one way. "Yes," I whispered before closing my eyes. Sleep was upon me within seconds.

My eyes slowly opened as I let them adjust to the sun. I had no idea what time it was. All I knew was that I slept through the night with no nightmares. My body felt relaxed and my mind was totally clear. It was then I noticed my fingers lightly moving up and down Preston's arm. He was still holding me the exact same way as when I fell asleep.

Smiling slightly, I closed my eyes and wondered what it would be like to wake up like this every morning in his arms. Of course, it was hard not to notice his hard-on pressed against me. I'd never been with anyone other than Trey. Sex with him was good, but I somehow got the feeling sex with Preston would be mind-blowing.

Opening my eyes, I gazed out the window and thought about Trey. I loved him, but I always knew I wasn't *in love* with him. No matter how hard I tried to be. And I knew he felt the same way about me. The only reason we were even together was because of TJ. It still hurt that he had cheated on me though; that he didn't feel like our marriage was worth the effort.

I pushed the thoughts from my mind and thought about Preston. His smile did things to me that I didn't want to admit to. His touch sent bolts of lightning racing through my body. No one had ever had that kind of effect on me. Not even Trey.

Then there was his laugh. Goodness, the man had a laugh that moved through my body like silk over your skin.

Of course, who could ignore that body of his. It was clear I couldn't. He was built perfectly. Not too big, but big enough to make a girl's body melt when he undressed in front of her. Abs that had you dreaming of running your tongue along them. An ass that... Oh dear God.

Stop thinking about his body, Harmony! I fought the urge to press back against him.

Could I risk opening my heart up to him? What if he hurt me? Was I even ready to let someone else into my heart when I still felt like I was still searching for myself? Something was missing... and I needed to find it before I could open my heart up to love again.

Pulling me in tighter against his body, Preston let out a sigh in his sleep. Yes. I could get very used to waking up every day like this.

Then a thought occurred to me. What if I'm never able to sleep again unless I'm in Preston's arms?

Shit. That could be bad. Or good.

Slowly lifting Preston's arm, I slipped out of bed. Looking around for my clothes, I saw a T-shirt of Preston's and picked it up and pulled it over my head. The T-shirt fell to my mid-thighs. I had no idea why I put it on. My pants and shirt were right there on the chair. Glancing back at Preston, my stomach fluttered. Oh dear, he was even handsome when he slept.

Shaking my head to clear my thoughts, I made my way out of the bedroom and downstairs. I was starving and prayed that Preston's aunt and uncle had left some food in the house before they took off for Ireland. I remembered the days of Jake living alone. He never had food.

Opening the refrigerator, I found eggs, bell peppers, mushrooms, salsa, and an onion—perfect ingredients for an omelet. Smiling, I thought back to the morning Preston made me breakfast and I'd had almost the same things.

Taking everything out, I searched for a skillet. Finding that, then olive oil, I got to work making Preston breakfast.

While the veggies sautéed in the olive oil, I glanced around the kitchen. Uncle John's house was adorable. It had a very nineteen-eighties feel to it though, with dark wood nearly everywhere and linoleum flooring. Little curtains that had daisies on them hung from the kitchen window above the sink. It felt cozy. I could see raising a small family in this house and being so incredibly happy.

When the clock on the mantel started dinging, I let out a small scream from the fright it gave me and quickly slammed my hands over my mouth. I sat there and counted the dings while I attempted to get my heart beating normally again.

Eight dings later and I stood there stunned. Preston and I had slept over twelve hours.

"Wow, I must have really needed the sleep."

Making my way back over to the stove, I began beating the eggs lightly. The air around me changed and the hairs on my body stood.

I stupidly prayed Preston hadn't gotten dressed. Silly girl.

"How did you sleep, Harmony?"

God I loved the way my name rolled off his lips. Glancing over my shoulder causally, I went to talk but nearly choked on my own spit.

Preston stood before me in nothing but jogging pants that barely hugged his hips. There should be a law against guys this hot making old sweatpants look so damn sexy.

"Um—"

Tilting his head, Preston's eyes roamed over my body. "Could you not find your clothes this morning?"

Lord, help me, he has a sexy-as-hell morning voice.

Giving him a slight smile, I repeated the only word that seemed to be able to come from my lips. "Um—"

Pushing his hand through his hair, Preston walked into the kitchen and over to the coffeemaker. His back was toward me and the way his muscles moved when he moved was beyond hot. And his ass—damn it looked good in those sweatpants. All I could do was stand there and stare. As if I had never seen a male body before. In my defense, I'd never seen a body so chiseled. He was perfect in every way. Rolling my eyes as I bit down on my lips, I pushed down the moan I wanted to let out.

He glanced back at me, and my eyes snapped up to his eyes. "Want some?"

I sure as hell do. I shook my head to clear my thoughts. "No, thanks. I don't drink coffee."

Preston jerked his head back and placed his hand over his chest. "What? You don't drink coffee? What is wrong with you?"

Letting out a nervous chuckle, I got back to making the omelet and ignored what my body was doing around him. It's not a big deal that there is a sexier-than-hell firefighter standing in the kitchen with you. Never mind he's half naked... and his ass looks *really* good in those old sweats. None of that matters. Focus. Focus. Focus.

"What?"

Turning to Preston, I asked, "What?"

Laughing he asked, "Why are you saying focus over and over?"

"I am?"

Preston walked closer to me as I stood my ground. Just friends. That's all Preston was. A friend.

Stopping right in front of me, I tried to give him a smile but I was afraid it would come out more as a moan. "You look awfully good in my T-shirt."

Oh God. I forgot I was half naked too. Pressing my lips together, I shrugged. "I guess I just wanted to still be wrapped up in—"

Preston reached up and rolled a piece of my hair around his finger as he asked in a whispered voice, "Wrapped up in what?"

Swallowing hard, I was about to say "you" when the doorbell rang ,and I jumped and took a step back. My heart pounded in my chest, and I held my breath. Closing his eyes, Preston turned and headed to the front door.

Letting out the breath I'd been holding, my shoulders dropped, and I leaned against the counter to get my wits about me. "Holy hell, what is he doing to me?" I whispered as I heard Preston talking to someone.

I turned and looked at the almost dried up eggs and turned off the stove. Focusing on looking for plates, I froze when I heard a female voice.

I'd only met her once, but I would never forget Sherry's voice.

"Don't tell me we don't have anything to talk about, Preston. You moved out. I had to find out from Sharp that you were here. Why did you leave our place?"

Preston let out a frustrated moan. "It wasn't our place, Sherry. It was mine. I left because I'm moving on and leaving the past in the past. What does it matter anyway, you moved in with whatever his name is."

Not really knowing what to do, I quickly found the plates and dished up the omelet while Preston talked to Sherry.

"I need a favor, Preston. I haven't told my parents that we broke up, and Daddy is having a holiday party on Martha's Vineyard in two weeks. I need you to come with me."

Preston laughed. "Why can't your new boyfriend go with you?"

"You know my father, Preston. He will not be expecting a new boyfriend, he will be expecting you."

"Sherry, you are so full of shit I can smell it from across the room."

Pressing my lips together tightly to keep from laughing, I took both plates and made my way out to the small dining room that was off the living room. I was pretty sure Preston and Sherry were still in the living room.

Rounding the corner, I walked to the table and set the plates down.

Letting out a frustrated sigh, Sherry said, "Fine. Daddy needs an endorsement from the Boston Fire Department and if his daughter shows up with a firefighter boyfriend, then—"

Clearing my throat, I leaned against the table. Sherry spun around and stared at me with her mouth hanging open.

"Breakfast is ready," I said with a smile. The smile that spread across Preston's face caused me to smile bigger.

"Harmony? What are you doing here?" Sherry's eyes moved over my body as her mouth dropped open. Spinning around on her heels, Sherry looked at Preston. "Are you *sleeping* with her?"

Preston looked between Sherry and me as he walked over to me. Pulling me into his arms he winked at me and said, "Yes, Sherry. Harmony and I have slept together."

Smiling like a kid in a candy store, I said, "Your eggs are getting cold." I wasn't sure why this tickled me so much. I knew what Preston had meant. We had slept together, twice now.

Letting go of me, Preston pulled out a seat and motioned for me to sit down. Sitting down, Preston pushed my chair in and leaned down and pressed his lips against my neck under my ear. "Thank you."

And just like that, he was gone and I was left breathless again. Picking up my fork, I stabbed my eggs and started to eat while Preston showed Sherry out. Before she left, she got the last word in. "I hope the two of you are happy living in this tiny little shithole of a house with your stupid paycheck to paycheck job."

My mouth dropped open and I stood up, ready to lay into her ass, but Preston slammed the door in her face.

"Oh my gosh. How dare she insult us like that!"

Laughing, Preston walked up to the table, sat down, and began eating his omelet. "She didn't really, Harmony, because this isn't our house, and we aren't really sleeping together."

Chewing on my lip, I slowly sat down. "Your job is more than what she makes it out to be, Preston. I hope you know that."

Giving me a smile that about melted my panties right off, he simply said, "I know it is."

Preston and I ate in silence. Standing, he took his plate and mine and brought them into the kitchen. "Let me do the dishes really quick and I'll take you home if you want."

I made my way into the kitchen. Preston moved about filling up the sink with water and soap while I leaned against the counter and watched his every move.

Turning toward me, Preston leaned against the counter and looked at me. My chest grew tighter as I worked up the nerve to say what I wanted to say.

Letting out a nervous chuckle, I said, "You're going to think I'm crazy for saying what I'm about to say."

"Try me," Preston said with a crooked smile that pulled on my heart.

"Last night was the first night since you stayed with me a few weeks ago, that I haven't had any nightmares.

I was relaxed, and I felt…" I shook my head and looked away as I whispered, "I felt safe."

"What do you mean safe?"

Shrugging my shoulders, I looked back at Preston as our eyes met. "I don't know if safe is the right word. Relaxed, comfortable, at ease maybe? All I know is I needed you to be there for me to feel that way, and I'm afraid to be alone, Preston, and that is not like me. I don't know what's happening but—" My voice cracked as the threat of more stupid tears started to build up. "I never used to be so damn weak."

Preston walked up to me and placed his hands on the sides of my face. "Come home with me for Thanksgiving. I'm leaving today and staying until Friday."

My eyes widened and my chest felt warm and tight. "You mean to your parents'? For Thanksgiving? Can you do that, can you just bring someone home like that without asking them first?"

Smiling, he said, "Yes. My mother would love to have you there. She's been dying to teach someone other than my baby sister all her recipes."

Looking down I thought about it. "Well, Jake invited me over to Sandy's parents' but I didn't want to feel like a third wheel and all."

Preston's thumb moved across my cheek and the trail of fire he was making with each movement was causing something deep down inside my stomach to pull and tug even more than before.

"Besides, you said you needed me near you to sleep. Country air, me close by you at night, what makes for a better recipe for sleep than that?"

The look in Preston's eyes was amazing. He seemed excited at the idea of me spending Thanksgiving with him. My head was telling me no, but my heart and my betraying body were screaming yes.

"Okay," I whispered.

Preston smiled and before I knew it, I was in his arms as he spun me around. Setting me down he turned me away from him and hit my ass as he said, "Now go get dressed because I'm only human and you're driving me fucking mad wearing my T-shirt."

Quickly making my way back upstairs, I stripped out of Preston's T-shirt the moment I walked into his room. Glancing at the bed I couldn't help but smile. Placing my hands on my stomach to calm the butterflies, I turned to grab my clothes when I decided I needed to take a shower. I could hear Preston on the phone downstairs talking to what sounded like his mother. Scooping up my clothes, I headed into the bathroom. Turning the shower on to hot, I removed my bra and panties and stepped inside the shower. The water felt like heaven as it poured over my body.

Now if only Preston would join me, everything would be perfect. No! Stop thinking that way, Harmony. Ugh. He was going to be the death of me.

Looking around, I saw a bottle of men's soap. Picking it up, I inhaled deeply, letting the smell invade my nose. "Preston," I said with a smile on my face.

"Yeah?"

The moment I heard his voice I froze. *What the hell? Is he in the bathroom?*

"Um, are you in here?"

"Yes, ma'am."

Dropping my mouth open, I stepped as far back in the tub as I could. "W-why are you in here?"

Laughing, he asked, "Why are you in here?"

"I'm taking a shower, Preston!"

"Well, I'm brushing my teeth, Harmony."

Not moving an inch I stood there and listened.

"Man, you sure are a quiet bather. Are you almost done? I want to jump in."

Placing my fisted hand to my mouth, I attempted to calm my breathing down. *Should I tell him to join me?*

No. No. Focus, Harmony!

"With me? You want to jump in here with me?"

Silence.

"Preston?" I slowly asked.

"Are you inviting me in there with you?"

"No!" I practically screamed. Quickly grabbing the soap, I poured some in my hand and frantically washed my body. My hair would just have to wait.

Turning off the shower, I stood there. Pulling the shower curtain back a bit, I peeked out. Preston was leaning against the sink wearing nothing but a towel. Pulling the shower curtain back quickly, I sucked in a breath of air and heard the jerk chuckle.

"Um, would you mind stepping out so I can get out of the shower?"

"How about if I just turn around?"

That bastard. I could hear the smile in his voice. "If you turn around, you'll be looking in the mirror... at me."

"Okay, if that's what you want."

Letting out a frustrated moan, I reached for the towel that was hanging up and dried off quickly. Wrapping it around my body, I pushed the shower curtain open. Preston's smile dropped and his eyes turned dark as he took in the sight of me in nothing but the towel.

It was hard as hell holding back my satisfied smile. I had to admit, the way he was looking at me made me feel sexy. Trey never looked at me the way Preston was looking at me this very moment. I felt empowered.

Tilting my head, I motioned for him to get in the shower as I walked toward the bathroom door. "It's all yours," I said with a purr in my voice.

Pushing off the counter, Preston turned and reached into the shower, turning it back on. Before stepping in he dropped his towel. I let out a gasp as I looked at his perfectly fit body and tight ass.

"God help me," I whispered as I grabbed my clothes and practically ran out of the bathroom.

Chapter
FOURTEEN

TAKING IT SLOW

Preston

AFTER STOPPING BY HARMONY'S PLACE so she could pack a small bag, we headed out of Boston and to my parents' house.

"So you grew up out here, huh?" Harmony asked as a few curls whipped around her face. She had insisted we drive with the windows down. It was an unusually warm day for November in New England. Sixty-five degrees and Harmony acted like it was a heat wave.

Sticking her hand out the window she took everything in while she wore a smile.

"Yes I did."

"Did you like growing up in a small town?"

Letting out a laugh, I nodded. "Yeah. There wasn't a whole lot to do so we got in trouble a lot."

Smiling, she kept her eyes on me as she asked, "What kind of trouble?"

Taking a quick peak at her, I shook my head. "Oh no. You'll pump me for information, then my parents will pump you for any dirt that you have on me. This is a no-win situation for me."

Laughing, Harmony dropped her head back against the headrest of the car. "I promise not to divulge any stories that you tell me."

Reaching my hand over to her, I held out my pinky. "Pinky swear?"

Giggling, Harmony wrapped her pinky around mine. Shit. I don't think I'll ever get used to the way her touch made my chest tighten or my stomach drop. I've never had that happen with any girl I've ever dated.

"I pinky swear."

Taking in a deep breath, I slowly blew it out. "Well, once we cut the tail off of a dead skunk and threw it under the seats of the school bus."

"Gross! That had to have smelled terrible."

Smiling, I nodded my head. "Yep. It did. It was my brother Weston's idea. We all got kicked off the bus for the rest of the year. My mother was pissed because she had to take us to school and pick us up after if we couldn't catch a ride."

Shaking her head, Harmony laughed. "Tell me another one."

I loved seeing Harmony smile and loved it even more when she laughed. She seemed so relaxed and carefree.

Like an almost twenty-one-year-old should act. Her eyes were beginning to get the light back in them, and I was surprised by how much I wanted to be the one to make that happen.

"Let's see. There was the time I talked my brother Finn into scaling down the wall of an old well."

Harmony sat up. "You did not!"

Laughing, I nodded my head. "Yep. We tied a rope around him, and Wes and I eased him down into the well."

"Preston, what if it would have collapsed?"

Shrugging my shoulders, I said, "I don't know. I guess we would have dealt with it. It was pretty stupid thinking back on it."

Punching my shoulder, Harmony said, "Ya think? My gosh, your poor mother. You boys must have worried her sick."

Thinking back to all the shit my brothers and I did; we probably were the reason our mother went gray early.

Pulling down the driveway to the house, I noticed Harmony had been rubbing her hands up and down her pant legs.

"Are you nervous?"

Nodding her head, she turned to me with the sweetest smile I'd ever seen. "I know it's stupid. I've never been over to any other family for their holiday dinner. Well, besides Trey's family. Before Trey, I usually spent the holidays with Berti."

Pulling up and parking behind my father's truck, I turned to her and asked, "Who's Berti?"

"Our maid. She was more like my mother than my own mother."

My heart physically hurt for Harmony. "You spent the holidays with the maid?"

Nodding her head, she whispered, "Yep." Then she smiled. "Well, when Jake was still home he would take me somewhere to eat. He had a credit card in my parents' name so he would take Berti and me out to eat. It was fun. Once he left for college, I was alone. Until I met Trey." Harmony glanced out the window and stared like she was in deep thought. "Sometimes I wonder if Trey wasn't just a substitute for Jake. Someone who was there for me when I needed them." Looking back at me, she gave me a weak smile. "That's terrible to say, isn't it?"

"Did you not love him?"

Her eyes lost that light and they turned dark and sad again as she chewed on her lip. "I loved him, but I wasn't in love with him, if that makes sense. I know he felt the same." Letting out a humorless laugh, she shook her head. "He cheated on me, so yeah, I'm not even sure he loved me at all."

Reaching over, I took Harmony's hand in mine. "He loved you, Harmony."

Smiling weakly, her eyes filled with tears. "We only got married because of TJ. We actually had broken up before I found out I was pregnant. I knew Trey wasn't the one, and with us going off to college I wanted to start fresh."

A tear slowly made its way down her face. "I feel so guilty, Preston."

Reaching over, I wiped her tear away. "Why?"

There was a knock on my window and Harmony and I both jumped. Quickly wiping away her tears,

Harmony smiled as she put up her guard to protect herself. She quickly opened the car door.

Angie was standing there jumping around like a nut. The moment Harmony stepped out of the car, Angie was running over to her.

"Oh my gosh! Another girl! You have no idea how happy I am!"

Grabbing Harmony's hand, Angie dragged Harmony into the house. Glancing over her shoulder at me, Harmony gave me a frightened expression as I laughed and gave her a reassuring smile. "I'll get the bags!" I called out.

Turning, I saw my mother walking toward me. "Hey, baby boy," she said as she kissed my cheek. "That looked like a pretty deep conversation your sister busted into."

Inhaling a deep breath, I smiled and shrugged. "When are Finn and Wes getting here?"

Narrowing her eyes at me, my mother smiled. "Smooth change of subject."

"I learned from the best," I said as I grabbed the bags and tried to make sense of everything. The emotions running through my mind, the feelings racing through my heart, and the way my body felt whenever Harmony touched it. It was all so damn confusing.

"Harmony's been through a lot, Mom, and she's still so young. I'm just trying to be patient with things. Take it slow, but—"

Kicking the car door shut, I stood in front of my mother ready to spill my guts.

"But you want more than friendship, and you're not sure how Harmony feels?"

My mouth dropped open as I barely shook my head. "How do you do that?"

Shrugging her shoulders, she gave me a wink. "It's a gift."

Wrapping her arm around my waist, we made our way toward the house. "Patience is the key, Preston."

Nodding my head, I said, "I'm trying, Mom. I really am."

Stopping before we reached the front door, my mother stood in front of me. "My biggest piece of advice to you Preston is to always follow your heart. Sometimes that is harder to do because our mind wants so desperately to lead the way." Placing her hand on my chest she smiled sweetly. "Your heart will never lead you down the wrong path, Preston. You just have to learn to listen to it."

Leaning over, I kissed her on the cheek. "How did you become so wise?"

She patted my chest. "Experience, my dear boy. Experience."

Sitting at the kitchen table, I watched as my mother and Harmony peeled potatoes at the sink. Angie stood next to Harmony as she rolled out a piecrust and talked about how amazing the winter formal dance was that she went to this past weekend. Harmony's laugh moved through my body and filled it with pure happiness. Almost as if I needed her near me just so I could breathe.

"So what kind of nurse do you want to be, Harmony?" Angie asked. '

"Neonatal nurse, I think," Harmony said as she set a peeled potato on the cutting board.

My mother turned to Harmony and smiled. "My best friend is a neonatal nurse."

Harmony's posture perked up. "Really?"

Nodding her head my mother said, "Yep, we met in nursing school."

Harmony's mouth dropped open. "You're a nurse?"

Laughing, my mom shook her head. "I was a nurse. Operating room."

"Oh wow! I didn't know that."

Nodding her head, my mother turned to me and said, "That was before kids. Once I had my children, they became my everything."

Harmony nodded her head. "I bet." Her voice sounded sad, yet I thought there was a bit of happiness trying to make its way out.

Setting the last potato down, Harmony turned to me and smiled. "Do you want to take a walk?" I asked.

"Oh Harmony, you'll love it here! Preston, be sure to take her to our secret spot!" Angie said as she dropped the rolling pin and frantically texted someone. My sister's attention span was short to say the least.

Harmony pushed off the counter and turned to my mom. "Did you need me to do anything else?"

Waving her hand, my mother shook her head. "Go have fun, sweetheart."

Standing, I motioned for Harmony to go first as I grabbed our jackets in case we needed them. As we walked out the back door Harmony took in a deep breath. "The air is so… clean!"

I agreed. "Yeah, it is. I love coming home to Charlton. Something about being out of the city is refreshing."

As we walked along, Harmony reached down for my hand and my stomach did about ten flips. *Does she even realize how much her touch affects me?* Things felt natural with Harmony and I was almost positive she felt the same way.

"Would you want to live somewhere like this? I mean, you know, when you decide to settle down and raise a family?" she asked.

Smiling, I looked straight ahead. "I couldn't wait to get out of here when I was younger. Now, all I want to do is come back." Peeking over to Harmony, I couldn't help but notice she was walking with a huge smile on her face. Looking straight ahead again, I continued talking. "So, yeah, I could totally see myself living on a piece of land here, building a house on it, and raising a family."

Bumping her shoulder with mine, I asked. "What about you?"

"Oh yeah. I could totally see myself living in the country. Trey wanted to live in the city. I wanted to move further out so that TJ could have a place to run and play. I grew up close to Boston, but we still had about seven acres of land. My father had to be close to Boston. I think my mother would have rather been in a four-story row house on Comm Ave. But for me though, I loved it. I would find myself walking around the gardens for hours just lost in thought."

We walked along the trail for a few minutes in silence. "How many acres do your parents have?"

"Twenty. My father lucked out and got it for a great price. Built the house for my mother with his brothers and father. My mom says we will have to take her out of the house in a pine box."

Laughing, Harmony stopped and looked over toward a large tree house that Finn and Wes had built years ago. "Is that a tree house?" Harmony asked as she made her way over to it.

My mind was flooded with images of Harmony sitting on a porch in a rocking chair, rocking a baby. Shaking my head to clear my thoughts, I followed. "Yeah, this is Angie's secret place she was talking about."

Harmony looked at me confused. "But it's right here along the path. How is that secret?"

Blowing out my cheeks, I released it and shrugged. "It's Angie, I don't question her anymore."

Covering her mouth, Harmony giggled. "Is that a swing?" she asked in an excited voice.

"Sure is."

The next thing I knew, Harmony was sitting on the swing motioning for me to push her.

Walking behind her, I grabbed the chains and pulled back and let go. Harmony dropped her head back and closed her eyes as she smiled. "I feel like I'm flying." Laughing, she said, "It's freeing."

Gently pushing her so she could swing, I asked, "So why did you buy a condo on Comm Ave. if you want to be outside of Boston?"

Her smile faded slightly as she brought her head up. "Seemed like the right thing to do at the time. Closer to school and work and something different."

Nodding my head, even though she couldn't see me, I kept pushing. "Are you going to buy a place in Boston close to the fire station?" Harmony asked.

"Probably. I haven't thought too much about it, to be honest. I'm not really sure where I see my future going right now."

Harmony dropped her head back again as I continued to push her. "Harmony, may I ask you something?"

"Of course you can."

Taking in a deep breath, I slowly blew it out. "Earlier, in the car you said you felt guilty. What do you feel guilty about?"

Harmony snapped her head forward and dragged her feet on the ground to slow down. She came to a stop and slowly stood up and turned to me.

Her eyes caught mine and all I saw was confusion and something that looked like fear. Looking down she whispered, "You."

Wrinkling my brow, I pulled my head back. "Me? What about me makes you feel guilty?"

Harmony looked back up and into my eyes. "It's how I feel about you, Preston. That's what makes me feel guilty."

My heart felt like it jumped into my throat. I was scared as hell for what she was about to say next. "H-how do you feel about me?"

A smile slowly started to form on the corners of her mouth as she dug her teeth into her bottom lip. Taking a step closer to me, Harmony placed her hands on my chest and slowly took in a deep breath as she closed her eyes. "I've never experienced these feelings I have toward you before. They thrill me and scare me at the same time."

My heart slammed in my chest, and I fought like hell to keep my grin from growing into a full smile. "And that makes you feel guilty?"

Nodding her head, her forehead dropped to my chest and I wrapped my arms around her. "With the holidays upon us, I miss TJ so much, but you make me feel so alive and sometimes I forget about him, and that makes me feel guilty. I'm scared, Preston."

Holding her tighter, I placed my chin on top of her head and closed my eyes. "Me too, Harmony."

Pulling her head back, her blue eyes captured my green eyes. "You do?"

Nodding my head, I placed my hand on the side of her face. "The feelings I have for you," I let out a small chuckle. "This is all new to me. I've never felt this way about anyone ever."

"What about Sherry?" Harmony asked in a whispered voice.

Smiling, I leaned down and brought my lips to hers as both of our breathing increased. Stopping short of her lips, I spoke. "My body feels so alive when I'm with you, Harmony. My heart feels… complete. I've never felt that before."

Closing her eyes, she whispered, "Preston."

Brushing my lips across hers, I kissed her gently. Letting out a soft moan that vibrated through my whole body, Harmony opened her mouth to me as I slipped my tongue in and moaned myself. She tasted like heaven. About to deepen the kiss, I heard someone clear his throat. Pulling back quickly, Harmony took a step back as she looked into my eyes. Her chest was heaving up and down as I attempted to get my heart rate back under control.

Her eyes were on fire and I wanted nothing more than to pull her back to me and finish what we started.

"Preston?"

Turning my head, I saw my older brother, Wes. Smiling, I quickly made my way over to him. I hadn't seen him since last Thanksgiving.

"Jesus H. Christ, look at you, Wes. Is that an expensive suit?" I said as I approached him. Laughing, he grabbed me and pulled me into a quick hug. Pushing me back at arm's length, he looked me up and down.

"Shit, I always knew you were going to be the better-looking brother."

Pushing him on his chest, I laughed. Turning, I motioned for Harmony. Smiling, she walked up and stood next to me. "Wes, I'd like for you to meet Harmony. Harmony, this is my brother Weston, but we call him Wes."

Placing her hand out to shake his, Harmony said, "It's a pleasure to meet you, Wes. Preston has spoken very highly of you."

Wes laughed and shook his head. "Really, that is a pleasant surprise. Usually he has some smart-ass things to say about me."

Looking between Harmony and me, Wes glanced back to me and raised an eyebrow and said, "So, I interrupted something when I walked up."

"It's not what you think. Harmony and I..." Turning to Harmony, I looked at her as I pinched my eyebrows together. What were we now? I just kissed her. We admitted that we both had feelings for each other. We had for sure moved past the friend status.

Giving me the sweetest smile, Harmony reached for my hand. "Preston and I are friends."

Forcing a smile, I turned back to Wes. I wasn't sure if I liked the fact that Harmony still thought of us as just friends. I certainly thought differently after the kiss we shared.

Holding up his hands, Wes grinned from ear to ear. "Hey, if that's what you want to call it. Finn is about ten minutes out if you guys want to head back up to the house."

"Sounds good!" Harmony said as she dropped my hand and headed back toward the house.

What in the hell? Harmony acted like she wanted to be as far away from me as possible and all I wanted to do was pull her into my arms and feel her lips against mine again.

Standing there like an idiot, I watched Harmony taking off toward the house. Wes placed his hand on my shoulder and gave it a slight squeeze.

"Dude, don't overthink it. I saw the way she was looking at you."

Taking in a deep breath, I let it out as I shook my head and said, "Yeah," as I tried to push the uneasiness I suddenly felt away.

Chapter
FIFTEEN

MORE THAN THANKFUL

Harmony

WALKING BACK TOWARD PRESTON'S PARENTS' house I tried to push away the look of disappointment in Preston's eyes when I had told his brother we were friends. Why had I said that? Why?

That kiss. Good lord that kiss was amazing. I can't even begin to imagine how far things would have gone had Wes not showed up.

Closing my eyes, I took in a deep breath and blew it out as I opened my eyes and put a smile on my face. Turning around, I saw that Preston and his brother were a good ways behind me talking. I didn't mean to take off like I had. I needed to put some space between us. We both just admitted to having feelings for each other and I needed to think things through.

Hearing someone drive down the driveway, I turned to look and saw a truck pulling up. Honking the horn, the truck stopped, and I saw Angie running out of the house.

A tall, dark-haired guy got out of the truck and caught Angie in his arms while he spun her around. Smiling, I was guessing it was Finn. As I drew closer, I noticed he was also a good-looking guy. *Man, this family has good genes.*

Stopping a few feet back, I watched Angie and Jenn greet Finn.

Wes and Preston walked by me and made their way over to Finn. The love in this family was amazing. My heart broke slightly as I realized the only person I had was Jake. Looking away, I stared off into the pasture as I chewed on my lower lip.

"Harmony! Come meet Finn," Angie called out.

Glancing back to the group, I smiled as Preston walked up with his brother. Finn gave me a quick onceover and smiled. His smile was almost as amazing as Preston's.

"Finn, this is Harmony, a *friend* of mine. She's spending Thanksgiving with us."

My smile faltered briefly as I peeked at Preston and saw nothing but coldness in his eyes.

Turning my attention back on Finn, I shook his hand and tried not to let my voice crack as I talked. "It's a pleasure to meet you, Finn."

"The pleasure is all mine. I see my baby brother's taste in *friends* has improved."

Everyone laughed as I let out a nervous chuckle. Preston smiled as he walked around me and headed into the house. Turning, I wanted to call out to him but I was frozen. I knew why he was upset with me. The look in his eyes spoke more than words ever could and I couldn't blame him. One moment I was hot, the next cold. All but dismissed the kiss and the feelings we had admitted for one another.

Placing her hand on my arm, Angie led me back into the house. "Tonight is game night! You better keep your eyes open; the boys like to cheat."

Giving her a slight chuckle, I said, "Got it."

The rest of the afternoon I spent with Angie and Jenn as we finished up some things for Thanksgiving dinner tomorrow. I hadn't seen Preston since dinner. As soon as he and the boys cleared the table, he'd excused himself along with Finn and they disappeared.

Drying off the last bowl, I stood and stared out the kitchen window.

"Harmony, would you like a cup of tea, darling? We can go sit on the back porch and talk." Jenn handed me a cup of tea as she mouthed *peace and quiet.*

"No way, Mom. It's game night! I'll go find the boys."

Rolling her eyes, Jenn shrugged. "I tried."

Giggling, I shook my head and said, "Even though Angie's just a few years younger than me, I feel like she has more energy than the Energizer Bunny."

"You have no idea," Jenn said as she shook her head. Standing she said, "Let's make our way to the dining room. Once the boys realize what game Angie wants to play the peace will be over."

Smiling, I took my cup of tea and followed Jenn to the formal dining room. I loved Preston's childhood home. It wasn't anything extravagant, yet it was classy and comfortable. It was a typically New England home with clapboard siding along with brick. The inside had wood floors throughout and warm, soft colors like beige and blue. I felt at home. Pictures of their family were spread throughout the house. There was a fireplace in the main living room and the formal dining room. Walking over to the fireplace in the dining room, I picked up a picture of Preston.

"I see his charming, good looks started early," I softly said.

"Oh lord, the girls that chased after that boy. His older brothers used to get so mad. The three of them could be standing there, and the girls would always approach Preston first," Jenn said with a lighthearted laugh. "I think it was the boyish good looks, and he certainly knew how to charm the ladies."

Smiling, I placed the photo down and then picked up what looked like Preston's senior picture. Good lord, he had only grown better-looking with age.

Running my fingers over the picture it felt as if my lips were tingling. Placing my fingers on my lips, I could almost feel Preston's lips on mine.

Hot breath hit my neck followed by, "Whatcha thinking about?"

Jumping, I quickly placed the picture back on the mantel. Preston stood there staring at me with an expression I couldn't read. He wasn't smiling, yet his eyes looked happy.

Opening my mouth to talk, I was startled when Angie began clapping her hands and talking.

"Okay! It's family game night. Monopoly is the game of choice."

Oh crap. I hate Monopoly.

Chewing on my lip, I whispered to Preston, "Can we vote on another game?"

"What's wrong, Harmony, Monopoly not your thing?"

Smiling, I shook my head. "Not really."

The next thing I knew we were all sitting around the table laughing our asses off as two hours passed by in a flash. Finn and Angie *really* got into the game and were in a dead heat for taking over the entire board. Jenn and I had long since dropped out of the game. Preston and Wes seemed to be making sideline deals against Angie.

"Well, look at this sight." The booming voice came from behind me and caused me to turn around.

My mouth dropped open as I looked at an older version of Preston. "Oh wow," I whispered.

Jenn leaned over and said, "I know. Now you see where Preston and the boys get their looks. He's been gone for two days helping a friend with a building project. Let me go say hello."

Blushing, I smiled at Jenn. Giving me a playful wink, she stood and walked over to her husband. He wrapped her up in his arms and lifted her off the ground as he kissed her. The act was so intimate that I turned my head, only to find Preston looking at me. Wes asked him something, causing him to pull his eyes away from me. My heart raced for some reason and I felt my body heat up.

Turning back to Jenn and Mr. Ward, I watched as they smiled and spoke softly to one another. So this was what love looked like. A true honest-to-God love. I wanted that desperately.

I peeked back over to Preston. My breath caught in my throat as I watched him throw his head back and laugh at something his brother had said.

It was in that moment I realized I wanted all of this, and I didn't want it with anyone else but Preston.

Jenn's voice pulled my gaze off Preston.

"Preston, would you like to be a good son and introduce Harmony to your father?" Jenn said as she motioned over to me. Preston jumped up and smiled.

Walking over to his father, they shook hands and Mr. Ward pulled Preston in for a quick man hug. Preston turned back to me as I stood and made my way over to where the three of them were standing. As I drew closer, Mr. Ward let out a whistle as he held out his hand for me. Placing my hand in his, Preston's father brought it up and placed his lips gently on the back of my hand as I let out a nervous giggle.

"All right, Dad, that's enough. She's mine."

I drew in a breath as, I looked at Preston while he and his father exchanged laughs.

She's mine.

My heart felt like it plunged to the bottom of my stomach.

Preston turned to me and placed his hand on the small of my back. Goose bumps raced across my skin and my heart melted at the simple gesture.

"Dad, this is Harmony. Harmony, this is my father, Mike."

"It's a pleasure to meet you, Mr. Ward."

Waving his hand at me, Preston's father shook his head. "It's Mike, Harmony. Please call me Mike."

Nodding my head, I said, "Mike it is."

He gave me a satisfied head nod, looked past me and the next thing I knew, Finn and Weston were standing around their father.

Preston stepped closer to me and placed his lips near my ear. "You look tired."

Stay strong, Harmony. His smell is not knocking you out of your socks, his hot sexy voice is not penetrating into the very depths of your soul, and his stunning green eyes are not piercing yours and beckoning you to him.

Parting my lips open, I fought to find the words to speak.

Shaking my head, I whispered, "I'm not tired."

Raising an eyebrow, Preston tilted his head and then smiled.

"Yes! I told you she wasn't tired, Preston," Angie grabbed my hands and pulled me toward the stairs. "Come on, Harmony. We're changing."

Looking back at Preston, he was grinning as he shook his head. "Changing for what?" I asked as I watched Preston until Angie had pulled me all the way up the steps.

"We're going dancing! The club is eighteen and older so you and I can go. Although Preston told me your birthday is tomorrow." Putting her finger up to her mouth she said, "Don't worry, he made me promise not to tell my mother because you didn't want anyone to know."

Before I even had a chance to protest, I had tried on three different dresses before Angie settled on a teal blue cocktail dress. She went on and on about how the teal brought out the blue in my eyes.

"Holy shit. You have killer legs. Wait until my brother sees you in this dress. He's gonna jizz in his pants."

My mouth dropped open as I let out a strangled laugh. "You did not just say that!"

Throwing her head back, Angie began jumping. "You're gonna be twenty-one in a few hours, Harmony! Aren't you excited?"

Shrugging my shoulders, I said, "I guess I am. I haven't really been thinking about it."

"Well, we're gonna dance our asses off. When was the last time you went to a club?"

Scrunching my nose up, I said, "Um, maybe high school."

Angie froze, then slowly shook her head. "I promise you, Harmony, you're gonna be finding your groove tonight, and I don't mean just dancing. Did I mention Preston's room is in the attic? Far away from everyone and most importantly, my parents' bedroom. It's on the first floor."

Looking at Angie with a confused expression, I asked, "What does that have to do with anything?"

Rolling her eyes she spun me around and quickly pulled my hair up and put it in a French twist. Pulling a few strands down she looked at me in the mirror.

"Harmony, do you have any idea how beautiful you are?"

Blushing, I looked away. Turning me around to face her, Angie looked into my eyes. "You have no clue how much my brother is over the moon for you, do you?"

Biting on my lower lip, I smiled. "You think?"

"Oh honey, I don't think... I know. And after tonight, you won't have any questions about it, and you will totally understand my reference to his bedroom."

Angie ran over to the closet and slipped on a pair of red high heels. She handed me a pair of black heels as she smiled a naughty grin. Angie and I were exactly the same dress and shoe size. Slipping them on, I turned and looked at myself in the mirror. I didn't even recognize the woman standing in the mirror. Somewhere between getting pregnant, married, and losing a part of myself, I had become a woman.

Glancing over my shoulder, I watched Angie put on lipstick. Smiling, I looked back into the mirror. Up until a few hours ago I didn't know what I was thankful for but now I know exactly what I am thankful for. This entire day as well as this family I was quickly falling in love with.

Chapter
SIXTEEN

ALREADY FALLEN

Preston

S ITTING ON THE SOFA TALKING to my father, my
brothers and I all waited for Angie and Harmony.

"Don't stay out too late, tomorrow is Thanksgiving.
And keep an eye on your sister."

Finn laughed, "Dad, this is Angie we're talking
about. The last time we all went out to this club, Wes
almost beat the living shit out of some guy for looking
at Angie the wrong way. I think between the three of us,
we'll keep our eyes on her."

My mother sat down next to my father and reached for his hand. "Now boys, let the poor girl have fun. She's been feeling down the last few days since her boyfriend broke up with her."

Dad jerked his head to look at my mother. "Let her have fun? Hell no." Turning and pointing to each of us he said, "You watch her like a hawk."

Wes laughed and said, "Better not count on Preston for that, Dad."

Looking at Wes, I pulled my head back and was about to ask why when he continued talking.

"I'm thinking his eyes are going to be glued to someone else all night."

Looking toward the stairs, my mouth dropped open when I saw Harmony. She was dressed in a teal dress that fell to the middle of her thighs. Swallowing hard, my eyes moved over her body. She was laughing at something Angie was saying as they walked down the steps.

Motherfucker. She's gorgeous. How would I keep guys away from her when she looks like that?

The top part of the dress was covered in sparkly shit but the way her breasts looked in the dress had my dick growing painfully hard.

"Son, you might want to at least close your mouth while you stare at her. It's more polite."

Looking at my father, I whispered, "W-what?"

He chuckled. "You're staring at Harmony with your jaw down to the floor, Preston."

Standing up, Finn slapped me on the shoulder. "Damn dude, either you stand up and walk over to her or I'm going to."

Jumping up, I pushed Finn out of the way and made my way over to Angie and Harmony. Stopping in front of my sister, I smiled and said, "You look beautiful, Angie."

Beaming, she said, "Thank you, PJ."

Turning to Harmony, my hands began to shake and that damn fluttery shit was happening in my stomach again. Taking her hands in mine, my eyes captured hers. "Harmony, you look gorgeous."

Glancing around the room, she blushed and looked back at me. "I haven't been dressed up since…" Shaking her head, she let out a nervous chuckle. "Thank you, Preston. Angie picked out the dress."

"It's beautiful," I whispered.

My mother walked up and smiled as she pushed a curl to the side of Harmony's face. "Oh Harmony, you look stunning. That color makes your eyes stand out. Let me grab you a shawl, it's chilly out."

My mother quickly went to her room while my father lectured Angie about being safe. Walking back out, my mother wrapped a black shawl around Harmony's shoulders.

"Oh, thank you so much, Jenn."

Winking, she nodded her head.

Angie clapped her hands to get everyone's attention. "Okay, since Dad is putting a curfew on me—which I still say is so unfair since I'm eighteen, but whatever—we should probably head out."

"I'll drive," Wes said as he kissed my mother on the cheek, followed by Finn. I couldn't take my eyes off Harmony. Finn hit me in the chest and asked, "Are you guys driving separate?"

Nodding my head, I said, "Yeah. I think we will."

Taking Harmony's hand in mine, I kissed my mother on the cheek and glanced at my father. He was giving me a look that I couldn't really read. Raising his eyebrow he said, "Be careful, Preston."

Smiling slightly, I nodded and said, "Yes, sir." I knew there was a hidden meaning in that, and I knew he meant be careful with Harmony. Just how he wanted me to be careful was the question.

Walking out to my car, I opened the door and held Harmony's hand while she got in. Jesus H. Christ. Her legs. Why had I not noticed before what amazing legs she had?

Shutting the door, I turned to see my parents standing on the porch. My father was watching me intently as I walked around the front of the car. Stopping at the door, I asked, "Is everything okay, Dad?"

Smiling, he said, "Yes, Preston. Have fun this evening and watch your sister."

"Will do, sir."

Getting into the car, I started it up and followed Wes down the driveway.

Clearing her throat, Harmony looked at me. "You look handsome."

Glancing down, I had on dress slacks, a button-down shirt with the sleeves rolled up and a pair of dress shoes that I borrowed from my father since my mother said I couldn't wear my sneakers.

"Thanks, I'm afraid you're going to steal the show this evening though."

Laughing, she shook her head as I looked straight.

"I don't dress up often so it was kind of fun. Angie really gets into the whole dressing up thing. She said she just wore this dress for her winter formal."

Nodding, I said, "Ever since she was little she has been the princess who loves to get dolled up."

Smiling, Harmony let out a chuckle. "How far is the club?" she asked as she looked out the window. Glancing over to her legs again, I held back a moan.

"Ah... about thirty minutes. We used to always go to this place. It's eighteen and up, but in a couple hours, you'll be legal enough to get hammered."

Letting out a laugh, Harmony held up her hands. "Oh no. I've decided drinking and I do not go together."

My heart was beating so hard in my chest I was positive Harmony would be able to hear it.

"Preston? Is everything okay?" Harmony asked as she placed her hand on my arm, causing a jolt of energy to rip through my body.

"Yeah. I was just thinking, that's all."

Dropping her hand, Harmony talked about all the great recipes she got from my mother. Before I knew it we were pulling into the club and I was praying like hell some asshole didn't catch Harmony's eye. She might have admitted to having feelings for me, but I wasn't so sure she wanted to do anything about it. Walking toward the club, the bass from the club was booming and Harmony smiled a beautiful smile. "I haven't gone dancing since before I had TJ."

"Really? Well then you have some making up to do, princess."

Harmony's eyes lit up when I called her princess and I took note of it. "I should probably get on your dance card now, huh?"

Biting down on her lip, Harmony walked closer to me and placed both hands on my chest. "My dance card is already filled, Mr. Ward."

I swallowed hard as my heart tripped over itself. "It is?"

Nodding her head slowly she reached up on her toes and brushed her lips gently across mine. "Your name occupies all the spots; I hope you don't get tired of me."

Wrapping my arms around her, I pulled her into me as she let out a gasp as my hard dick pressed into her stomach. "I could never get tired of you, Ms. Banks."

Harmony's eyes glassed over with tears as she whispered, "Do you promise?"

Wrapping my hand around the back of her neck, I pressed our lips together and kissed her with as much passion as I could.

"Oh holy hell, dude! I thought you would at least be able to control yourself until after we got into the club," Finn yelled out.

"Don't mess up her hair, Preston!" Angie yelled out.

Harmony and I laughed as we pulled back from each other. "You ready to get your dance on?" I asked.

Nodding her head, she laced her arm around mine and we headed into the club. The bouncer looked at Harmony's license and smiled. "Three more hours, I'm going to give you a wrist band and stamp. Once it gets past midnight you can drink."

"Okay," Harmony said as she looked up at me and grinned.

Finding a way to a table, Finn clapped his hands and then pointed to Angie. "Behave, don't leave with anyone, don't take a drink from anyone, and check back in with one of us every hour. We'll all meet back here at one to see how everyone is feeling."

Angie held up her hand and said, "I see my friends, later big brothers." Turning to Harmony, she leaned over and whispered something that made Harmony's cheeks turn bright red.

Giving me a wink, Angie took off.

"What did she say?" I asked Harmony, who looked shocked as hell by whatever my sister had said to her.

"Um… nothing. It was ah… nothing at all."

Tilting my head, I gave Harmony an incredulous stare. Holding up her hands she laughed. "I swear, it was nothing."

"One drink, then we'll go dance. What do you want?" I asked as Harmony glanced around the club.

"Diet Coke."

Laughing, I said, "Seriously? You don't want a drink?"

"Preston, no! He told me I had to wait until midnight."

Good God this girl is too good to be true. Her innocence had to be one of the most attractive things about her. "Diet Coke it is."

After fighting the crowd at the bar and two really drunk girls trying to get my attention, I made my way back to Harmony who was sitting at the table talking to Wes. Setting her Diet Coke down on the table, I sat down next to her. Wes glanced at me, then back to Harmony. "Have you always wanted to be in nursing?"

Nodding her head, Harmony said, "Yeah. I think it all started when my older brother Jake decided he wanted to be a doctor. I didn't think I was smart enough for medical school, so I thought nursing would be a great pick."

Wes was about to ask something else when a brunette walked up and asked him to dance. Grabbing his bottle of beer, he got up, wrapped his arm around her waist and led her out to the dance floor.

Taking a quick look around the club, I saw Finn all up on a girl as they danced. Pointing to him, I said to Harmony, "I'd bet you a hundred bucks he's already told her he is a firefighter."

Laughing, Harmony took a sip of her soda. "It is rather sexy. The whole firefighter thing."

Lifting my eyebrows, I smiled. "Really? Well would you like to dance with one?"

Chewing on her lower lip, she asked, "Are you asking me to dance?"

Standing, I held out my hand. Placing her hand in mine, I pulled her up and prayed like hell she didn't notice how sweaty my hands were. I had no idea why I was so nervous. That's a lie. The more Harmony and I opened up to each other, the more nervous I became.

As we walked out to the dance floor I saw at least three guys eye-fucking her. Bringing her closer to me, I grabbed her hand and spun her out as she laughed. Pulling her back to me I kissed her quickly on the lips. "I want every asshole in this place to know you're mine."

Harmony's eyes darkened as she pushed her hand up into my hair and pulled my lips back down to hers. I wasn't sure how long we stood there and kissed. Someone bumped my arm, causing me to pull away. Turning, I looked at Finn who was laughing.

"Dude, the dance floor is meant for dancing, not kissing."

The song changed and "Beg For It" began playing. Harmony raised her eyebrow and said, "You wouldn't make me beg for it, would you, Mr. Ward?"

Pulling her to me, I placed my lips against her ear and said, "I think hearing you beg might be a major turn-on."

Harmony gave me a naughty smile and began dancing. *Holy shit.* Not only was she beautiful, but she could dance too.

I looked up and prayed for strength.

Harmony moved her hips in a sinful way as I smiled and moved right along with her. Turning around, Harmony pushed her ass into me as I grabbed her hips and closed my eyes while a moan slipped out.

Fucking hell. This girl is driving me mad with desire.

Turning back around, Harmony wrapped her arms around me as she kept moving against me. My hands moved over her body as we danced close together.

The song changed to Sam Hunt's "Make You Miss Me." Pulling Harmony into my arms, we slowed the dance down. I wasn't sure where all of this would lead, but I hoped like hell Harmony was on the same path as I was.

Her head rested on my chest as we danced. Pulling back some, she looked into my eyes. I quickly became aware of my heartbeat as the hairs on my arms raised. Harmony's eyes were laced with passion and fear. Placing my hand on the side of her face, I slowly stroked her soft skin with my thumb as her breathing quickened.

Placing her hand over mine, Harmony closed her eyes. "Don't let me push you away. Promise me you won't let me push you away."

My knees felt weak as my eyes searched her face. Opening her eyes, a single tear rolled down her face. I brushed it away as I said, "I promise you."

When the song finished, I walked Harmony back over to the table. "Do you want a drink?" I asked. She gave me a smile that quickly grew.

"Are you trying to loosen me up, Preston?"

Before pulling her chair out, I leaned over and gently kissed her as I whispered against her lips, "Trust me, princess, I have a much better idea of how I would loosen you up."

Harmony grabbed onto my arms as she appeared to steady herself. "I think I'll take that drink now."

Harmony and I had sat at the table for at least an hour simply talking. We mostly talked about my job and her schooling as she nursed the Bud Light I had set in front of her an hour ago.

Every now and then, Angie would make an appearance to check in. Wes had all but disappeared, and I was pretty sure he was hooking up with the girl he had been dancing with since we got here. Finn was standing at another table talking to about six women. Somehow I had a feeling he'd end up with at least two of them tonight, knowing Finn.

Angie came running over and hugged Harmony and said, "Happy twenty-first birthday, Harmony!"

Standing up, I reached for Harmony and pulled her up. "Let's dance, old lady."

Throwing her head back, Harmony walked out onto the dance floor as she moved her hips while she danced with Angie.

"Hands On Me" started playing and Harmony spun around and pointed to me. "Oh my God! I love this song!"

Placing my hands on her hips we began dancing pretty provocatively, grinding our bodies together. My hands were all over her as Harmony licked her lips and ran her hands over her own body.

Fuck me. Hottest damn thing I've ever seen is Harmony rubbing her hands over her own body. I'm gonna have to take a cold shower when I get home.

Turning, she backed up against me and tilted her head, exposing her neck to me. My lips were all over her skin as she ran her hand through my hair.

When the song changed to a slower song, Harmony melted into my arms. Holding her close to me, we danced in silence. I quickly learned that one of Harmony's favorite things to do was bury her face in my chest. I was pretty sure I enjoyed it as much as she did.

Looking up at me, I saw something change in Harmony's eyes. It was as if she was letting down the wall she had built to guard her heart. I tucked some strands of her hair back and looked deeply into her eyes. I decided to take my mother's advice and listen to my heart for once.

I drew in a deep breath and slowly let it out. Ignoring the way my heart thundered in my ears, I softly said, "Harmony, I'm falling in love with you."

The smile that spread across her face left me breathless. Her cheeks began to glow as she closed her eyes. Pressing her lips tightly together, she opened her eyes. When I saw the tears I wasn't sure what I should do. Reaching up, I placed both my hands on her face as I leaned over and kissed them away.

"Please talk to me, princess. Don't disappear on me."

Shaking her head, Harmony's eyes lit up as she said, "Preston, I'm falling in love with you, too. I… I'm pretty sure I've already fallen."

My heart knocked against my chest and a rush of emotions I'd never experienced before rushed through my entire body.

"Let me make you mine, Harmony," I whispered against her ear.

She only needed to say one word back to me, and I prayed like hell she would.

Chapter
SEVENTEEN

IT WAS ALWAYS YOU

Harmony

THE MOMENT HE SPOKE THE words, my heart grew larger in my chest and I felt such a sense of happiness. I'd only experienced that once before in my life and that was when TJ was born. Preston was falling in love with me. Preston wanted to make me his.

I was excited and scared all at once. I'd never been with anyone else but Trey.

Damn it. Why weren't we back in Boston? I'd be begging Preston to take me home and make love to me.

Preston was about to say something when Angie walked up to us. "Preston? I'm not feeling so great."

He dropped his hands from my face and took a hold of Angie. Concern laced his eyes as he looked her up and down. "What's wrong? Did something happen?"

"No, no, it's nothing like that. I think I'm just tired and it hit me. Finn is wrapped up in trying to hook up with someone and Wes... hell, I think Wes left with someone."

Attempting to hide my smile, I glanced over to Finn. He was for sure working it.

"Yeah, Wes told me he was leaving with Mandy."

"Mandy? His girlfriend from high school?" Angie asked.

Chuckling, Preston nodded his head. "Yep. I didn't recognize her but that's who he was indeed with."

"Gag me," Angie said as she turned and headed over to Finn. Preston grabbed my hand and led me over to the table where I grabbed my shawl and Angie's. She must have been telling Finn we were leaving because he looked over and gave Preston a thumbs-up, then made some motion with his hand to Preston as Angie walked back over to us.

"Bastard," Preston mumbled as he placed his hand on my lower back. The butterflies in my stomach took off at the simple gesture. "Let's go."

Glancing back over my shoulder, I noticed Finn had his arm draped around one of the girls and they appeared to be leaving as well. Turning back to Preston, I asked him, "What was that hand gesture he did to you?"

Shaking his head, Preston said, "It was nothing."

"It was something. What was it?"

Preston looked at me and smiled. "When we were in high school and used to go out, we had a signal we would give each other if we were… um… if we were…"

"If they were about to get lucky," Angie busted out.

Pressing my lips together, I held back my smile. "Oh, I see. So did that mean Finn was getting lucky?"

Preston smirked. "Yeah, Finn is for sure getting lucky."

Looking straight ahead, I said, "Huh. I guess Wes gave you the same signal."

"Yeah, he did when he said he was leaving and for me to make sure Angie got home okay."

Angie let out a huff as she marched to the car. "I'm not a child, ya know. I can take care of myself."

Angie opened the car door and then slammed it shut. Preston walked me to the passenger side and whispered, "Angie's ex showed up with another girl."

"Oh no, poor Angie."

Preston smiled. "She's better off, he was an asshole."

I let out a light laugh. Once I was in the car, I wondered how many of poor Angie's boyfriends her brothers and father had scared away.

Feeling my body move, I slowly opened my eyes. Preston was carrying me into his house and up the stairs. Jenn had already arranged for me to be in the guest bedroom. I couldn't believe how exhausted I was.

How many times will this poor man have to carry me to a bed?

Opening the door to the guest bedroom, Preston walked up to the bed and slowly set me down on it. He walked back to the door and slowly shut it. My heart pounded in my chest at the thought of Preston making love to me.

He made his way back to me and held out his hands as I put my hands in his. He gently pulled me up. "Turn around, Harmony," he whispered.

Turning, I glanced back over my shoulder to see Preston licking his lips as he unzipped the dress. Pushing it off my shoulders, he leaned over and kissed my shoulder as he made his way over to my neck.

"You're so beautiful," Preston whispered against my sensitive skin. Goose bumps erupted across my body as I let out a soft moan.

His fingers softly moved over my arms and tiny electric bolts zipped across my skin everywhere he touched.

Preston's touch did the most amazing things to my body. My stomach dipped as if I was on the ride of my life.

His hands slowly made their way up to my shoulders where he gently turned me to face him. Placing his hands on the sides of my face, he leaned over and kissed me. My arms grabbed hold of him as my knees went weak.

The kiss was soft, gentle, yet full of passion. Pulling his lips away he spoke against my lips. "Where are your pajamas?"

Disappointment flooded my body as I frowned. I knew we were in his parents' house and to expect him to make love to me in their guest room was crazy. Swallowing hard, I pointed to my bag. Preston turned and walked over to the bag and opened it. Pulling out a pair of Victoria's Secret pajamas, he turned and walked back over to me.

My eyes moved over his body. I could see his muscles moving under his shirt, and I had to push the blooming desire deep down. Smiling, he said, "Turn around, princess."

Doing what he asked, I turned and waited to see what he was going to do. When his fingers touched my back, I jumped. His skillful fingers had my bra undone within seconds. Sucking in a breath of air as his fingers moved across my bare back, I closed my eyes and pressed my lips together. "Lift your arms."

I'd never moved so fast in my life. His fingers moved gently up my right side all the way up my arm as I whispered, "Preston."

He put the shirt on as my stomach clenched and my body began to weave slightly as I dropped my arms after the shirt was on. Preston turned me around and slowly bent down. His hands moved slowly down my legs I as lifted one leg and slipped the pajama shorts over one foot. Repeating the incredibly sexy motion with his other hand, he lifted the other leg. Slowly pulling the shorts up, Preston lifted my shirt some as he kissed around my belly button. My head fell back as I whispered, "Oh God, Preston."

Holy hell, I can't even imagine how I would feel with him making love to me. My body was practically trembling under his touch. He stood and reached around my body, taking my hair down then ran his fingers through my long blonde hair.

"Harmony, everything about you turns me on."

My eyes captured his and I tried to find my voice. His gaze was on fire with a passion that had my heart stumbling all over the pace. "Preston," was all I could pull from my mouth. Leaning over he pressed a soft kiss against my lips as he whispered, "Will you be able to sleep without me?"

With a nod of my head, I whispered, "I think so. I know you're close by so…"

He leaned his forehead to mine, drew in a long deep breath, then exhaled before he whispered, "Sleep well, princess."

With that he turned and walked out of the bedroom as I stood there a trembling, turned-on mess. Letting out the breath I hadn't even realized I was holding, I fell back onto the bed.

My hands moved across my body as I let out a small laugh and traced my lips with my fingertips. Never would I have imagined someone turning me on by putting my stupid pajamas on. The look in his eyes was burned into my soul.

Harmony, everything about you turns me on.

Biting down on my lip, I let out a frustrated moan and rolled over and looked out the window into the darkness.

Angie's words flooded my mind. *Did I mention Preston's room is in the attic? Far away from everyone.*

Closing my eyes, I wasn't sure how long I laid there before I got up and slowly made my way out into the hall. Angie had pointed to the attic door that led up to Preston's room after we had gotten ready for the club, so I knew which door led to him.

Could I do this? Would Preston think differently of me if I went up to his room? What about his family?

Turning, I walked back to the guest room but stopped when I heard the faint sound of music. Spinning back around, I pressed my ear to the door. I could barely hear it coming from the attic.

Chewing on my lip, I slowly placed my hand on the doorknob and held my breath as I turned it. When it opened, I let out a shaky breath.

You can do this, Harmony. It's time to move on.

Slowly making my way up the stairs, I stopped at the top. My eyes widened when I looked at Preston's room. It was huge. Hearing water, I glanced around and noticed another door. They must have put in a bathroom up here. I walked further into the giant room and smiled when I saw a shelf that contained trophies. Picking one up, it said first place and had the name of a soccer tournament on it. Setting it down, I looked around as I made my way over to the door. Leaning against it, I let out a sigh. What I wouldn't give to have the courage to open the damn door?

I pushed off the door and made my way around Preston's room as Maroon 5's "It Was Always You" began playing. The words flooded my mind as I continued to look around at all of Preston's things.

The more the song played, the more I realized that the only thing I wanted was Preston Ward. I wanted his touch, his smile, his laughter, and more than anything, his love.

Forever.

Running my fingers across his desk, I made my way over to the side of his bed. Smiling, I placed my hand over my mouth when I saw *Pride and Prejudice* sitting on the side table.

I reached for the book as I whispered, "Oh my, that certainly explains a lot." Opening the book, I could tell it had been read often. Running my fingers over the pages, I closed my eyes and imagined Preston lying in bed reading. There was something incredibly sexy about that image playing in my head. What were the odds Preston would have my all-time favorite book sitting on his bedside table? Setting it down, I went to turn, but immediately felt his presence behind me. I froze. My stomach pulled hard with desire and my breathing picked up.

Somehow I managed to speak. "I couldn't sleep so —"

His hands gently grabbed my arms as he slowly turned me around. Letting out a gasp, my eyes wandered over his perfectly toned muscular body. The only thing he had on was a towel wrapped around his waist.

Swallowing, my gaze landed on his lips as I licked mine before I snapped them up to see his heated eyes on me. They looked beautiful as they were filled with what I had always dreamed of seeing in a man as he looked at me. Love. Passion. Desire.

His hands moved to the bottom of my shirt as he slowly lifted it over my head. My chest burned as Preston dropped the shirt on the floor next to us. His mouth fell slightly open as he looked at my breasts. Closing his eyes he mumbled, "So perfect."

Opening his eyes again, his hand came up to the side of my face as I placed my hand over his. "Preston, I've never been with anyone other than Trey. I'm not sure I —"

"Don't say anything, Harmony. Please, let me love you."

Oh. My. Goodness. I have to be dreaming.

"I'm scared," I whispered.

"I'm scared too, princess, but I promise you I'll be slow and gentle with your body." Preston kissed me gently as Chase Rice's "Ride" began playing. *What timing for this song.*

Preston gave me a naughty smile as he dropped to his knees and slowly took my shorts off. I stepped out of the shorts and sucked in a breath when Preston moved his hands up my legs. My head fell back as I felt a rush of wetness between my legs.

Preston pressed his lips against my panties, and I looked back down to him. *Can you pass out from being so turned on?*

Preston slowly pulled my panties down. *Breathe, Harmony. Breathe.*

Sitting back on his knees, Preston just stared as I lifted my feet and stepped out of my panties. Standing before Preston completely naked should have had me trembling with fear but that wasn't what I felt. The way he took in my body made me feel… beautiful. Cherished. *Loved.*

Preston placed his hands on my legs, and my body erupted with goose bumps. Swallowing hard, I closed my eyes and concentrated on breathing.

Then I felt his lips on my skin. "You're so beautiful, Harmony."

Smiling, I pushed my hands into his hair.

"Preston," I whispered as I felt him move his lips up my body.

"Open your eyes, princess."

Doing as he asked our eyes caught and I drew in a breath of air as Preston's eyes turned dark. Cupping his hands on my face, he gently placed his lips on mine.

I'd never experienced a kiss like that. He ran his tongue along my bottom lip and I moaned in pleasure. Preston was clearly much more experienced than I was.

What if he is disappointed? What if I do something wrong?

Trey and I had good sex, but Trey never was one to… experiment with other things. We had very vanilla sex and not because that was what I wanted.

I placed my shaking hands on his chest and froze. I swallowed hard and looked up into his eyes.

"Put your hands wherever you want them to go, princess."

I slowly moved them down to the towel. Preston kissed me again as I pushed the towel off his waist. Moving my hand down, I took his hard dick in my hand and moaned into his mouth at the same time he did.

Holy crap. Preston was much more endowed than Trey was. It felt like it was my first time again as my body shook with anticipation.

He drew his lips slightly back and whispered against mine, "Your touch drives me crazy, Harmony."

The feeling was very mutual. "I want you; I need you so badly."

Before I knew what was happening, Preston lifted me in his arms and placed me on his bed. He picked up my foot and kissed the inside of my ankle and my body arched as I drew in a deep breath.

"I'm going to kiss your body everywhere, Harmony. I plan on memorizing every inch of you by morning."

Each time Preston touched me a rush of pure pleasure swept over my skin, and I had to fight to contain my moans. The feel of his lips and hands on my body had my head thrashing back and forth while my hands grabbed his sheets to steady the sensation I was flying. It wasn't going to take me long to come.

Preston's hands spread my legs slowly open as he whispered, "Open yourself to me, princess."

Oh. My. God. I've died and gone to heaven. Doing as he asked, I lifted my head and watched Preston's hands move up my thighs with his lips trailing behind them. His hands moved up my body and to my stomach as Preston settled between my legs.

Biting down on my lower lip, I fought to keep from crying out in pleasure. Preston kissed around my clit as I lifted my head and watched him. His hands caressed my stomach as I whispered his name. "Preston, oh God."

His eyes moved up to mine as he smiled and licked across my clit. Gasping, I dropped my head back down. "I've never —"

"Never, Harmony?" Preston asked as he gently placed kisses everywhere but where I needed his lips to be. Lifting my hips, I silently begged him for more. Thrashing my head back and forth I said, "No. Never."

My body jumped as Preston's hands moved and he opened me to him. The moment his mouth came down on me, I felt the buildup happening.

Oh my… this was going to be amazing. My hands moved through his hair as I pulled his head into me more. Grabbing a handful of his hair, I hissed through my teeth, "Oh God yes!" I'd never felt so pleasured in my entire life.

Preston slipped his fingers inside me as my eyes rolled to the back of my head and I saw stars. Slamming my hand over my mouth to contain my moans of pleasure, I rode out my orgasm as Preston sucked and licked me through the most incredible orgasm I'd ever had.

The room felt like it spun. I hadn't even realized Preston was moving farther up my body and had a nipple in his mouth. My body trembled as my hands ran across his muscular back. He took his time as he gave each nipple the same attention. Was it possible to have an orgasm just from his sucking on my nipples? The sensation started to build in my toes as I moaned his name over and over.

Preston's lips moved up my chest to my neck as he kissed gently across my jaw and over to my ear.

Whispering into my ear, Preston said, "Harmony, I'm going to make love to you now."

Gripping onto his strong arms, I felt the tears building. Trey never took the time to talk to me while we made love. It was always a rushed experience. He never adored my body like Preston had been doing. I was overcome with so many sensations.

My voice was shaky as I closed my eyes and whispered two words. "Yes, please."

Then his warmth was gone. Opening my eyes, I watched as Preston reached into his side drawer and grabbed a condom. I wanted to feel him, without any barriers. I wanted this experience to be raw. Lifting on my arms, I got my first real look at Preston's dick.

Holy shit. I was going to be sore as hell. Preston tore the condom open and was about to put it on when I said, "Preston, wait."

Stopping, he looked at me. His face dropped as he stared at me. Inhaling a deep breath, I asked, "Have you always practiced safe sex? I mean, even with Sherry?"

Nodding his head, Preston said, "Yes. I've never had sex without a condom."

Chewing on my lower lip, I looked away quickly and tried to gather the courage for what I was about to ask of him. "I've only been with Trey. Once I found out he had an affair I was tested. I'm clean."

Preston smiled. "Okay."

He began to roll the condom on and I sat up more. "No, Preston. I want to feel you. All of you. I want this to be us being together as one."

Stopping, his mouth dropped open as he whispered, "What?"

I was positive my poor lower lip would be bruised and swollen tomorrow with the way I was abusing it. "If you're not comfortable with not wearing a condom, I totally understand, I just… well… I don't really know why I asked. Never mind, I'm so sorry I even suggested—"

Preston smiled as he quickly moved back over me as I fell back against the pillow. "Harmony, do you even realize how amazing it would be to make love to you with no barriers between us? I can't even imagine it and honestly, I'm afraid I'll come the moment I push in."

Heat swept over my cheeks as I looked away. Placing his finger on my chin, he brought my eyes back to him. "Are you on birth control?"

Nodding my head, I whispered, "Yes."

"Harmony, are you sure you want this?"

"Yes, Preston. I've never been more sure of anything in my entire life."

Preston moved over my body again as I spread my legs open more to him. Cupping his hands on both sides of my face, his eyes boar into mine. "You're so beautiful. I've never in my life met anyone as amazing as you, Harmony. I melt every time you look at me."

I was positive my heart had never hammered so hard in my chest. I was sure Preston heard it. Tears formed in my eyes as I closed them and felt a single tear fall. Feeling Preston's lips on my cheek, a small sob escaped my lips. Opening my eyes, I attempted to talk without my voice cracking.

"You make me feel like a princess and not only when you call me that."

Pressing his lips to mine, Preston kissed me as he teased my entrance with his dick. My body shook with anticipation. Barely pulling his lips from mine, Preston whispered, "You are a princess, Harmony. You're my princess."

And there it was. My heart tumbled and I completely gave myself to Preston as he pushed into me.

Arching my back, I let out a whimper. "Relax, Harmony."

Closing my eyes, I did as he asked while he slowly worked himself in. Words could not even begin to describe the way I felt. Pain mixed with pleasure as Preston pulled out and pushed in deeper.

"I'm all the way in," he gasped out. "Harmony, you feel so amazing."

Wrapping my arms and legs around Preston, I whispered the one thing that scared me more than anything. "I'm yours, Preston. Completely yours."

Chapter
EIGHTEEN

YANKEES FAN

Preston

D ON'T MOVE. IF I MOVED I would surely come. Never in my life have I ever experienced such a rush of pleasure.

Harmony wrapped her arms and legs around me and whispered, "I'm yours, Preston. Completely yours."

My heart about burst from my chest as she spoke those words. I wanted more than anything to whisper in her ear that I loved her, but I wasn't sure how that would make her feel. I had told her I was falling in love with her, but how different would it be to actually tell her I loved her.

Slowly moving in and out, I let out a moan. Fucking hell, it felt so damn good. Harmony's fingers slowly glided across my back as she moaned in pleasure.

"It feels so good. Please go faster. I want more of you."

My eyes about rolled into the back of my head. I placed kisses along her neck until my mouth covered hers and I moved faster.

The feel of her body clenching mine as we moved together was so fucking amazing.

Wrenching her mouth away, her eyes met mine. "Yes! I'm so close, Preston."

Gritting my damn teeth together, I prayed like hell I wouldn't come before her. Never having sex before without a condom I had no idea what in the hell I was missing out on. Then again, I think it had more to do with being with Harmony than anything else.

Her pussy squeezed around my dick as I let out a low growl from the back of my throat. "Baby, you're so close. I feel you squeezing down on me. It feels so fucking good."

Harmony met me thrust for thrust. "Don't stop."

Her body began to shudder as she fell apart. Her gaze never left mine as she cried out, "I'm coming. Oh God, Preston."

I pressed my mouth to hers as I swallowed her cries of pleasure while I felt her pulsing around my dick.

Son-of-a-bitch, I'm not going to last much longer.

Once her body stopped shaking, I picked up the pace and began pulling out and pushing in harder.

"Yes! Preston, harder. Faster."

Oh Jesus, she clearly had no idea what she did to me.

My balls pulled up and I could feel the sensation drawing closer. I was going to come hard.

I pushed in harder as Harmony sucked in a breath. "Harmony, oh God, I'm going to come."

"Preston, I'm coming again!" Harmony came at the same time I had. It felt like she squeezed every drop of cum out of me as we both fell together.

Holy Mother of God. I had never come so hard or so long in my life.

Coming to a stop, I stayed buried deep inside her as my dick continued to twitch. Our breathing was erratic and as soon as I could manage to speak, I placed my mouth next to her ear and whispered, "Harmony, you destroyed me. I've never… experienced anything like that before in my life."

Wrapping her arms around me tighter, she spoke in a voice I'd never heard from her before. She sounded… content. "Preston, please don't move. I want to stay like this a little longer."

Looking into her eyes, I could see she was feeling the same things I was.

I placed my hand on the side of her face and gently rubbed my thumb across her delicate skin. "Take a shower with me, princess. Let me take care of you."

Her eyes widened again and I could tell she hadn't been used to this kind of love making. What a fucking idiot her husband must have been not to worship her like she deserved to be. If Harmony was my wife, I'd spend every damn day showing her and telling her how much I loved her.

Nodding her head, Harmony let out a nervous giggle. "Okay."

Pulling slowly out of her, I missed her warmth immediately. I leaned over and gently kissed her before reaching down and picking her up. Letting out a small squeal, Harmony covered her mouth and widened her eyes. Laughing, I said, "Don't worry. No one can hear us."

Burying her face into my neck, she whispered my name. I loved the sound of my name coming from Harmony's lips.

Walking us into the bathroom, I reached in and turned on the shower. Once the temperature was right, I walked us into the shower and slowly slid Harmony down my body.

"I think you like carrying me around, Mr. Ward."

I rubbed my noise against hers.

"What I love is your body close to mine."

My dick was already trying to come back up as I watched the hot water cascade down around Harmony. Reaching down for my shampoo, I poured some into my hands and motioned for Harmony to turn around. Smiling, she quickly spun on her heels as I washed her hair.

"That feels so amazing."

She turned and faced me as she placed her hands on my chest and chewed on her lower lip. Leaning down, I pulled her lip from her teeth and sucked on it as Harmony held onto my arms.

We quickly got lost in our kiss as I picked Harmony up and walked her against the wall of the shower.

"I want you again, princess, but I have to be honest with you."

Her eyes were burning with desire. "Always be honest with me, and I'll do the same."

Swallowing hard, I said, "I want to fuck you. Hard and fast."

Her lips parted open as she nodded her head and slowly smiled. "I think I would like that. A lot."

Smiling, I lifted her leg pushed into her as she let out a small cry.

"I'm sorry, I'll try to control myself."

She shook her head. "Don't. I want all of you. Please, give me all of you."

Doing as she asked, I pulled out and pushed back in.

"Yes," she hissed as her nails dug into my back. "More. Preston, more!"

I moved hard and fast as Harmony dropped her head against the back of the shower. I lifted her, my hands grabbing her ass. I lost myself in her and she in me.

"I'm going to come," she breathed out.

"That's it, come for me, princess."

The moment she fell, I went right along with her.

Ten minutes later, I was carrying Harmony back to my bed. Her body was weak and tired as she whispered against my neck how amazing she felt.

I drew back the covers and placed Harmony down and then crawled in next to her. Wrapping my arm around her, I melted into her body.

Her breathing slowed to a steady pattern. Once I was sure she was asleep, I whispered, "I love you, Harmony."

Closing my eyes, I dreamt of Harmony and a little blonde curly-haired girl running around the house I built just for them both.

Walking into the kitchen I was stopped dead in my tracks. Harmony was standing next to my mother, wearing one of her aprons, laughing as she mashed potatoes.

This is what I have been wanting. This is the girl I would walk into a jewelry store and buy that engagement ring for. This is the girl I wanted to start a family with.

Smiling, I walked over to my mother and Harmony. Giving my mother a kiss on the cheek, I turned to Harmony and did the same.

My mother turned around and pointed to the cabinets and said, "Preston, will you set the table in the formal dining room."

My mouth dropped open. "But... football is on, Mom."

Giving me that look that told me I had better stop talking and walk to the cabinet, I let out a frustrated sigh and said, "Yes ma'am."

Pressing her lips together to contain her smile, Harmony looked back down at the mashed potatoes. My mother walked up to me and kissed me on the cheek. "That's a good boy." Turning, she reached into the oven and pulled out a pumpkin pie. The smell filled the kitchen and Harmony and I both let out a groan. Laughing, my mother put the pie in the middle of the island.

Wiping her hands off, she leaned against the counter and looked between Harmony and me. "I was telling Harmony how beautiful she looked today."

Harmony's eyes captured mine and she smiled the most beautiful smile ever. Smiling back, I said, "She does." Harmony had her hair braided to the side and had on jeans and a baby blue shirt that made her eyes even more insanely blue. We laid in bed for a few hours earlier this morning talking before Harmony crawled on top of me and took me to heaven and back.

"She has a... *glow*... about her. Wouldn't you say, Preston?"

A beautiful flush swept over Harmony's face. Walking up to her, I placed my hands on the sides of her face and ran my thumbs over her skin as her lips slightly parted. We hadn't talked about letting anyone know what had happened between us, but I needed to kiss her. Right at that moment, I needed to kiss her.

Brushing my lips across hers, I gently kissed her. I drew my head back and said, "She certainly does, Mom."

Harmony smiled and shook her head slowly. Dropping my hands, I took a few steps back when I heard Wes and Angie heading into the kitchen. Giving Harmony a wink, I turned and finished gathering all the dishes for the table. Taking a peek at my mother, I saw tears in her eyes. Quickly gaining her composure, she shouted orders out to everyone as I attempted to keep myself from asking Harmony to go back up to my room.

Everyone began bringing out the plethora of food my mother, Angie, and Harmony had cooked. Dad brought out the turkey and got ready to carve it. The smells of the turkey mixed with all the other smells had me ready to eat. Everyone groaned in frustration when Dad stood up and cleared his throat and got ready to give his yearly speech. Harmony had met my grandmother and grandfather earlier, and my grandfather was stuck on her like glue.

Glancing over to Harmony, I was taken away by her laughter. Granddad was saying something to her that had her laughing. Covering her mouth, Harmony shook her head and looked across the table at me. Her eyes looked so happy. My heart was soaring above the clouds. I never wanted the day to end.

"Now, I know how much everyone loves my yearly speeches," my father said as everyone mumbled in disagreement around the table. Harmony giggled as she watched my father.

"This year is going to be different though. I have not prepared a long speech."

Angie clapped as my father shot her a dirty look. "Sorry, Daddy. I got kind of excited at the thought of actually eating Thanksgiving dinner before it got cold."

Glaring at her my father pointed to her and said, "Watch it, young lady." Smiling an innocent smile, my sister blew him a kiss. Looking around the table, my father cleared his throat. "This Thanksgiving I think has been one of my favorites so far. Seeing my children happy is probably the greatest thing to be thankful for. Of course, it doesn't hurt that we've all had a little… Harmony… come into our lives.

Everyone laughed as Harmony rolled her eyes and shook her head as she laughed. "Sorry, I couldn't resist. Honestly, it's been an honor having you with us this year, Harmony."

Harmony's smile faded some as her voice cracked when she spoke. "Thank you so much for allowing me to be a part of your family holiday."

Angie reached for Harmony's hand and took a hold of it. "You brought a breath of fresh air to us all."

Looking down, Harmony let out a nervous laugh. "I… I'm not sure what to say… but thank you."

My father clapped his hands and said, "Alright, let's do this. It's give thanks time." Leaning over the table, I told Harmony, "Everyone has to give thanks for one thing that has happened to them this year."

Harmony nodded her head and gave me a smile.

Finn was the first to give his thanks. Followed by Wes, Angie, my grandparents, and my mother. Everyone looked at me as I stared at Harmony. Pulling my eyes from her, I glanced around the table as I grinned like a lovesick fool.

"Preston, you're up!" Angie said.

Clearing my throat, I stood and said, "I have a lot to be thankful for this year."

"You can only pick one," Angie said as she chuckled.

Harmony's eyes met mine as they danced with light. "I'm thankful for the New York Yankees."

Everyone at the table let out a gasp. Harmony continued to stare at me as she narrowed her eye and tilted her head.

"That's blasphemy, Preston James Ward!" My father shouted as my brothers both said I needed to be kicked out of the house.

Granddad laughed as he looked at Harmony and shook his head. Standing, he waved his arms around and said, "Leave the boy alone. He has his reasons."

My father stood up and pointed to me. "Well, it better be a damn good reason or I am disowning you!"

Smiling, I nodded my head. "You would have had to see her in the Yankees baseball cap, Dad, to understand."

Glancing over to my father he stared at me like I was insane. "See who?"

Turning, Granddad spoke to Harmony, "Harmony, darling, it's your turn."

Standing, Harmony never took her eyes off me. "I'm thankful for Preston. If it wasn't for him... I'm not sure where I would be right now."

My heart stopped as I looked into Harmony's eyes. I was stunned into silence at Harmony's words as she smiled and sat back down. I don't think she will ever realize how important those words were that she'd spoken.

Everyone sat at the table in silence. Sitting down my father leaned over to my sister and said, "Please tell me Harmony is not a Yankees fan."

Holding Harmony's hand, we walked along the worn-out path in peaceful silence. I had no desire to be anywhere else than right where I was.

Harmony began humming, which was something I'd never heard her do before. Letting out a deep contented sigh, she began to speak. "I've never experienced such an amazing Thanksgiving. Your family is wonderful, Preston."

Smiling, I nodded my head. "Yeah, they are pretty amazing."

"My heart felt so empty a few days ago. I wasn't sure I was going to be able to make it through this knowing TJ wasn't here, but I did. Thanks to you and your family."

Pushing me slightly on the shoulder, she gave me a look that only a mother can give. "I wonder how your mom found out it was my birthday. I mean, she had to have known a few days ahead of time to order that amazing Italian cream cake. Which happens to be my favorite cake ever."

Shrugging my shoulders in an innocent way, I said, "I can't believe she ordered that cake! What a crazy coincidence." Laughing, we both shook our heads, as we looked straight down the path again.

"It was a beautiful and delicious cake though. Her friend did an amazing job on it," Harmony said as she leaned her head on my shoulder as we kept walking.

Nodding my head, I said, "Yeah, she did."

Stopping, I turned to face Harmony. "Tell me what you're thinking right this second."

She looked away. "I'm thinking about how this feels like a dream. Guilt is starting to settle in because I feel the happiest I've felt in a very long time. I'm also thinking how my heart feels — complete. That's the only word I know to use to describe it and that scares me."

Placing my finger on her chin, I brought her eyes back to mine. "Why does that scare you?"

Tears formed in Harmony's eyes as she closed them, then opened them again, only to let them release a tear to roll down her beautiful face. "It scares me because I heard what you whispered to me last night, Preston."

My heart slammed in my chest. Damn it. I'm pushing her into this too fast. Shit. Shit. Shit.

"I heard you say that you loved me and... and — "

Slamming my lips against hers, I wrapped my arms around her as she did the same. I wanted to pour as much into the kiss as I could. The last thing I wanted to do was push Harmony away.

Pulling my lips back, I spoke softly, "Harmony, please don't feel like you have to say anything in return to me. The last thing I want to do is push you into something or push you away."

Shaking her head, she smiled as she placed her finger to my lips. "I love you, Preston."

I was pretty damn sure my heart stopped. My knees went weak and I wanted to yell at the top of my lungs how fucking happy I was.

"I'm pretty sure the moment I knew I loved you was the moment I opened my eyes and saw we were at Fenway Park. I've just been so scared to let it happen. The thought of losing someone else I love… it scares me to death, and I'm not sure how to work through that."

She loves me. Harmony loves me.

Entwining my hand through her hair, I pulled her closer to me as I gazed into her beautiful blue eyes. "We'll work through it together." I slowly shook my head as I went on. "I wish I could turn back time. I would have found you sooner so that I could have loved you longer."

A single tear rolled down her face as she sucked in a breath. Reaching up, I wiped her tear away and softly said, "By the way, you should know, I'm a huge Patriots fan."

Laughing, Harmony threw her body into mine as I wrapped my arms around her and picked her up.

"Preston, take me home. I want you to make love to me."

Chapter
NINETEEN

LIFE MOVES ON

Harmony

PRESTON RUSHED BACK TO HIS parents' house, practically pulling my arm out in the process. Walking in through the back door, everyone turned to look at us.

"Hey!" Preston said with a quick wave.

"Where's the fire?" Angie asked as she threw her head back and laughed. Preston stopped and looked at her while I attempted to hold back my chuckle.

"Like I've never heard that before, Angie," Preston said as he gave her a soft push.

Sitting down on one of the stools at the kitchen island, I was about to say something when Preston turned and looked at me with a shocked expression. "Why are you sitting there? Shouldn't you be packing?"

Standing up, I pressed my lips together and nodded my head as I made my way out of the kitchen and up to the guest room. Taking the stairs two at a time, I raced up them. The sooner I packed up the faster I'd be in Preston's arms again.

Grabbing my bag, I quickly packed my things up.

"So, you sure are in a rush."

Jumping, I spun around and let out a nervous chuckle when I saw Angie standing in the doorway. "Oh, hey."

"I thought you were staying a few days. You know, take in that fresh country air."

"Um," I said in almost a whisper.

Shit. What in the heck am I going to tell Angie? Oh hey, I want to leave so I can have sex with your brother and not worry about your parents hearing?

Chewing on my upper lip, I tried to think of an excuse. "Well… I um… we need to —"

Looking behind Angie, I smiled when I saw those green eyes. "You need help packing up, princess?"

My stomach dipped the moment Preston called me princess. Slowly shaking my head, I said, "Nope, I don't have much to get."

Pushing his sister out of the way, he walked into the room and slowly started to close the door on Angie.

Angie's mouth dropped open as she put her hand on the door. "Excuse me, I was talking to Harmony."

"Well it's my turn now, little sister." With one hard push the door closed and Preston locked it.

Turning to me, Preston smiled. My heartbeat must have increased tenfold just from that smile. "Preston," I whispered as he made his way over to me.

Wrapping me up in his arms, he brought his lips to mine and kissed me. "Jesus, Harmony. I've had a taste of you and it's all I can think about. You are consuming my thoughts."

Giggling against his lips, I spoke. "I feel the same. I need to feel you inside of me."

Grabbing my hair, Preston pulled my head back, exposing my neck to his mouth. Kissing along it, I let out a low deep growl as I felt Preston's hard dick pressed into my body.

"Soon, baby. I'm going to pack my bag and soon we will be back in Boston."

Dropping his grip on me, Preston took a step back as I jutted my lower lip out. Walking backward toward the door, he slowly shook his head. "What are you doing to me?"

Placing my fingers over my lips, they felt as if they were tingling still. "The same thing you're doing to me apparently."

Preston flashed me a drop-dead sexy smile before he turned, unlocked the door, and raced toward his room in the attic.

Quickly racing to the guest bathroom, I grabbed everything and threw it into my bag. Taking in a deep breath, I glanced at myself in the mirror.

"Oh my." Leaning in closer, I took a good look at myself. The last time I looked at myself closely in the mirror I had bags under my eyes, my face was too thin and my eyes looked blank. The reflection I saw in the mirror was of someone happy. My eyes were a sparkling blue again and I saw life in them. My face had color and I looked like I had gained a few pounds.

Smiling, I quickly wrapped my hair up in a bun and applied a light shade of pink to my lips.

I closed my eyes and thought back to what Jake had said to me on the phone a few weeks back.

"Harmony, it's time to start living again. It's time to get your sparkle of life back. If you would only allow your heart to open again."

Taking in a deep breath, I slowly blew it out. "It's hard, Jake. I've lost so much and to open it again and risk losing it all over. I'm not sure I can."

"I know, Harmony. I know. But trust me, the moment you let that wall you've built around your heart fall, you will never regret it. Would you rather spend the rest of your life sad or live each day with someone who made you feel alive?"

Wrapping my arms around my body, I thought about last night and how amazing Preston had made me feel. The idea of how much I needed Preston still scared me, but that wall had finally fallen and I couldn't wait to start over with him. I closed my eyes and grinned when TJ's smile appeared. My heart would forever have a piece missing. I knew that there would always be a part of me forever lost. But Preston had given me hope. He'd filled a void I had long since had.

Life was moving on.

A week had passed since my birthday and things couldn't have been better. Preston had stayed with me at my condo every single night when he wasn't on shift. I felt so alive. Even my friends from school and work said they saw a difference in me.

My phone vibrated in my pocket, and I pulled it out to see it was Jake.

"Hey!" I said with a smile.

"Hey, back at you. You've been radio silent the last week. When do I get to take my baby sister out to dinner and drinks to celebrate her twenty-first birthday?"

Laughing, I said, "Sorry. I've been kind of busy."

"Hmm, let me think about this. I sent Preston a text a couple days ago asking if he wanted to hang out on one of my many rare days off, and he said he had been really busy. You're busy. That leads me to the conclusion that you're getting busy together."

My face heated as I continued to throw a load of laundry into the washer. "I'm not even going to give you the satisfaction that I heard that."

Laughing, Jake said, "I knew it. Harmony, I can hear it in your voice, sweetheart. You sound… happy."

I leaned against the washer, and my smile weakened as the guilt came flooding back with the thought of me being happy without TJ in my life. I pushed it to the side and walked into the kitchen and checked on the roast I was making for dinner. The smell of rosemary filled the air. Preston would be getting off later so it would be a late dinner but that didn't matter. It could sit in the crock-pot on warm.

"Jake, I am happy. Preston has this way of making me feel like I'm the center of his world and I'm not used to that."

"He better fucking make you feel that way or I'll kick his ass. Doesn't matter that the guy can probably bench press me ten times, I'll still pound his face if he hurts you."

Giggling, I took out a peach cobbler from the oven and set it on the cooling rack as I leaned over and smelt the heavenly smell of sugar and peaches. "Stop it. There will be no ass kicking or face pounding."

Jake mumbled something to someone then continued talking, "I hope not. I really like his uncle's pub."

Laughing, I shook my head. "How is Sandy?"

Jake became very quiet all of a sudden. "Jake? Is everything okay between you guys?"

"Yeah. Everything is great. I um... well I... I kind of..."

"Holy hell, spit it out already."

Blowing out a deep breath, Jake said, "You can't tell anyone this. Promise?"

Crossing my fingers, I said, "I promise."

"Uncross your fingers, Harmony."

Damn it.

"Fine, I promise."

Blowing out a few quick sharp breaths, Jake said, "I bought an engagement ring. There, I said it."

My mouth fell open. "Shut up! When are you going to ask her?"

"Christmas. Do you think she'll be surprised?"

"Yes! I think she will be very surprised. Oh Jake, I'm so happy for you."

"Thanks, Harmony. I've been kind of waiting until things settled down with you and all."

Wait. What? What does he mean he has been waiting for things to settle down with me?

"What do you mean?" I asked.

"Well, you know, I didn't want to ask Sandy too soon after the um... well... I didn't want to feel like I was kicking you while you were down."

My heart dropped to my stomach. Jake had put off asking Sandy to marry him because of me?

I was about to say something when I heard someone calling out for him. "Hey, sis, I've got to run. Remember! Don't tell Sandy anything! I love you."

Trying to find my voice, I said, "I won't. I love you too."

The line went dead and I stood there staring out the window. Setting my phone down, I made my way over to the sofa and sat down. I was stunned that Jake would wait for me. Was I that pathetic after the accident? So frail and fragile that my own brother wouldn't think I would be happy for him?

Standing up, I decided to go for a run. Changing into my running gear, I headed out and started pounding the pavement. I wasn't sure how long or how far I ran but by the time I got back, I saw Preston's car parked in my spot. Smiling, I raced up the stairs and into my condo. Opening the door, I called out his name. "Preston?"

I saw part of his uniform lying over the sofa and that familiar pull in my lower stomach started building. Mmm... something about Preston in his uniform turned me on.

Making my way into the bedroom, I heard the shower going. Smiling, I quickly stripped out of my running clothes and snuck my way into the bathroom. Preston was standing in the middle of the shower, his head leaned back, eyes closed and hot steaming water running down his sinfully perfect body.

Quietly stepping into the shower, I wrapped my arms around him and kissed his back. "I missed you."

Turning, Preston placed his finger on my chin and lifted it so we were face to face. "I missed you more. I couldn't sleep damn it. I wanted to have you in my arms listening to your soft breathing lull me to sleep."

I placed my hand on the side of his face. "Let me wash you."

I took the soap from and his hand and slowly moved it over his body. First his arms, then his legs. Licking my lips as I watched his dick grow harder, I wished like hell I had the courage to take him in my mouth. Cleaning his chest, I glanced down at it again.

Fuck it. I'm going for it. Setting the soap in the container, I rubbed along Preston's chest as he dropped his head back. Dropping down, I quickly took him into my mouth.

"Fuck!" Preston hissed through his mouth. Taking him as deep as I could, I worked my hand up and down his shaft as I sucked and licked his dick.

Preston let out moan after moan as he laced his fingers through my hair and began moving his hips. I remembered something about one of the girls at work saying to play with their balls and apply light pressure to their backside. Lifting my hand, I played with his balls and then slowly moved my finger back.

Sucking in a breath of air, Preston pulled me up, lifted me into his arms and backed me into the shower wall. Slowly sinking me down on him, I sighed in relief. Dropping my head back against the wall, I let out a whimper of need.

"Harder! Preston, harder!" I screamed out.

Preston quickly picked up the pace as I felt my orgasm growing. "Yes!" I screamed out as my orgasm hit me. The waves of pleasure rolled across my body as I squeezed down on him.

One last push and Preston let out a low rumbled grunt as he pressed his lips to mine and lifted me higher.

He hit my sweet spot again as I gasped into his mouth as another orgasm started. Pulling away he panted. "Fucking hell, you're squeezing my dick and getting out every ounce of cum I've got."

I loved when Preston talked dirty to me. Smiling, I wrapped my legs around him tighter as we stood there for a few minutes. I loved that he was never in a rush to pull out of me. The connection we shared was amazing and I cherished it each and every time we made love.

Pulling out of me, he slowly let me down. "Jesus, you have no idea how much I needed that."

Grinning, I purred, "Me too."

Quickly finishing up the shower, we both dried off and soon found ourselves in bed where Preston slowly made love to me.

I made small circler motions on his chest as I listened to Preston's breathing.

"What are you thinking about?"

Smiling, I said, "How perfect this is." Moving my head, I rested my chin on the back of my hand as it lay on his chest. "About how happy I am and how happy you make me."

Reaching down, he pulled me up closer to him where he pulled my lower lip into his mouth and gently sucked on it. "You make *me* happy, Harmony Banks. Don't ever forget it."

Before we got lost in yet another kiss, I pulled back and whispered against his lips, "Are you hungry? I made a roast and a peach cobbler."

Pushing me off of him, I laughed as Preston jumped up, got dressed and called over his shoulder, "Meet you downstairs, baby."

Sitting up, I pulled my knees into my chest and smiled. I made a note to myself to call my brother and tell him he needed to ask Sandy as soon as possible to marry him. Life was too short to wait.

"Harmony! Come on before I eat the cobbler first!"

Giggling, I jumped up and threw on one of Preston's T-shirt and rushed to the kitchen.

Yes. I'm happy, and I wasn't going to feel guilty about it. I'd give anything to have my baby back, but Preston had taught me that I could be happy once again and that TJ would always be with me.

Chapter
TWENTY

CHOICES

Preston

SITTING AT THE TABLE I couldn't concentrate. "Ward, what the fuck? Are you going to play or stare off into space?"

I glanced around the table. Nodding my head, I said, "Right, sorry.

Um… I'll take two cards." Pulling out two cards, I put them down on the table and slid them to the center of the table as I picked up the other two cards.

Smiling when I saw the queen of hearts, I shook my head.

Sharp took one look at me and threw his cards in the middle of the table. "Aw, hell no. I know that smile. I'm out." Soon, everyone was out except for the captain and me.

"You ready to show what you think you've got son?" Captain Ryan said with a smirk on his face.

"Bring it," I said with a grin.

Captain laid down his cards and everyone yelled out. Taking a look at it, I said, "Damn, three of a kind and a pair. Cap's got a full house."

Cap pulled the pile of chips toward him when I said, "But… I believe my girl is with me tonight." Spreading my cards down, I laid out a Royal flush. "The queen of hearts was all I needed, and damn Cap, you dealt it straight to me."

Rolling his eyes, Cap got up and pushed his chair back. "Ward, I want to talk to you in my office. Now."

Everyone laughed as I scooped up my chips and started high-fiving everyone. Sharp walked up to me and shook his head. "Damn, you know you pissed off the Cap when he loses at poker and wants to talk to you in his office."

Laughing, I nodded my head. "Right?" Placing my winnings in my hat, I took off toward the captain's office.

I knocked and poked my head in. "Cap, you wanted to see me?"

He motioned for me to sit down. Setting my cap full of winnings in the chair next to me, I sat down and smiled as I waited for him to start speaking.

When he leaned back in his chair and stared at me for a few minutes, I got a bit worried. "So, how did those counseling sessions go?"

Oh fuck.

Shrugging my shoulders, I said, "Sir, I never went to them."

Shaking his head, he pursed his lips and narrowed his eyes at me. "You have a reason why you never went?"

"I didn't think it was necessary." Raising his eyebrow, I threw in, "Sir."

Clearing his throat, he let out a breath and began talking. "Preston, we've all lost people. You've lost people before you lost Harmony's son. You don't find it strange that you couldn't save her son's life, you became involved in her life, and now you're practically living with her?"

Moving about in my seat, I cleared my throat. "Sir, who told you I was living with her?"

"Uncle John."

Rolling my eyes, I let out a frustrated sigh. "Sir, I'm not really sure that this has anything to do with me not going to those sessions."

Leaning forward, he said, "I've seen it happen, Preston. Firefighter can't save the life of a loved one, or the victim is burned badly because you couldn't get them out in time. What happens? The guilt eats you alive and you find yourself pulled toward that person out of guilt."

Standing up, I pointed down to him. "I do not love Harmony because I feel guilty about her son. Do I wish she had never lost him, hell yes I do. Do not sit there and tell me how I feel, Cap. My feelings for Harmony are unlike *anything* I've ever experienced. Fate brought us together, in a really fucked up way, but I believe in my heart she and were meant to be together."

Sitting back in his chair, Cap nodded his head. "If she asked you today to walk away from this job, would you?"

Without even thinking, I answered, "Yes."

Raising his eyebrows, he asked, "Really? Like that you would walk away?"

"I love her, and I'll do whatever I have to do to make her happy."

There was a knock on the door and Captain Ryan looked around me. "One second!" he shouted as he looked back to me. "You're like a son to me, Preston. Your daddy brought you to this station since you were little. I watched you grow up with my own eyes. I only want you to be happy."

I exhaled. "She makes me happy, Cap. The happiest I've ever been in my life."

Standing, he reached across his desk and shook my hand. "Good enough for me, Preston. Now get out of here and go win some more."

Smiling, I grabbed my hat and headed out. Stopping at my bunk, I pulled my phone and found Harmony's name.

Me:	Hey, princess. How is your day going?
Harmony:	Good! I painted the hallway a silver blue gray kind of color.
Me:	I can't wait to see it. I love you, Harmony.
Harmony:	Is everything okay?

Smiling, I ran my finger over her name. I would lay down my life for her. There is nothing that I wouldn't do to make her happy.

Me:	I miss holding you in my arms.
Harmony:	Me too. I couldn't sleep last night with you gone ☹ Are we still getting a Christmas tree tonight?
Me:	Hell yeah, we are.

Smiling, I decided to have a little bit of fun with my girl.

Me:	Is that whole wearing the Yankees shit bet still on?
Harmony:	Yes! Don't even think about it Mr. Ward.
Me:	What if I made you another bet, would you be game?
Harmony:	Sounds fishy?!?!?

Letting out a chuckle, I got ready to bring out the big guns. Harmony had been having a dream about her and me the last week and I was hell bent on making it come true.

Me:	What if I can make your dream come true?

I waited for what seemed like forever for her to respond.

Harmony:	If you can make that happen, I'll let you out of your bet

The alarm went off stating a minor car accident. Fist pumping, I stood up and sent her another text.

Me:	Yes! Got to go. Alarm went off. I love you!
Harmony:	Please be careful and I love you too!

Smiling, I dropped the hat and took off. Only twelve more hours to go and I'd be home with Harmony wrapped in my arms.

Sharp walked up and hit me on the foot as I glanced up from the book I was reading. "What's up?" I asked as I gave him a head bob.

"What did the Cap want?"

Rolling my eyes, I waved it off. "Nothing. Butting into my personal life."

Falling down onto his bed, he crossed his legs and rested his head in his hands. "He was asking me if I'd been around you and Harmony. What my thoughts were on your relationship."

Sitting up, I dropped the book to my side. "What the fuck? Are you kidding me?"

"Nope, don't get pissed, Ward. He thinks of you as a son. He was worried."

"What did you tell him?"

Glancing my way, Sharp gave me that damn smile of his. "I told him I'd never seen you look at a girl like you looked at Harmony. I also told him I'd never seen you so happy."

Smiling, I reached my hand out and Sharp slapped it. "Thanks for having my back, dude."

He let out a gruff laugh and said, "I was only speaking the truth. I'm glad to see you happy, Preston. I know how much you want to settle down and have a family. I sure as shit didn't see that happening with Sherry."

"Me either."

Then I sighed. And of course, he caught it.

Sitting up, Sharp looked at me. "What is it?"

Shrugging my shoulders, I let out a sigh. "I want to start a family with Harmony. I just don't want to push her. I mean, we've only been together officially for a month, before that we were best friends." Pushing my hand through my hair, I let out a laugh. "Jesus, it's all I think about. Dream about really. It's the same damn dream, over and over. Harmony chasing a little girl around in a house I built out in the country."

Giving me a weak smile, Sharp said, "That doesn't sound bad, Ward."

Smiling like an idiot, I nodded. "No, it doesn't sound bad at all."

The alarm rang for a three-alarm fire. Jumping up, we both took off. Hopping into the truck, Sharp leaned over and shouted, "We have choices in our life that sometimes we aren't sure of, Preston. The best way to know which choice to make is to follow your heart."

I stared at Sharp with a stunned expression. "Who the hell are you and what in the fuck did you do with Mitch?"

Throwing his head back, Sharp let out a rumbled laugh as we pulled up to the three-alarm fire. Stepping out of the truck, we saw the structure and said, "Holy shit."

Flames engulfed the building. Cap came walking up shouting orders. "Fourth floor. There's a family trapped. Let's move people. Now!"

After getting on our breathing apparatus, we headed into the building. Smoke surrounded us as we made our way to the stairs. Stopping on the fourth floor, I thought

I heard someone screaming. Yelling for Sharp, I pointed down the hall and quickly made my way to the last apartment on the left. Following our safety standards we checked everything out before opening the door. Sharp and I quickly made our way around the apartment. The smoke was getting thicker from the fire on the floors above us. A woman was sitting in the corner trying to keep the three kids' mouths covered the best she could.

"We need to move fast. Cap said the structure is going," Sharp shouted to me.

Looking down, I noticed the small little boy up next to his mother. My mind flashed back to Harmony's accident as I stood there frozen.

Hitting me on the arm, Sharp yelled, "You've got to grab them, Preston! We need to get them out of here now!"

The ceiling caved in around us as Sharp grabbed the mom and one of the kids and started out of the building. Picking up the other two kids, I turned to follow when a large piece of the ceiling fell in front of us, trapping us in the room.

Hearing the screams of the mother on the other side, all I could think of was Harmony.

"The thought of losing someone else I love… it scares me to death."

Chapter
TWENTY-ONE

SHATTERED HEARTS

Harmony

S TEPPING OFF THE LADDER, I smiled at my work. "It's perfect," I whispered. I'd been painting since early this morning and I was exhausted. I wanted it finished before we went out and bought a Christmas tree though.

The gray blue walls in the hallway brightened up the whole living room. Maybe I should paint the whole place this color. It's calming. Soothing. Yeah, that's what it was. Soothing.

Heading into the kitchen for a drink, I attempted to wash the paint off my hands. "Good lord, I've got more paint on me than I do on the walls."

Picking up my phone to see if Preston had texted back, I sent him a text.

Me: Thinking about you. Love you.

When he didn't respond, I let out a worried sigh. He must be on a call. My heart dropped slightly as I pushed away the worried feelings that were bubbling up inside me.

Walking into the living room, I was about to get back to painting when my doorbell rang. Heading over to the door, I looked to see who was there. When I saw Anne and Dan, Trey's parents, standing at my door, I sucked in a breath of air.

What in the hell are they doing here?

I hadn't seen them since I sold the house. Dan and Anne had signed the house over to me and told me to keep all the equity made in the sale of the house. I had been speechless by the gesture. When Dan told me it was the least he could do, I saw something in his eyes, I just couldn't put my finger on it.

Pushing the intercom, I attempted to speak without having my voice crack. "Hey, Dan and Anne. Come on up."

Holding my hands up, I tried to get them to stop shaking. I drew in a deep breath and plastered on a fake smile, I opened the door and greeted them.

"Anne, how are you? Dan, it's so good to see you both."

Anne kissed me on both cheeks and gave me a sweet smile. "Harmony, darling I've missed you."

Dan leaned over and kissed my cheek and gave me a wink. "Harmony, I love the place you settled on."

Smiling, I looked around. The picture on the mantle caught my eye at the same time it caught Anne and Dan's. Walking up to it, Anne picked it up and smiled as she ran her fingers across the glass.

"This was the last time the three of you were over at the house. Dan snapped this picture and sent it to Trey."

Nodding my head, I softly spoke. "Trey gave it to me for Mother's Day."

The picture showed TJ on Trey's shoulders. Trey had his arms wrapped around me as we both looked up at our little boy. My heart hurt as I looked away. Preston was the one who found the picture and put it on the mantle. Watching him place it on there, I fell in love with him even more.

"Would you like a cup of coffee or tea?" I asked as I motioned for them both to sit down.

"Coffee would be great," Anne said as Dan nodded in agreement.

After making the coffee, I placed three mugs on a serving tray and carried them out to the living room. I set it down on the coffee table and took a seat across from them and placed my shaking hands on my lap. "So, why are you here?"

The moment the words came out of my mouth I regretted them. It sounded cold hearted. "Not that I'm not happy to see you and all. It's just... well... I..." Rolling my eyes, I shook my head as I let out a slight chuckle. "I'm sorry, I guess I'm nervous is all."

Anne gave me a tender smile as Dan nodded his head and then cleared his throat. "Harmony, Anne and I felt it was best to come talk to you, after that day at the office and what you discovered. We weren't sure how long to wait. You pulled away from us, and we both totally understood you had your reasons why."

I moved about in my seat. I couldn't decide if I wanted to sit or stand up and pace back and forth. Why were they bringing this up six months later? I wanted to forget the day I found out Trey had been unfaithful. It was in the past. Why bring it up now?

"Dan, I should apologize for my... outburst that day. The reason I've kept my distance is, well, I guess I don't really have a reason that really makes a whole lot of sense. I just needed it to move on."

Shaking his head he held up his hand. "Please, there is nothing for you to apologize for, Harmony."

Anne's eyes began to form tears and I glanced between the two of them. Feeling a sickness build in my stomach, I dropped my mouth open. "You knew, didn't you?"

Anne broke down in tears. Standing, I looked at them both. "You knew Trey was cheating on me and you let it happen? We had a child together for Christ's sake!"

Dan closed his eyes and motioned for me to sit down. "Harmony, please. Please just let us speak. Hear us out sweetheart, and then you can lay into us all you want. You can't possibly make us feel any worse than we already do."

Narrowing my eyes at them both, I wanted to tell them to get out. The only thing holding me back was my strange curiosity about the whole thing. How could they know their son was cheating on his wife and allow it to happen right under their noses?

Inhaling a deep breath, I pushed it out quickly. Dan spoke again. "Yes. We knew of the affair but found out a few months after it had started. Margie had come to work for the company about six months before the… accident. Trey saw her one day in the cafeteria and made arrangements to have her transferred to work as his assistant."

My heart physically hurt. I wasn't sure I wanted to hear anymore. Turning my head, I stared out the window as I pulled out my charm and held it for a few seconds before putting it back into my pocket. "One evening, I was staying late and saw Trey's office light on. I walked in on them… um… together."

My eyes snapped back to Dan. "Margie immediately left and I laid into Trey. I was disappointed to say the least."

"Imagine my feelings," I said barely above a whisper. Anne wiped a tear away as she sat there next to Dan.

"I cannot imagine, Harmony." Turning to Anne, he took her hand in his.

"A few days after that, Trey told his mother and I that he was going to ask you for a divorce."

It felt like the floor fell out from beneath me. "No," I whispered as Anne cried again.

"Anne and I told him he needed to take a step back and think long and hard about it. You both had a child and that he had a responsibility to you both. You had each sacrificed things for your marriage."

Closing my eyes, I fought to hold back tears. I was so over crying. *Trey was going to leave us. How could he? How could he leave his own child?*

"How long before the accident did he say he was leaving me and his son?" I coldly asked.

"Harmony," Anne whispered.

Attempting to contain my anger, I shouted, "You brought this all up! How far before the accident?"

Dan looked away as he said, "Three months."

I sucked in a breath.

"The morning of the accident Trey called me. He was crying and I could barely understand what he was saying. Once he calmed down, he told me he was going to have Margie transferred to another department that was located at our other office in South Boston. He also said he was going to tell you everything about Margie and the affair and beg you to forgive him. Something had happened that morning. I... I can't remember exactly what it was. He said you looked at him and it reminded him of the love you shared."

"W-what?" My mind spun. Was that what Trey was going to tell me in the car right before the accident? That he was having an affair but wanted to work things out? Shaking my head to clear my thoughts, I stood.

"Why are you telling me all of this, Dan? Why now when I've finally put it all behind me? Why?"

Looking away, Dan swallowed hard. "I needed you to know that Trey really did love you, Harmony. It's just that you both married so young, and we all know the only reason you got married was because of the baby."

Feeling anger rush through my veins, I stood up. "Yes, Dan. We all know. The only difference between your son and me is that I remained faithful to the vow we took. I stayed true because I did love him. It might not have been the path we would have taken otherwise—" I drew in a deep breath and paused for a moment before I went on. "I. Stayed. Faithful. Had I met someone and developed feelings for them, I would have told Trey. I wouldn't have *fucked* around behind his back."

Anne stood and looked at me. "Harmony, please. He is still our son and our hearts ache for him."

My mouth gaped open as I stood there stunned. "And you don't think the last six months *my* heart hasn't ached. You don't think I haven't woken up almost every single night re-living the worst moment of my life? Seeing my child smile at me the moment before he died? Hearing my own husband telling me how his job was more important than I was right before his life ended? Don't stand there and tell me your heart aches. The only reason you came here today was to set your guilty conscience free. Are you even telling me the truth or is this some sick way to make your son seem like the good guy?"

When neither one of them said a word, my hand came up to my mouth. "Oh my God, you just lied to me. It was all a lie."

Anne broke down crying.

"He was going to ask me for a divorce, not say he wanted to work things out."

"I'm so sorry, Harmony. We didn't want you to feel like he didn't love you," Anne said as she wiped her tears away.

Walking over to the door, I opened it. "Thank you for stopping by and getting your guilt off your chest."

"No, Harmony it wasn't anything like that, we—"

"Please, I'm asking you nicely to leave, and I would appreciate it if you would never contact me. There is nothing we have to discuss." Closing my eyes to keep the tears from falling, I whispered, "Please just leave."

Opening my eyes, I stared at them. Anne and Dan looked at each other and slowly walked toward the door. Anne stopped in front of me and gave me a weak smile. "Harmony, we didn't mean to upset you. We only thought—"

Pinching my eyebrows together, I shook my head. "I'm pretty sure I could have lived out the rest of my life not knowing that Trey was going to divorce me, Anne."

Her mouth opened to speak but she quickly shut it and started for the stairs. Dan stopped in front of me but didn't utter a word before he turned and walked away.

Closing the door, I counted to thirty and then slid down to the floor and screamed.

I wasn't sure how long I sat there before I jumped up and grabbed my purse.

Preston. I need to see Preston.

Racing out to Comm Ave., I flagged down a cab. Jumping in, I said, "Firehouse 37 on Huntington."

"Yes ma'am."

Two minutes later we were stuck in traffic. "What's going on? Is it a wreck?" I asked.

Shaking his head, the cab driver said, "Fire in an apartment building. There are like four fire trucks there."

My heart stopped. Preston would be there. "How far down is it? I see the smoke."

No. Oh dear God, please keep him safe.

"Two blocks."

Reaching into my wallet, I pulled out a twenty and handed it to him. "I'll get out here and walk. Thank you."

As I made my way I could see Engine 37 and Ladder 26. Firefighters were running everywhere.

"It's going to go! Get those firefighters out of there now!"

Frantically looking around, I saw Captain Ryan. It was his voice shouting out the command.

Pushing my way through the crowd, I tried to get closer. "Excuse me, my boyfriend is in there. Please, excuse me!" I shouted as I made my way to the barricade. My face turned ashen as I saw firefighters rushing from the building. Some were carrying people as they ran out. My heartbeat raced, nearly exploding as I felt a pain in my chest.

"Preston," I whispered. "Please, don't be in there."

Captain Ryan walked up and I heard his call. "Sharp, Ward. You need to vacate now!"

I sucked in a breath when I heard Preston's voice. "We've located the family, sir. One adult woman, three small children. Fourth floor east."

"Ward, I'm ordering you, out now. The whole building is about to go."

Nothing.

"Sharp, do you copy?"

Nothing. Placing my hands on my stomach, I felt like I was going to be sick. "Copy sir, I've got the woman and one small child. The roof collapsed between me and Ward."

No. Preston, no!

At that moment, Captain Ryan turned and saw me. Walking over to a police officer he said something and quickly walked away. Looking back toward the door, I saw Sharp coming out helping a woman and holding a small child. The police officer walked over and motioned for me to go with him.

"Ma'am, it's best if you wait in my car."

Stopping, I grabbed his arm. "What? I'm not waiting in your car. My boyfriend is in that building. I want to know what is happening!" I yelled out.

His eyes turned compassionate. He was about to say something when there was a loud explosion on the top floor of the building. Grabbing me he pushed me down and covered me up. All I heard were screams coming from everywhere.

"It's going. Get these people back!" someone yelled. Standing, the officer helped me up. "Are you okay, miss?"

Tears streamed down my face as I looked back to the building. The whole fourth floor was in flames. Wrapping his arm around me he led me away as I yelled, "No! Please no. Preston! Please don't do this to me again!" I screamed out.

Just before he brought me over to an ambulance, I saw someone coming out of the building. He was carrying two small children. I instantly knew it was Preston.

Dragging the police officer to a halt, I screamed out, "Preston!"

Looking at me, his eyes caught mine. "It's him! Thank you, God. Thank you!"

Turning to the police officer, I threw myself at him as he patted my back. "See, I told you everything would be okay."

Pulling back, I glared at him before turning back to where Preston was. He was carrying one of the kids to an ambulance as he coughed. An EMS working took the child from Preston and told him to get oxygen. Walking toward me, Preston smiled and I broke down in tears and ran to him. Slamming my body into his, I held him as tight as I could.

"Preston. You're okay! You're okay!" It was the only thing I knew to say and I kept saying it over and over.

Finally someone pulled Preston away and led him to an ambulance where he was put on oxygen for a few minutes and checked out by EMS.

Standing by the police car, my eyes moved between the fire and Preston. I knew the moment the EMS said he was okay, he would go back to fighting the fire. Glancing back at the building, I was shocked it was still standing. The fire was starting to get contained, but I had no idea how long it would take to get it to a hundred percent containment.

My arm felt a rush of energy run through it as Preston touched me. Turning, I fought to hold back my tears. "Preston."

Pulling me to him, Preston moved his lips to my ear. "I'm okay, princess. I promise you I'm okay."

Holding him tighter, I said, "Please don't go back in. Preston, promise me you won't go back in!" My voice was laced with fear and panic.

Rubbing his hand up and down my back, Preston said, "I promise you. I'm not going back in but I do have to get back and help." Pulling back and holding me out at arm's length so he could look at me, he said, "Look into my eyes, Harmony."

Doing as he asked, he smiled that smile that melted my heart. "I promise you. Do you believe me?"

Nodding my head, I said, "Yes."

I wasn't even sure how long I had been standing there watching the fire and keeping an eye on Preston.

When another engine showed up to relieve Engine 37, I breathed out a sigh of relief. When a different police officer asked me if I needed a ride home, I shook my head and said no. "I live just a few blocks down Comm Ave."

Preston walked up to me and pulled me into his arms. He was covered in soot and smelled of smoke.

"I love you, Harmony."

Feeling my heart ache again for the hundredth time today, I forced myself to answer him back. "I love you, too, Preston. So very much."

"I'll be home in a few hours. Do you want to come to the station and wait, or are you going home?"

Swallowing hard, I said, "I'm going home. I'll see you there. I mean, you're done, right? You're not going back in or—"

Placing his fingers on my lips, he said, "Shh. Harmony, I promise, I'll be home soon."

Nodding my head, I held onto his hand until he walked too far for me to hold it. Turning, he headed back to the truck and my heart broke in two.

Again.

Walking back to my condo, I knew what I had to do to save my heart. By doing it, I also knew it was going to completely shatter it in the process.

Chapter
TWENTY-TWO

LOST AND ALONE

Preston

I STOPPED AT THE DOOR and drew in a deep breath before I opened the door to Harmony's apartment. It was dead silent as I slowly walked in. I had sent her a text letting her know what time I'd be home.

"Harmony?"

"I'm in the kitchen."

Letting out the breath I was holding, I headed to the kitchen. The small table in the nook was set with two plates, two glasses of wine and candles. Harmony was pulling out lasagna. My mouth instantly began watering. Turning, she smiled but it didn't touch her eyes.

"Hey."

Smiling back, I leaned against the counter. "Hey."

Swallowing hard, she looked around at all the food. There was lasagna, a huge salad, and a chocolate cream pie. "I didn't make the pie but I know it's your favorite."

Grinning, I looked at her. "What's with all of this? Are we celebrating Christmas a couple days early?"

Letting out a nervous chuckle, she shook her head. "It's me being thankful that you're okay. I was really... scared today."

My heart broke as I watched her fight to hold back her tears. Walking around the island, I pulled her into my arms and held her while she cried.

"Shh, it's okay, princess. I'm okay. Not a scratch on me."

Grabbing onto my shirt, she pulled it as she made a fist and sobbed more into my chest. "I love you, Preston. Please know I love you so much."

Placing my finger on her chin, I lifted her face up as I leaned over and kissed her. Picking her up, I carried her into the bedroom and gently slid her down my body.

Her eyes looked sad, empty almost as I undressed her. Closing her eyes, she sucked in a breath as I ran my hands across her body. When she opened them again, she lifted her hand and ran the back of it down the side of my face.

My body trembled as Harmony undressed me. Her blue eyes finally burned with desire as she smiled.

Standing in front of each other naked, Harmony reached for my hands and brought me over to the bed where she slowly laid down. Everything about the moment was beautiful. Kissing her from her ankle up to her lips, I took my time loving her. My hand moved down her body as I slipped my fingers between her legs and began working her into an orgasm. Arching her back, Harmony called out my name as I moved over her. Settling between her legs, I slowly pushed in as I kissed her. It wasn't lost on me how she started crying. I was going to do whatever I could to let her know I was okay. That I would never leave her.

Wrapping her arms and legs around me, I slowly made love to Harmony as we whispered against our lips how much we loved one another.

Pulling out of her, Harmony rolled over as I pulled her into my body. I hadn't realized how tired I was until I slowly drifted off to sleep. I drew her close to me, afraid to let go of her.

Whispering against her bare back, I said, "Harmony, you're forever mine."

Her voice cracked as she replied, "Forever yours, Preston."

Light beamed from the window as I rolled over and looked at the clock. Shit. It was nine-thirty in the morning. *Fuck.* I must have needed that sleep. I sat up and looked around the room.

"Harmony?" I called out as I scrubbed my hands down my face.

Throwing my legs over the bed, I got up and made my way to the bathroom. I splashed water and my face then froze. The silence in the condo made me feel uneasy.

Heading back over to the dresser, I pulled open the top drawer and pulled out a pair of sleeping pants and a Boston Red Sox T-shirt. Slipping it over my head, I stopped and looked around. Fear and panic set it in as I went downstairs and walked into the living room.

"Harmony? Are you here?"

Silence.

Walking into the kitchen, I looked around. Harmony had put everything away. Glancing over to the table I couldn't help but notice the plates were still out. The candle had been blown out but there was a piece of paper on the plate where I sat.

Swallowing hard, I walked over and picked it up. Unfolding it, I noticed my hands were shaking.

Dear Preston,

I'm so sorry to do this to you. I thought I was able to handle opening my heart again, but yesterday proved to me why I had built that wall in the first place.

I don't know any other way to deal with all of this. Please know that I don't want to leave you, because I love you more than anything. I've never felt a love like this before, and I don't think I ever will again. I can't tell you the countless times I've daydreamed of us getting married and starting a family together. The thought of losing you... I would rather die than lose you too, Preston. I love you too much to ask you to give up something you have dreamed of since you were little. I would never ask you to pick.

You are the only person who has ever loved me so completely. Thank you for last night. Thank you for giving me the happiest moments of my life. I will treasure you and our love forever.

I love you,

Harmony

My whole body shook as I read the letter for the fourth time. Shaking my head, I dropped the letter and ran through the condo. Racing up the stairs I screamed out for her.

"Harmony! Harmony, please don't do this! *Harmony!*"

Running back to the kitchen, I looked for my cell phone. Grabbing it, I found Jake's number and hit call. My heart felt as if it was being torn straight from my chest as I fought to drag in air.

"Hey buddy, what's going on?"

"She's gone! Jake, where is she? You have to tell me. I won't lose her. I can't lose her! She's my entire life!"

"Wait, what are you talking about? Preston, calm down. I can hardly understand you. Who's gone?"

Closing my eyes, I doubled over as I dragged in a few deep breaths. "Harmony! She's gone. She left me a note saying she couldn't be with me anymore. She left!" Dropping to the floor, I cried out, "Jake, she left."

"Are you at Harmony's, Preston?"

Forcing air into my lungs, I barely whispered, "Yes."

"Don't leave. Sandy and I are on our way."

Dropping my cell phone to the floor, I pushed my hands through my hair and looked up as I screamed, "Harmony!"

Sitting on the sofa, Sandy held my hand as Jake read Harmony's letter again. Standing, he pushed his hand through his hair.

"Fuck!" Jake shouted as Sandy jumped, not expecting Jake to yell out like he did.

Closing my eyes, I dropped my head back onto the sofa.

"I get that she freaked out about what happened to you yesterday," Jake said. "But I can't see her leaving because of that."

Sandy dropped my hand as she stood up and walked over to Jake. "Jake, Harmony has suffered so much hurt and loss, I don't think it's too farfetched to say Preston almost dying yesterday caused her to freak out."

Letting a sigh, I said, "I didn't almost die."

Turning, Sandy glared at me. "Preston. You were in a building that blew up right in front of her. Harmony overheard them saying you were trapped. In her eyes, you almost died."

Wiping a tear from my cheek away, I turned to look out the window. This was my fault. I should have known my job probably scared her to death. Damn it. I should have known.

The doorbell rang. We looked at each other before we all quickly ran over and hit the camera. There was an older couple standing there.

"Who in the hell are they?" I asked.

Jake shook his head as he said, "Dan and Anne. Trey's parents. What the hell are they doing here?"

Hitting the button to let them in, Jake opened the door and waited for them to reach the top stairs. Stopping at the top of the stairs, they both looked at me, and then over to Jake and Sandy.

"Jake, how are you doing?" Dan asked before glancing back over to me.

"Um, Harmony isn't here if you're looking for her," I said, trying to keep my voice sounding normal.

Clearing his throat, Dan nodded his head. "Well, I wasn't sure if she would see us again or not."

Pulling my head back in surprise, I asked, "Again? When did you see her?"

"Yesterday."

My heart dropped. "Yesterday? When, what time were you here?"

Dan shook his head as he shot me a dirty look. "I'm sorry. You are?"

Jake stepped between us. "This is Harmony's boyfriend, Preston."

Anne gasped. "Oh no. Oh, Dan, I told you it wasn't a good idea coming to see her." Closing her eyes she turned away from everyone.

Stepping around Jake, I asked again. "What time were you here yesterday?"

Dan shook his head as if trying to clear his thoughts. "Early afternoon. Around one."

Looking at Jake, I said, "That was around when we went out on the call. It was before Harmony was there."

Turning back to Trey's parents, I cleared my throat. "What did you say to Harmony? Did you get her upset or talk about TJ and Trey?"

Looking down, Dan cleared his throat. "We did, we... we talked about Trey."

Now Jake stepped forward. "What about him?"

"We felt it was best if Harmony knew the whole truth about the affair." Anne started crying harder as she turned around and shook her head.

"I knew we should have left things alone. There was no reason we needed to tell her Trey had wanted a divorce. Then Dan lied and she realized it. She was so angry with us."

Sandy, Jake, and I all said at once, "What?"

Holding up his hands, Dan talked. "I thought if we told her he changed his mind and wanted to stay with her it might make her feel better."

My mouth dropped open. "Why would you tell her all of that? What possible reason did you have to tell her that?"

Swallowing hard, Dan looked at Anne. "I wanted her to know my son was a good man. The way Harmony left that afternoon at the office, all she knew was that Trey had been cheating on her. I wasn't sure if he had asked for the divorce or not, but I didn't want her to think of him as betraying her. I thought it would help her move on."

Making my way over to Dan, I went to reach for him when Jake pulled me back. "You did this! You planted more hurt into her heart just to make your own self feel better about your son! You fucking did this! Right when she was finally moving on you had to show up!"

Sandy walked up to me and stood in front of me. "Preston, you're upset. Calm down. We can't find Harmony if you're screaming and shouting."

"Wait, Harmony is gone?" Anne asked with shock laced in her voice. It was then I realized how red and swollen her eyes were. Like she had been crying for hours.

Stepping away, I scrubbed my hands down my face and let out a frustrated moan.

Sandy nodded as she said, "Yes, she left a note for Preston saying she couldn't risk losing him. There was a fire yesterday and somehow Harmony ended up there and found out Preston had been trapped in the building. It freaked her out."

Sandy walked up to me and placed her hands on my arms. "Wait, this might explain why Harmony was there. She probably was heading to the fire station to see you after Trey's parents left. She saw the fire and made her way there."

Sitting down in the chair, I placed my head in my hands. "Fuck. Of all the times she had to show up on scene and it was yesterday."

Jake started talking to Dan and Anne. Asking them places where they thought Harmony might have gone. Neither of them had any clue.

"Was there anywhere that Harmony and Trey used to go to as a couple? You know, like a special place she might have mentioned?" Sandy asked as she walked back over to Jake and Trey's parents.

"No, not that I'm aware of. I honestly don't think she'd go somewhere they went together. Maybe somewhere that made her think of TJ? If we think of anything though, we will be sure to call you, Jake." Anne stated.

"Great, let me give you my cell phone number. If you think of anything, please call me right away."

Jake walked Trey's parents out as I stood at the window and looked out at the snow that was beginning to fall.

Harmony. Where are you?

Chapter
TWENTY-THREE

COASTAL MEMORIES

Harmony

P ULLING UP TO THE FRONT of the hotel, I put the car in park. Opening the door, the valet gave me a smile and wink. I wanted to roll my eyes, but I smiled back politely.

"Are you staying with us this evening, ma'am?"

Nodding my head, I handed him my keys as I turned and opened the back door and grabbed my two bags.

"Allow me, ma'am," the bellhop said as he took the bags from my hands. Following him into the hotel, I took a deep breath of ocean air. I was exhausted from driving and nearly fell asleep on the ferry ride over here.

Making my way up to the front desk, I attempted to put on a smile. "Good afternoon. Welcome to The Nantucket Hotel and Resort. Do you have a reservation with us?"

Nodding my head, I pulled out my wallet and handed her my driver's license as well as the American Express card that my parents had given me a few months back. I swore I would never use it, but now I didn't care. I knew my father's company would pay the bill each month and never think twice about it.

The hotel clerk was typing away on her computer when she finally smiled. "Mrs. Banks. There you are."

Giving her a weak smile, I said, "Ms. Banks."

"Excuse me, I'll make that correction right now. Have you stayed with us before, Ms. Banks?"

My stomach felt sick as I thought back to Trey asking me where I wanted to go on our honeymoon.

"Nantucket! I've always wanted to go there," I said with a smile.

Laughing, Trey shook his head. "Nantucket? Hell, Harmony. We can go there anytime. Let's go somewhere good. I mean, if my parents are footing the bill, let's go all out. You know once the baby is born we won't be doing anything. We'll be tied down with working and going to school."

Shrugging my shoulders, I said, "I guess so. Where do you want to go?"

Trey picked me up and spun around. "Cancun! I've already had my father's secretary make all the travel plans. I can't wait to see you in a bathing suit."

Smiling, I wrapped my arms around Trey and buried my face into his neck.

"Cancun sounds perfect," I said with a forced smile.

"Ms. Banks?"

Shaking my head to clear my memory, I let out a small chuckle. "Sorry, daydreaming. Um, no, I've never stayed here before. I've never been to Nantucket."

Giving me a polite smile, she looked back down at the screen. "Oh, I see you'll be staying in our Point Suite room. And it looks like you're here for at least a… oh… at least a month."

"Yes. Until I can figure out some things, I'll be here for a bit."

"Well Christmas in Nantucket is beautiful."

My heart broke at the thought of not spending Christmas with Preston. "I'm looking forward to it," I lied as I balled my fists and then flexed my hands back open.

After collecting a bit more information, the front desk clerk handed me back my license and credit card along with the key card to my room. She gave me some additional instructions for breakfast, lunch and dinner. Glancing around the hotel lobby, I smiled at all the Christmas decorations. My heart instantly hurt when I thought of Christmas without TJ.

Following the bellhop to the elevator, I forced myself to breathe. Inhale for four, hold for four, exhale for four, hold for four. Once I was in my room, I tipped him and shut the door. I looked around as I walked further in. It was large with a small kitchen to my right, and a large king-size bed to my left. In front of me was a small sitting area and dining room. Beyond that were French doors that led to a balcony.

I opened the curtains to reveal a gorgeous view of the ocean. It didn't take long for my legs to give out and for me to fall on the floor in a jumbled up crying mess. Lying there, I buried my face in my hands and whispered his name, over and over.

"Preston."

Rolling over, my eyes adjusted to the small amount of light coming from the crack in the curtains. I sat up and threw my legs over the bed and stretched. I had pretty much stayed in my room for the last two days and didn't step outside once. This would be my first Christmas alone.

No watching TJ rip open his presents, or Jake trying to guess what I got him. I closed my eyes and wondered if Preston had found the wrapped gifts in the hall closet.

I picked up my phone as I got up and headed into the kitchen. Grabbing the jar of Nutella and a spoon, I dragged in a deep breath as I looked down at my phone. I had turned it off the morning I left Boston. Chewing on my lower lip, I debated if I should turn it on. Letting out a sigh, I turned it on and watched as it booted up.

Sucking in a deep breath, I saw I had over a hundred text messages. Opening them up, tears formed in my eyes when I saw seventy-three of them belonged to Preston. Twenty belonged to my brother and six were from Anne.

Closing out my messages, I opened my voicemail. Call after call was from Preston. I didn't dare listen to them. Backing out, I opened my messages and hit Jake's name.

Me: I'm okay. I need some time alone to figure things out.

It wasn't even thirty seconds later and Jake was texting me back.

Big brother: Harmony! Thank God. Please call Preston! He is freaking out.

Me: Please tell him I love him. I can't talk to him right now.

Big brother: Sis, I'm begging you to call him. He's a mess. He has been going to the pub every night after driving around Boston looking for you. Harmony, you are destroying him by not calling.

Closing my eyes, Preston's words from the first time we made love flooded my mind. *You have destroyed me, Harmony.*

I fought to hold back my sobs.

Me: Jake, please. I need some time to think.

Big brother: About what? If you would just give him a chance. Harmony I know how much you love him. Don't walk away from him.

Me: I've got to go. I love you, Jake. Merry Christmas. Kiss Sandy

After hitting send, I quickly turned my phone back off. Setting it on the table, I decided to go exploring. Almost everything would be closed today, but that was okay. I needed to walk and clear my mind.

I jumped into a hot shower and quickly washed my hair and soaped up. My mind drifted to Preston making love to me in the shower. Pushing those thoughts away,

I turned off the shower, dried off and got dressed. Pulling my wet hair up, I put on my New York Yankees baseball cap.

Taking another look around the room, I grabbed my phone and shoved it into my purse. As I walked toward the elevator, I watched as a little boy ran up and quickly pushed the button for down. His mother and father were right behind him.

"Sorry, he loves to push the button," the mom said in a tender voice.

Smiling, I said, "No worries. I don't mind at all."

Stepping into the elevator I watched as the dad picked up the little boy and began telling him a story. Leaning my head back, I closed my eyes and got lost in a memory of TJ.

Standing at the kitchen sink, I rinsed off the grapes I had cut up. I looked down to see TJ holding up his favorite book with that smile that melted my heart.

"You want a story, big guy?"

Laughing and jumping, TJ yelled out, "Tory time! Tory time, Mommy!"

Reaching for his hand we walked into the living room and snuggled up on the sofa together as I read his favorite book to him. Standing up, TJ wrapped his arms around my neck as he kissed me on the cheek.

"I wuv you, Mommy."

"Miss? Um, are you getting off on the ground floor? Miss?"

Snapping out of my memory, I jumped and let out an awkward laugh, "Yes, sorry. I was lost in thought."

Giving me a polite smile, she nodded her head and said, "Merry Christmas."

"Merry Christmas," I replied as I watched the young family walk away.

Forcing the tears back down, I turned and headed for the boardwalk. Maybe a walk on the beach would help clear my head. I regretted not drying my hair the moment I stepped out into the cold wind. I made my way down the beach and noticed someone else walking ahead of me. Not paying too much attention, I turned left and he turned right. Wrapping my coat tightly around me, I pulled the baseball cap down further as I lifted the hood of my coat over it and pulled the ties down, hoping to block out some of the wind. Sitting down, I looked out over the ocean.

I let the sounds of the waves clear my mind as I fell back onto the sand and closed my eyes and quickly got lost in another memory.

"Well damn! Look at you, hot momma!"

Spinning around in the two-piece bathing suit, I giggled as Trey's eyes moved over my body. His eyes landed on my stomach where my five-month pregnant belly was taking center stage.

"Jesus, Harmony. You look fucking hot in that swimsuit."

Feeling my cheeks flush, I looked away. "Really? I feel kind of funny in it."

Walking up to me, Trey placed his hands on my stomach and leaned over and kissed it. Standing back up, he looked into my eyes. "Nah, you look great."

I was about to say something when I felt a flutter in my stomach. Almost like gas moving through.

Taking a hold of my hands, Trey led me out to the beach. We were just steps away from the water, and we even had our own private cabana on the beach. Lying a blanket down, Trey pulled me down to sit next to him. Laughing, I looked out over the crystal blue water. *Glancing over to Trey, I wanted to ask him if he was happy. We both knew we had probably gotten married for the wrong reason, but there was no doubt about us loving each other. Now we had something in common that would forever tie us together. Feeling the flutter again, I placed my hand on my stomach and fell back onto the sand.*

There it goes again. Then it hit me. Oh. My. Goodness. The baby is moving.

Letting out a giggle, I turned to look at Trey who was now lying back as well with his eyes closed. "Trey?"

"Yep?"

"The baby just moved."

Sitting up, Trey looked down at me. "What?"

Nodding my head, I said, "Yep. She's moved about four times now."

Standing up, Trey reached down and pulled me up. Lifting me in his arms, he spun me around before setting me back down. "Wait one second. She?"

Giggling, I nodded my head. "Or he."

Smiling, Trey placed his hand over my stomach. "I can't wait to feel him... or her."

"Ms. Banks? Are you in need of a blanket?"

Opening my eyes, I shielded them from the sun as I looked up at the bellhop who had brought up my bags the other day. Sitting up, I smiled and shook my head. "No, thank you. I'm about to head back in."

Nodding his head, he turned and headed back up toward the hotel. Standing, I brushed the sand from my pants and walked back toward the boardwalk. In the distance I saw a lighthouse. Stopping, I stared at it as I pulled the charm out of my pocket and looked down at it.

Everything happens for a reason.

Closing my eyes, I put the charm back in my pocket and looked over to the lighthouse again. "The Great Point Light House. It's amazing to see in person."

Jumping at the sound of a male voice, I spun around to see an older gentleman standing there. It was the same guy I had seen walking in front of me earlier.

Holding up his hands, he laughed. "I didn't mean to startle you."

"It's okay. I'll, um, make a note to head over and check it out."

Nodding, he gave me a polite smile and headed back to the hotel.

Watching him walk up the boardwalk, I couldn't help but notice the emptiness in his eyes when he had talked to me. I wondered if that was what people saw when they looked into my eyes.

As the older man walked into the hotel, I let out a sigh and began up the boardwalk. Once I was inside, I glanced around and saw nothing but couples and families. Smiling slightly, I made my way into the hotel café.

The hostess smiled. "Table for how many?"

Holding up one finger, I said, "One."

As she walked me into the restaurant I saw the older man sitting alone in the corner. At least I wasn't the only one spending Christmas day alone.

Chapter
TWENTY-FOUR

WAITING ON YOU

Preston

STANDING AT THE WINDOW, I gazed out as the snow slowly fell. Feeling my mother's hand on my shoulder, I smiled slightly. "Preston, dinner is ready."

I turned and followed her into the formal dining room. Stopping at the table, I looked at the seat Harmony had sat in at Thanksgiving. Uncle John was now occupying it as he talked my father's ear off about the Patriots' last game.

Pulling the chair out, I sat down and stared down at my plate. I felt my sister bump my shoulder. "She's going to call. She has to. It's Christmas."

Attempting to smile, I gave her a quick nod and then looked back down at my plate. My father stood up and hit the side of his wine glass to get everyone's attention. I didn't feel like looking at him. I didn't feel anything. My chest ached where my heart was, my stomach had felt sick, and my head pounded. Evidence of how much I had to drink at the pub last night. Finn ended up having to come and pick me up.

We stopped at Harmony's and quickly packed up what I could. I was half drunk out of my mind as I wandered around her condo. When I opened the hall closet to see if my coat was in there, I saw all the presents.

Grabbing my coat, I shut the door and headed out the door with my bag. There was no way I was planning on going back to that condo. I felt lost and alone without Harmony there.

"Now, let's all stand and give one hope for the upcoming year," my father said as he looked around the table.

Tuning everyone out, I sat there in a daze. Where was she? What was she doing? Who was she with? My mind raced as I kept coming up with all these scenarios.

"Preston, it's your turn," Angie whispered.

"Just pass over me," I said, barely above whisper.

Clearing his throat, my father's voice boomed across the room. "Preston James, it's your turn."

Looking up at him, I shook my head, "I'm going to pass on the Christmas traditions this year, Dad. I don't really have much to look forward to in the new year."

"Preston," my mother said as she stood. "For your father."

Glancing around the table, everyone had their eyes on me. My mother gave me pleading eyes. I stood up and pushed my chair back, causing it to fall backward.

"The one thing I'm looking forward to next year is…" Glancing down to Uncle John, I let out a laugh. "Saint Patrick's Day, a day when I get drunk and don't have to answer to anyone."

"Preston!" my mother and Angie both said as once.

"Excuse me, I'm not much in the mood for eating." Leaning down, I picked up the chair and pushed it in, and then headed up to my room, but not before I stopped in the living room and grabbed a bottle of rum from my father's liquor cabinet.

Once I was in my room, I sat down in the chair and stared at my bed. Taking a shot of rum, I could almost feel her hands moving across my body as she softly moaned into my ear.

My phone buzzed in my pocket but I ignored it. I had lost count on how many times I sent her a text or called and left her a message. Harmony Banks did not want to talk to me. Letting out a laugh, I pulled out the phone number that was shoved into my pocket from last night.

Karen Mitchell. From what I could remember, she was pretty cute. Finn said he would have banged her had she given him her number. But she gave it to me. Said she had the perfect cure for a broken heart.

Tossing my head back, I laughed. "Fuck." Holding up the rum bottle I said, "This! This is the perfect cure for a broken fucking heart."

Opening the bottle, I drank straight from it until I finished it off. Standing up, I stumbled to my bed and fell face-first on it. Finally, I had drunk enough booze to pass the fuck out.

Sleep would finally come.

One Month Later

WIPING DOWN THE BAR, I looked up when the door opened. Uncle John walked in and gave me a smile. "You're here early."

Shrugging my shoulders, I simply said, "I was thirsty."

Walking around the bar, my uncle gave me a push. Not just a small push, but a push so hard it caused me to lose my balance and fall on my ass.

"What the fuck, Uncle John?"

Walking up to me, he pointed. "Don't get up. Sit there for a second while I talk to you."

Not moving an inch, I sat there, frozen. I'd seen my uncle beat the shit out of men twice my size. No way in hell was I gonna move.

"Are you finished yet?"

Tilting my head, I looked at him. "Excuse me, sir?"

Slowly shaking his head, he let out a breath. "Are you done walking around with your goddamn head stuck up your ass, trying to drown your problems in alcohol?"

Looking away, I shook my head. "I don't know what else to do."

Laughing, he gave me a kick.

"Ouch. That hurt, Uncle John!"

"Good! Maybe it will wake your ass up. You don't know what to do? Son, you find her."

Standing up, I wiped my ass off and rolled my eyes. "I don't know where she is. I have no damn clue where to even think to find her."

Frowning, my uncle narrowed his eyes at me. "Is that so? Maybe you don't love her like you thought you did."

It felt like someone had just punched me in the gut. "What?"

Taking off his coat, Uncle John hung it up and then walked over and poured him a draft of Guinness. Taking another glass, he filled another one and slid it down the bar to me. Grabbing it, I took a drink.

"There once was this Irish lad I knew. Couldn't have been more than twenty at the time. Fell deeply in love with a girl named Abby. Abby got spooked and ran off. O'Ryan wasn't going to have it. He packed a bag and began searching for her. Took him four months before he finally found her. It took some winning her over, but O'Ryan ended up marrying her and they popped out six kids."

"How did he know where to look?" I asked as I watched my uncle down his beer. Wiping his mouth he looked at me like I had just asked the stupidest question ever.

"He knew all of her favorite things. Her favorite places. He kept going until he found the one where she was."

Pulling my head back, I let my uncle's words sink in. "Favorite places, huh?"

Nodding his head, he pulled out his phone and showed me a picture. "Seems to me there was a beautiful young lady who you brought in a few months back. First thing I noticed was all of the New York Yankees shit she had on."

Smiling, I let the memory of that day fill my body with warmth. "Uncle John, she's been gone over a month. What if —"

Holding his hand up, he shook his head. "I've seen the way she looks at you, Preston. She's waiting for you to find her. She may not know it, but she's waiting. Stop and think, Preston. She told you where she was, you only need to remember."

Chapter
TWENTY-FIVE

LETTING GO

Harmony

S TANDING ON THE BEACH, I closed my eyes and inhaled a deep cleansing breath. The time I had spent on Nantucket had been good for my soul, but terrible on my heart. I hadn't slept more than four hours a night and woke up at least twice a night sweating. The nightmares hadn't return, thank God, but the feeling of loss seemed even greater.

Sitting down on the cold sand, I glanced over my shoulder to the lighthouse. I'd come to the lighthouse almost every day since coming to Nantucket a month ago. I wasn't sure why; it was as if it was drawing me to it. There was something there for me to find, I just hadn't found it yet. What in the hell was I searching for?

Standing, I slowly made my way back to the hotel. As I walked I noticed couples walking hand in hand along the beach. Families running and playing chase with their kids as their laughter echoed off the waves crashing on the shore.

Wrapping my arms around me, I buried my face into my scarf as I walked back to the boardwalk. A little girl ran up to me letting out a squeal. "It's Princess Elsa from Frozen!" Stopping, I quickly turned and looked behind me. The next thing I knew I had little arms wrapped around my legs. Laughing, I glanced down as big brown eyes stared up at me.

"Why hello," I said with a giggle.

Smiling the biggest grin I'd ever seen she said, "Wow. It's really you. Let's sing 'Let It Go'!"

I blinked down at her confused. "Um—" Glancing around I saw a couple walking up laughing.

"In her defense, you do kind of look like Princess Elsa," the father said with a chuckle.

Reaching up, I played with my braid as I smiled back down at the little girl. My heart ached with thoughts of TJ, but something else happened as I looked into her brown eyes. It was as if she was searching my soul and trying to tell me something. Bending down, I tapped her nose and said, "I love the movie *Frozen*, but alas, I am not Princess Elsa."

Jutting out her lower lip, she stomped her foot on the ground. "Drat. Can I still tell my friends at school I saw a princess?"

My heart melted as tears formed in my eyes. Preston's whispered words from the last night we spent together flooded my thoughts.

"I love you so much, princess. I'd climb the tallest tower just to hold you in my arms forever."

"Someone once told me I was a princess. If he said it, it must be true."

Jumping around, the little girl took off running again as her father went after her.

"Hey, don't run off! Pumpkin!"

Laughing, she called out, "Daddy, try to catch me."

I turned back to the mother and smiled. "She's adorable. Her daddy sure does love her."

Nodding her head, I saw the happiness dancing in the mother's eyes. "Thank you. Her father died a few years back and Scott has been so patient waiting for her to open up to him. Really he's been patient with both of us."

Swallowing hard, I looked back at them. The dad was spinning the little girl around as she laughed. "I'm so sorry for your loss. She seems very happy though."

A soft laugh slipped from her mouth before she said, "She is happy. I'm so glad I took the leap of faith and opened my heart again to love. It's an incredible feeling once you let the walls that you built after such heartache fall down."

My head jerked back to look at her. "What?" I whispered.

"Opening my heart again to love was a huge leap of faith for me. I knew I needed to do it not only for me but for my daughter as well."

Fighting to keep my tears at bay, I asked, "How did you do it? How did you move on without feeling... guilty about being happy or afraid you'd lose that love again?"

"Oh, I felt guilty and I was terrified. My mother told me to ask myself if it had been me that passed and my husband was left with our daughter, would I want *him* to be happy?" Looking down, she smiled. "I would. I wouldn't want my husband to live the rest of his life without love."

Nodding my head, I glanced back out at the little girl running around laughing. Watching her was freeing. Something moved through me as I watched this family live out their second chance at love and happiness.

I looked back at the mother as I whispered, "Love really does heal all wounds, doesn't it?"

Smiling, she said, "Love is such a powerful thing. Once we allow it into our hearts, it's amazing how it heals not only the heart, but our soul as well. We never forget," she said as she placed her hand over her heart. "but we do heal." Glancing back out to her husband and child, she let out a small chuckle. "I loved my husband, but Scott has made me realize that there is that one true soulmate out there for all of us. That doesn't mean my love for my first husband was less, it only means I've been blessed with a greater love." She looked at me and smiled. "I guess everything really does happen for a reason."

Reaching in my pocket, I felt the charm. My life would never be the same without my son in it, but I knew deep in my heart, love was healing the pain of losing TJ and Trey.

My lower lip trembled as I rubbed my fingers against my charm and whispered, "Yes, it certainly does. If you'll excuse me. Enjoy your day."

Smiling the sweetest smile the mother nodded and said, "Every princess deserves her happily ever after. Follow your heart."

I stared at her for a moment before I quickly walked down the boardwalk and into the hotel. My breathing felt so labored as I struggled to bring in air.

"What if I was too late? What if Preston no longer wanted me?"

Reaching my room, I shut the door, took off my coat, and slid down the wall until I hit the floor. Burying my face in my hands, I cried out, "Oh God. What have I done?"

My head dropped back against the door as I tried to calm myself down. After getting my breathing back under control, I walked over to the small kitchen area and pulled out the Nutella and a spoon.

Taking a bite of Nutella, I looked down at my phone. *Preston.*

Setting the Nutella down, I wiped my tears away as I turned my phone on. I hadn't had it on since Christmas and it was now the last week of January. I had used a prepaid phone each time I called Jake. Knowing how upset he was with me, I had only called him three times. Each time was less than two minutes. Enough for me to tell him I was okay and that I loved him. Each time he would beg me to call Preston.

Finding Preston's number, I hit dial and held my breath.

Voicemail. It went straight to voicemail. Closing my eyes, a small sob escaped my lips as my chest felt like a heavy weight had been placed on it. Setting my phone down on the side table, I walked over to the window and looked out.

"Preston." I whispered. "I love you so much. I'm so sorry."

Stepping out onto the balcony and not even caring I was freezing, I glanced down the beach toward the lighthouse. My heart tripped over itself. A man stood on the beach, looking out over the water. The moment his hand pushed through his hair, I drew in a deep breath.

Preston? An instant rush of adrenaline raced through my veins as I screamed out. "Preston!" Turning, I rushed to grab my coat. My hands were trembling as I kept saying his name over and over.

Throwing the door open to my room, I ran down the steps, not waiting for the elevator.

Running through the lobby, I called out, "Excuse me! Please, he's going to leave! Excuse me, coming through!"

People quickly stepped out of my way as I pushed out the door that led to the beach. Racing down the boardwalk, I prayed like hell that he was still standing there.

Please God. Please, give me this second chance. I beg of you!

Hitting the sand, I came to a stop. He was standing at the edge of the water looking out. The wind was now blowing harder as a front moved through and the temperature seemed to be dropping fast. Smiling, I screamed, "Preston!"

I'd never run so fast in my life as I called out his name. My eyes never left him as he stood there, not moving from the shoreline as he looked out over the ocean.

"Preston!"

The wind howled as the waves crashed on the shore. Preston lifted the collar of his jacket and turned to leave. Stopping, I screamed out as loud as I could. "Preston!"

Stopping, he turned and looked at me. I started to cry when I realized it was really him.

Run. Run to him, Harmony.

"Preston," I whispered as I took off running again. Preston smiled and stood there, waiting. Not even slowing down, I slammed into his body as he wrapped his arms around me.

"You came for me," I cried as I buried my face in his neck. "I love you, I love you, I love you so much. I'm so sorry I ran. Please forgive me."

Preston wrapped his arms around me tighter, not saying a word. Please don't let him hate me. Then a terrible thought came to my mind. What if he wasn't looking for me? My heart would shatter into a million pieces if that were true.

"Oh princess, I've been searching everywhere for you."

Crying even harder, I wrapped my arms around his neck tighter. "Please don't ever let me go. Please, Preston!"

"Never, baby I'm never letting you go ever again."

It felt as if Preston had held me forever before I slid down his body. He placed his hands on the sides of my face as he wiped my tears away. He pressed his lips to mine. "Harmony," he whispered as he kissed around my lips, my face, along my jaw and over to my neck. Reaching my ear, he whispered, "I was so lost without you."

My heart stopped momentarily knowing that I had hurt him. My chin trembled as I looked into his beautiful green eyes. Opening my mouth to talk, I felt sick. Closing my eyes, I drew in a shaky breath.

"Please forgive me. I was so scared and the thought of losing you was more than I could bear." Shaking my head, I wiped my tears away. "But now I know, I'd rather have you in my life than live this life without you in it. My life is complete with you. Without you... I'm nothing."

Preston's eyes searched my face. "Harmony, I want everything with you. Marriage, kids, rocking chairs on a porch out in the middle of the country. I want to own your heart forever and I promise you, I'll never give you a reason to run again."

My heart melted as my stomach fluttered. "I want all of that with you too, and it wasn't you that made me run. It was my own fears and insecurities that I let creep into my head. Trey's parents stopped by that day, the day of the fire."

Nodding his head, he whispered, "I know. They came back the day you left to apologize."

Rolling my eyes, I looked out over the water. "As soon as they left, I went to you. You were the first person I thought of. The first person I needed to get to. The cab driver was stuck in traffic and when I knew it was a fire, I guessed your station would be there. And then..." My voice cracked. I stopped to take a cleansing breath and calm my heart down.

Pulling me into him, Preston held me tightly. "Harmony, I know. I can't even imagine what it must have been like for you, but I promise you won't ever have to worry about that again."

I drew back and narrowed my eyes at him. "What do you mean I won't ever have to worry about that again?"

A sense of dread filled my body, as the realization of what Preston was about to say hit me.

"I'm no longer working at the fire station. I quit."

Shaking my head, I grabbed onto Preston's coat. "No! I don't want you giving up something you love doing. I swear to you, I won't ever run again. I'm not going to say I wouldn't worry, but please don't do that. Don't walk away from something you've always dreamed of."

Smiling, Preston ran the back of his hand down my face. "Harmony, you're the only thing I've ever dreamed of. Besides, I've already lined up another job."

Butterflies danced in my stomach as Preston's words soaked in. *"You're the only thing I've ever dreamed of."*

I prayed I wasn't dreaming and that Preston was really here. Smiling, I asked, "Do you have to get back to your new job right away?"

Shaking his head, he gave me a naughty smile. "Nope."

Reaching up on my toes, I brushed my lips across Preston's as I bit down on his lower lip. "Good, because we have a lot of time to make up for."

Giving me a naughty smile, Preston said, "Please tell me your place is close by."

I giggled as Preston kissed the tip of my nose. "The Hotel Nantucket is where I'm staying."

Preston pulled his head back and looked at me with a stunned expression. "You're shitting me. I've got a room there."

Fate certainly had a way of working things out, and I was positive destiny played her hand with Preston and me as well.

Taking my hands in his, Preston gave me the most gorgeous. "It's me and you forever, princess. There's no way I could ever let you go... even if I wanted to. I'll spend every day giving everything I have to you and only you."

I needed to do one last thing so that I could finally let go of the past to move on to the future.

"Will you help me do something?" I asked.

"Of course I will."

Reaching into my pocket, I pulled out the charm and held it in my hand. The charm had been my talisman as I grieved for the loss of my husband and son. It had comforted me, been my strength when I needed something to guide me. Now, it was setting me free from the pain and guilt.

Preston ran his finger across the charm as my entire body shuddered. How did I luck out with such an amazing man?

"It's time for me to let go of the past, so I can move on with the future. I thought I needed this charm to hold TJ and Trey close to my heart. I realized over these last few weeks I didn't need it. They'll forever and always be in my heart."

Preston closed my hand around the charm and something incredible moved between us. It was like I could feel the power of my heart healing as it moved across my body. Looking into Preston's eyes, I smiled. "I love you. Thank you for not giving up on me."

Shaking his head, he whispered, "Never." Taking my hand in his, we walked up to the shore. Opening my hand, I looked at the charm. My heart felt heavy, but at the same time it felt like a weight was being lifted off my chest.

Squeezing my hand shut, I whispered, "I'll forever love you both."

Reaching back, I threw the charm as hard as I could. The moment it touched the water I turned to Preston and cried as he held me tightly within his arms. I wasn't sure how long we stood there before I felt someone pulling on my jacket. Looking down, I smiled when I saw the little girl from earlier.

"You found your prince," she said with a huge smile spread across her face.

Turning to Preston, I nodded my head as I smiled. "I certainly did."

And just like that she took off running to her parents.

"What was that all about?" Preston asked.

Shaking my head, I said, "Nothing. Let's go back to the hotel. I'm freezing."

Wiggling his eyebrows up and down, Preston said, "I know a way to warm you up." I wrapped my arm around his waist and we started back to the boardwalk. Making our way into the hotel we stopped at the elevators and stared at each other.

"I think we should stay here for a few days," I said with a wicked smile.

Raising his eyebrow, he pulled me to him. "Your place or mine?"

My body was on fire as I thought about Preston holding me while we made love. "Mine," I whispered.

Kissing the tip of my nose, he hit the elevator and said, "Let me grab my bag and put it in your room and then I'll check out."

Pulling my head back, I looked at him and asked, "When did you check in?"

Grinning from ear to ear he walked me into the elevator as it opened. "I checked in earlier and the first thing I did was walk down to the lighthouse. Something was drawing me to it. I hadn't been there very long before you showed up."

My mouth dropped open. "We must have just missed each other. I've been going down there every day at the same time."

Placing his hand behind my neck, he pulled me closer to him as he whispered against my lips, "I'm sorry I took so long."

Closing my eyes briefly, I opened them and looked into his eyes and asked, "How did you know to come here?"

Laughing, he said, "I didn't. When I finally had some sense knocked into me, literally, I went back to your condo. I walked around for about two hours until I saw the Chatten painting of the seaside. Then it hit me where you were. I started hitting places that had lighthouses. Two nights ago I was sitting at a hotel bar and I heard this couple talking about a lighthouse on Nantucket. That's when it hit me and I remembered your dream of me taking you to Nantucket. I knew this had to be the next place I searched for you."

The elevator door opened and I slowly backed out as I took his hands in mine. "I'm glad you found me."

Preston picked me up and threw me over his shoulder as he quickly walked to the door to his room. "Duck your head, baby."

Shutting the door to his room he put me down and grabbed the sides of my face and kissed me. Backing me toward the bed, my legs hit and we both smiled against each other's lips.

Taking a step back, Preston took his coat off and then ripped his shirt over his head. Following his lead we were soon naked with our hands moving across our bodies.

Preston guided me down onto the bed and we quickly became lost in each other. Arching my back, I softly called out his name as he whispered in my ear, "You will never miss my touch again."

Smiling, I pushed Preston over as I rubbed against his dick and raised my eyebrow. "You know, since you officially didn't bring me to Nantucket, the bet is still on."

Preston's eyes widened in horror as he slowly shook his head. "You wouldn't."

Giggling, I leaned over and sucked his lower lip into my mouth as we both let out a moan.

With a wicked smile, I said, "I even bought us matching T-shirts to wear!"

Rolling his eyes, Preston lifted his hands up to the sky and called out "Why?"

My smile faded some as my eyes searched Preston's handsome face. Laughing, he shook his head as he looked at me. "Tell me what you're thinking."

"I'm thinking you're my forever."

Sitting up, Preston wrapped his arms around me as he spoke softly in my ear. "And you're my forever. I'm never letting you go."

"I'll never leave again. I swear."

Chapter
TWENTY-SIX

CELEBRATIONS

Preston

S ITTING IN THE CORNER, I watched Harmony talking to Sandy and another girl. Her smile was infectious, and I couldn't help but grin every time she did.

Someone hit my leg that was resting over my knee. Looking, I saw Jake standing over me. Pulling up a chair he sat down and gave me a knowing smile. "So, you guys got back last night, huh?"

Shrugging my shoulders, I brought my beer up to my lips and took a sip. Smiling, I gave him a wink. "We decided to stay in Nantucket a few extra days."

"Uh-huh. Well I'm glad you finally snapped out of it and went looking for her."

Staring at Jake, I asked, "Did you know where she was?"

Shaking his head, he tipped his beer back and finished it off. I couldn't help but notice how tired he looked. Sandy had said that Jake's residency was kicking his ass.

"I didn't have a damn clue where she was. I even thought about hiring a private detective. Want to know who knew exactly where she was? You're gonna shit your pants."

Narrowing my eyes, I shook my head as I said, "I have no clue."

"My parents."

Pulling my head back in shock, my mouth gaped open. "Huh? How? Why?"

"They were there and saw Harmony. I guess Harmony had an American Express card that my father gave her after the accident. She never used it, so when my father's secretary saw the bill come across, she brought it to him. My parents took a trip there and stayed a few days to make sure Harmony was okay. She never knew they were there, and they never fucking thought to tell me."

"Wow," I said as I pushed my hand through my hair. "But I thought your parents didn't want to have anything to do with Harmony."

"Yeah, me too. I did some digging around. My father's company was the one that came in with the highest bid on Harmony and Trey's house."

I watched Harmony as I asked, "Does Harmony know?"

"Nah, I figured my parents are keeping it a secret for a reason so who am I to say anything."

The way she was flying her hands around while she talked had me let out a chuckle. "I think she would like to know that her parents really do care though, don't you?" Turning back to Jake, I saw he was watching his sister.

"She seems so happy, Preston. Life is moving on for her, and I don't want to upset her."

Nodding my head, I finished off my beer and stood up. Slapping Jake on the back, I said, "Dude, it's getting late. It's now or never."

Nodding his head, he jumped up and began taking in deep breaths and blowing them out. "Right. Now or never. I've got this." Cracking his neck from side to side, he clapped his hands together and rubbed them back and forth as he kept repeating, "I've got this."

"Jesus, dude. Just go do it. My God you've warmed up enough."

"Fuck you, Preston. Wait until you do this with Harmony. Then we'll talk about how easy it is."

My heart dropped at the thought of asking Harmony to marry me. I almost did it in Nantucket, but it felt too soon. I needed to stick with my plan and be patient.

Inhaling a deep breath and blowing it out quickly, Jake turned to me and smiled. "Here goes nothing."

Giving him a thumbs up, I nodded and said, "Go get her, tiger!"

Jake walked over to Sandy and whispered something in her ear. Nodding her head, she said something to Harmony and then walked with Jake to the center of the room.

Harmony glanced over and smiled when she saw me. Motioning with my finger for her to come to me, her smile grew bigger as she quickly walked over to me and said, "I think Jake is going to make a speech. Sandy was talking about the house they just bought! I bet it's going to be about that."

Harmony leaned her body into mine as she looked at Jake and Sandy. Resting my chin on the top of her head, I said, "Nah, I don't think that's it."

Once Jake got everyone's attention, he smiled. "First I want to thank everyone for coming to Sandy's birthday party, even though she told me she'd kill me if I threw her a party, she seems to be having fun."

Everyone laughed. Getting everyone to settle back down, Jake talked again. "I wanted to go ahead and give Sandy her birthday present now."

"What's the present?" Harmony whispered.

Smiling, I waited for Jake to make his move. The moment Jake got down on one knee and Sandy realized what he was doing, her hands came up to her mouth as she began crying. Harmony pulled forward and said, "Oh my God! He's asking her to marry him!" Jumping, Harmony slammed her hands to her mouth to keep from crying.

"Sandy, you are my only reason for living each day with a smile on my face. I want to seal the deal so that I know I'll be waking up every morning to your beautiful face. Will you marry me?"

Laughing, I rolled my eyes and shook my head at his mention of sealing the deal. Sandy laughed as she dropped to her knees and threw her arms around Jake.

Turning, Harmony threw herself into my arms as she

cried happy tears for once. Pulling back she let out a giggle. "He said seal the deal."

Laughing, I leaned over and brushed my lips against hers. "Are you happy?"

Nodding her head, she said, "Yes! I'm so glad we were here for this. Thank you."

Placing my hand on the side of her face, I brushed my thumb across her wet cheek. "I hope that from now on your tears are nothing but happy tears."

Harmony's eyes lit up with desire. "I have a feeling they will be."

***

"Preston, when are you going to take this off?" Harmony asked with a giggle.

The taxi was pulling up outside the pub and I was having a hell of a time keeping my excitement down. My heartbeat was out of control and my hands were sweating like a son-of-a-bitch.

"Almost there."

Jumping in her seat, Harmony clapped her hands together. "I don't get one hint?"

Laughing, I said, "No. Be patient."

Letting out a frustrated groan, she flopped back against the seat. Once the taxi stopped she sprang forward. "Are we there?"

Handing the taxi driver money, I thanked him while I opened the door and took Harmony's hand. Sliding across the seat, I helped her out of the taxi. Standing outside the pub was my entire family along with Jake and Sandy.

Looking up at the sign, I'd never felt so happy in my life. Fighting back the tears, I smiled as I silently read the new name of the pub, *Flanagan's Pub.*

Placing my lips against Harmony's ear, I whispered, "Ready?"

Nodding her head, she said, "Yes!"

Taking the blindfold off, Harmony laughed when she saw everyone standing outside the pub wearing New York Yankees T-shirts. Placing her hands over her mouth she laughed until she had tears.

"W-what are you guys doing here?" Harmony asked as she walked up to my parents and hugged them first. Making her way down the line, she kept asking why everyone was wearing Yankees T-shirts.

Uncle John shrugged and said, "The new owner is making us wear them."

Harmony's smile faded some as she shook her head. "New owner?" I saw the confusion move across her face as she looked between Uncle John and me. "Oh John, you didn't sell the pub, did you?"

Nodding his head he pulled Aunt Sue into his arms. "I did. Sue and I want to travel some, and I'm too old to run this place. It's on the shoulders of the young pup now."

Harmony turned to me and walked my way before stopping. Turning, she glanced up at the sign and let out a gasp as she read it. Snapping her head back to me, the most glorious smile spread across her face. "Preston?"

Nodding my head, I let out a chuckle. "I am indeed the proud new owner of Flanagan's Irish Pub."

Dropping her mouth open, Harmony ran into my arms and frantically kissed me as everyone erupted in cheers. Wrapping her legs around me, she held onto me tightly as she said, "You told me you were going to be managing a new store opening in Boston!"

Smiling, I said, "I didn't want to ruin the surprise."

Harmony's eyes lit up as she said, "I'm so proud of you, Preston James Ward. I'm so very proud of you!"

"I would never have done this if it hadn't been for you, Harmony."

Pulling her head back and wearing a stunned expression, she asked, "Me? What in the world did I have to do with this?"

Brushing a piece of her blonde hair back, I said, "You showed me how to live in the moment. To never take anything for granted." Sliding down my body, Harmony kissed me gently while I still held onto her.

"Let's celebrate!" Harmony shouted.

Looking back at everyone, I yelled out, "Drinks are on the house!"

Uncle John yelled out, "No! Drinks are *never* on the house!"

Four hours later, Harmony and I were putting everyone into cabs. My parents were staying with Uncle John and Aunt Sue so they didn't have to drive home so late. "Goodnight, Mom. Thanks for coming and celebrating with us."

Kissing me gently on the cheek, she stared at me with a loving look. "I'm so happy for you, Preston. It means so much to your father and I that you followed your heart. Flanagan's is going to be even better than before."

Kissing her softly on the cheek, I whispered, "I hope so, Mom."

Slipping into the back of the taxi, she lifted her hand and waved good-bye as the taxi pulled away.

Harmony looked exhausted. "My goodness! You Irish sure can drink. I'm pretty sure I'm toasted."

Laughing, I dropped my arm around her shoulders and guided her back into the pub. Looking around the pub, my heart raced excitedly as I barely spoke above a whisper. "I can't believe this place is mine. I have so many ideas I don't even know where to start."

Harmony bit down on her lower lip. "I do believe we need to break the pub in."

My dick jumped as I watched a very tipsy Harmony attempt to walk backward while pulling her shirt over her head. At least she was trying to pull it over her head. It got stuck halfway and she spun around while screaming out in panic. "Oh my gosh! I'm stuck. I'm stuck in my shirt!"

Walking up to her, I took her in my arms and pulled the shirt over her head. Next came her bra. Reaching around her back, it took two fast movements and it was off and on the floor.

Lifting her eyebrow, Harmony pursed her lips out and shook her head. "Why, Mr. Ward, aren't you the talented one."

Smiling, I dropped and pulled her skirt down. Moaning when I saw the lace thong, I slipped my fingers in her panties, and gave a quick pull, eliciting an excited squeal from Harmony as her panties fell from her body.

"Wow, that was freaking hot!" Harmony said with a giggle.

Standing before me was the most amazing, kind-hearted, beautiful, innocent woman who I was madly in love with. I couldn't wait to show her my next surprise.

"You're looking at me like you want to eat me!" Harmony said as she attempted to hold her laughter in but failed miserably.

I waggled my eyebrows while I quickly stripped out of my clothes. "Eating you sounds pretty damn good."

Harmony pressed her lips together and swallowed hard. "That… does sound… pretty good."

Harmony backed up to a table and stopped. Lifting her up, she laid across it as she kept her eyes locked on mine.

"Your eyes remind me of the ocean, Harmony. I find myself lost every time I look into them."

"Preston. You say the most romantic things to me."

Giving her a smirk, I said, "Spread your legs open, Harmony. I'm taking what's mine."

Letting out a whimper, Harmony did as I asked. Pulling her to the end of the table, I licked and sucked her pussy until her screams of pleasure echoed around the bar. Pulling her up, I took her off the table and turned her around so she was bent over the table. Her breasts were pressed against the wood table as she grabbed the sides and looked over her shoulder.

"I'm taking you hard and fast. Hold on."

Pushing my dick into her, Harmony hissed "yes" through her teeth as she dropped her head. It didn't take long for us both to call out each other's names as I poured my cum into her. Leaning over her, I kissed her back gently and then pulled out of her.

I spun her around and picked her up into my arms. My uncle had a full bathroom added next to his office. Shit. My office now. I made a mental note to take Harmony in there next. Resting her head on my chest she let out a contented sigh and said, "We have a lot more tables to go."

Smiling, I kissed her forehead and headed into the bathroom. After cleaning up, I called a taxi. Harmony and I were soon wrapped up in each other's arms as we lay in our bed.

Silently saying a prayer of thanks, I couldn't believe how one dream after another had been coming true. I only had two more things on my wish list that I needed to check off.

Marrying Harmony and starting a family.

Smiling, I drifted off to sleep and dreamt of the little blonde-haired girl running around.

Chapter
TWENTY-SEVEN

PRINCE CHARMING

Harmony

G LANCING AT THE CLOCK, IT was almost two.
Preston was going to meet me in the break room of
the hospital for lunch. I was exhausted and pretty sure I
was getting the flu. Sitting down at the nurse's desk, I
placed my hands in my head and took in a deep breath.
I didn't want to complain to Joel about having to work
double shifts this week. After all, I was the one who
walked out on the hospital for over a month.

Feeling someone rub my back, I lifted my head only
to see Chuck standing there. Sitting up, I glared at him.
"Chuck? What are you doing in L & D?"

Shrugging his shoulders he gave me a wink and walked off. My body got a chill as I watched him walk away. I made a mental note to talk to Preston today about work. Ever since I went to Nantucket, nursing didn't seem to be a priority in my life anymore. Helping Preston follow his dreams with Flanagan's was at the top of my list now.

Standing up, I held onto the counter and whispered, "Whoa."

Becky, a nurse who had been working here for five years, walked up to me and grabbed my face gently as she looked into my eyes. "Harmony, something is not right."

Nodding my head, I said, "I agree. It's called double shifts, a hot boyfriend who likes to wake me up in the middle of the night to make slow, passionate love to me, and not eating in six hours. That and I think I'm getting the flu." Glancing over I saw another nurse, Rachel, walking up to us.

Rachel laughed as she walked behind the desk. Shaking her head, she made a tsking sound. "You are not getting the flu. I already know what's wrong."

Sitting back down, I glanced between both nurses. Becky looked at Rachel and said, "No!"

Rachel nodded her head. "Yes."

"Holy shit, do you think?" Becky asked.

My head snapped over to Rachel as she threw her head back and evil laughed. "What in the hell are the two of you going on about?" I asked with a confused look on my face.

Becky turned to me and tilted her head and sighed. "Awe, look Rach, she doesn't even have a clue yet. How cute is that?"

Rachel smiled. "It is cute. I remember those days."

Rolling my eyes, I turned away from them and dropped my head onto the desk. "I don't have time for this. My brother is getting married and Jenn wants to go dress shopping. I've never heard of a three-month engagement. Why they are getting married in May is beyond me. No one can plan a wedding that fast!" Stopping myself from talking, I thought back to my marriage to Trey. "Okay. Well it can be done but still. What's the hurry?"

Rachel leaned against the counter and said, "Unless she's pregnant."

Laughing, I lifted my head and looked at Rachel. "Please, Sandy is the most put-together person I've ever met. She would never forget to take her birth control pi—"

Lifting an eyebrow and tilting her head, Rachel smiled. "You were saying, Harmony?"

Dropping my mouth open, I slowly stood up. "Oh shit. Oh fuck."

"Oh I'm pretty sure you've done plenty of that since you got back with your hot ex-fireman now-turned-even-hotter Irish pub owner."

Covering my mouth, I let out an internal scream. Stupid! Stupid! Stupid! Turning, I placed my hands on the counter and dragged in a deep breath. Letting it out I said, "How could I be so stupid?"

"When did you run out of them?"

Closing my eyes, I said, "The end of December. It was near TJ's birthday. I was so upset I stayed in bed the whole day."

"Last period?"

Shrugging my shoulders, I said, "They've been so off since the accident. Even with being on birth control it wasn't uncommon for me to skip a month or two."

Becky walked up and held up a pregnancy test and smiled the biggest smile I think I've ever seen on her face.

"Crap," I mumbled.

Becky raised her eyebrow and said, "No baby, you piss on it."

Grabbing it out of her hand, I pushed past her as Rachel and Becky laughed. My phone buzzed and I pulled it out of my pocket.

Preston: Hey princess! I'll be there in twenty.

Walking into the ladies room, I hit reply as my hands trembled.

Me: Okay! Love ya!

Stay calm Harmony. Take a deep breath in and blow it out. You're not pregnant. Nope.

I pushed the stall door open, pulled my scrubs and panties down and peed on the stick. Holding my breath, I set it down on a piece of tissue paper as I flushed, pulled up my panties and scrubs and grabbed the test. Setting it down next to me, I turned on the cold water and splashed my face.

Wow. Is it hot in here? I'm burning up. See, that just proves I'm getting sick. I'll call in my prescription tomorrow and start taking the pill again. Everything will be fine.

Smiling, I nodded, as I stood tall and confident. "I've got this!"

Grabbing the test, I put it up in front of my face and read the results. A wide grin spread across my face as my pulse picked up and I felt a million flutters in my stomach.

Looking in the mirror, I let out a nervous giggle as I shook my head. Spinning on my heels, I made my way out of the restroom and headed to the break room. I was careful to avoid Becky and Rachel at all costs.

Pushing the door to the break room open, I came to an abrupt halt when I saw Chuck. Glancing over to me, Chuck smiled. "Hey Harmony."

Giving him a forced smile, I walked over to the water cooler and got a drink. I heard his chair slide across the floor as I held my breath.

The moment he touched me I jumped and took a few steps back.

"Harmony, how long are we going to play this game of you pretending like you're not interested in me?"

Glaring at him, I said, "It's not a game, Chuck. I'm really not interested in you. Now please back up and give me my space."

"Oh Harmony. You're so pretty. Let me show you what it's like to be with a real man."

My heart thundered in my ears and I barely heard the words he was speaking. "Please stop this and leave me alone."

Reaching his hand up he stroked my face as I attempted to push him away. He leaned closer to me as if he was going to try and kiss me, but he was quickly jerked back by someone.

Preston.

"What in the fuck do you think you're doing, asshole?" Preston said as he pushed Chuck back.

Chuck straightened his scrubs. "Who the hell are you? This room is for staff only."

Preston took a few steps toward Chuck as he backed up and hit a table. "I'm her boyfriend, fucker. If I ever so much as see you look her way, I'll pound your face so far into the ground your mother won't know who you are."

Chuck looked at me and then back to Preston. "If you'll excuse me."

He started for the door as I rushed over to Preston. "Thank God you came when you did. I've never been so scared in my life."

Preston held me close to his body as he spoke in a calming voice. "He wouldn't have been stupid enough to do anything here. Anyone could have walked in at any moment."

Burying my face into his chest, I held back my tears. I had promised Preston my tears would only be happy tears. I would not cry over this. "Take me home, Preston."

"You still have thirty more minutes."

Shaking my head, I looked into his eyes as I smiled softly. "What would you think if I said I wanted to find a new gig?"

Pulling his head back, Preston smiled from ear to ear. "I would say I have the perfect place for you."

"I want to be with you at the pub. Not here. I don't feel like this is the journey I'm supposed to be on. My place is by your side."

I'd never seen Preston smile as big as he did when he heard those words from my lips. "Seriously, Harmony? You'd do that? I mean, would you be happy, because I only want you to do what makes you happy?"

Nodding my head, I kissed him quickly. "I can always go back to nursing school. Right now, my focus is on us."

Preston lifted me up and spun me around as he laughed. "You just made me the happiest man in the world, Harmony."

"What are you waiting for, Mr. Ward?"

Giving me a knock-me-over grin, Preston took my hand and led me out of the break room. "What about work? Don't you have to tell anyone?"

Nodding, I started to head over to the nurse's station with Preston walking behind me.

Clearing my throat, Becky and Rachel both looked up and smiled, especially when they saw Preston.

"I'm not feeling well, ladies, so I'm gonna head on home. I'll call Joel in the morning." Lifting my hand, I wiggled my fingers as I waved good-bye.

"Call me!" Rachel said as Preston and I made our way to the elevator.

Stepping into the elevator, I smiled as I looked at Preston. "Everything from this point on is going to change, Preston. Are you ready for that?"

Wrapping his arms around my waist, he looked down at my lips and then back into my eyes. "I've always thought it was kind of nice to shake things up a bit every now and then."

I wrapped my arms around his neck and winked. "Good. Oh by the way, thank you for being my Prince Charming."

Laughing, Preston kissed my forehead and said, "Always."

Two weeks had passed since I told Preston I wanted to leave my job. Yesterday was my last day and there was something very freeing about it. After my shift was over, I went to Frog Pond and spent an hour lost in my thoughts. Memories of TJ filled most of those thoughts as I put another part of my past behind me.

Now I was sitting in Preston's car as I rubbed my hands across my jeans. "Okay Preston, this is twice you've put a blindfold on me and taken me somewhere. The last time was pretty big."

Reaching for my hand, Preston pulled it to his lips and kissed the back of it. "It's a surprise I've been working on since last December."

Feeling my stomach drop, I took in a deep breath and slowly blew it out.

"We've been driving a long time. Are we going to your parents'?" I asked with excitement lacing my voice. "Oh it's a beautiful April day. Please tell me we're going to your parents' place." It was the first week of April and we were having unseasonably warm weather for April fourth.

Squeezing my hand, he said, "Nope."

"Ugh, just tell me already."

The car came to a stop. "Don't peek, Harmony. We're here."

Bouncing in the seat, I clapped my hands as I heard Preston open his car door. Less than five seconds later, my door was opened and Preston was helping me out of the car. My senses were heightened since I couldn't see. Taking in a deep breath through my nose, I smelled flowers. The sounds of birds singing caused me to smile. There was something magical about where we were. I could feel it rushing over my skin.

Taking my arm, we began walking. The ground was soft and the air smelled clean. Fresh. Biting down on my lower lip, I said, "We're in the country."

Preston stood behind me as he pulled the blindfold off to reveal the most picturesque rolling hillside. It almost looked like a painting. My eyes scanned across the countryside until they landed on a giant sign hanging between two trees.

Welcome Home Harmony

Sucking in a breath, I spun around and then stumbled back as I saw Preston kneeling down on one knee.

My heart dropped to my stomach and I immediately cried as I whispered, "Oh, Preston."

"I only have two dreams left that I need to come true, princess."

A sob escaped my lips when I noticed he had on a New York Yankees T-shirt but paired it with a Boston Red Sox hat. Shaking my head, I let out a giggle as a feeling of pure love rushed through my veins. I loved this man more than the air I breathed.

Finding my voice, I asked. "What are your dreams?"

Removing the baseball cap and taking my hand in his, he slipped a princess cut diamond onto my finger as a tear slowly rolled down his cheek. "The first one… is for you to agree to be my wife."

Dropping to the ground, I whispered, "Yes," as I kissed him. Pulling back, I looked into his eyes and asked, "And the second dream?"

Placing his hands on my face, he gently swiped my tears away with his thumbs. "To start a family with the only woman I've ever loved."

A sob burst out from deep in my chest. I nodded my head as my eyes searched his face. His brown hair was messy as usual, but sexy as hell. Glancing down to his lips, I let out a contented sigh. Those lips have given me pleasure in so many different ways. Finally, I looked into his beautiful green eyes. Placing my hands over his, I said, "I've already got that one taken care of."

Preston's eyes widened. "W-what?"

Pressing my lips together, I rubbed them back and forth as I built up the courage to speak without crying. Then I remembered my promise.

Happy tears only.

"I'm pregnant, Preston."

Preston's eyes lit up like nothing I'd ever seen before. I held my breath as I waited for him to say something. "Harmony, we're going to have a baby?"

I held his stare as my stomach jumped all over the place. Nodding my head, I whispered, "Yes."

Preston quickly stood up and pulled me into his arms as he spun me around. Finally coming to a stop, he pushed me back at arm's length and looked my body up and down. "We're having a baby?"

Laughing as I wiped my tears away, I nodded and said, "Yep. I hope you're not angry."

Preston's smile dropped as he shook his head as tears rolled down his handsome face. "God no. Harmony, I've never been so happy in my entire life."

Reaching over, I gently wiped his tears away.

Preston slid his hand into my hair and pulled my neck back by a handful of hair. Kissing me along my neck he spoke between kisses.

"You. Destroy. Me. Harmony."

Smiling, I closed my eyes as I felt his lips shower me with love. Finally coming to my senses, I said, "Wait! This place. Preston, is this ours?"

Nodding his head, he turned me to face the countryside again. "Yes. It's ten acres and we're only about twenty-five miles from the pub. My father bought this piece of land the same time he bought the land where they're living now. I offered him a price for it, and he accepted it. Whenever you're ready to pick out a house, I plan on building it for you. Finn, Wes, and my father all offered to help."

My hand came to my mouth as I softly said, "Oh, Preston. I don't know what to say."

He drew me into his arms. "Tell me you love it."

Smiling until my cheeks hurt, I cried out, "I love it! I love it! I love it!"

Kissing me gently on my lips, Preston smiled as he picked me up and threw me over his shoulder. Slapping my ass he said, "Time to break the new place in, baby."

Lying in Preston's arms on a blanket under a tree, I lazily ran my fingers up and down his arm as I looked out over the beautiful countryside. My heart had never felt so content.

Preston's breathing was steady next to me as his hand lay perfectly across my stomach. Taking in a slow deep breath, I held it for a moment and slowly let it out as I placed my hand over Preston's.

Slowly drifting off to sleep, I dreamt of a little girl with blonde curly hair running around a tree as Preston and I chased her.

"Love is such a powerful thing. Once we allow it into our hearts it's amazing how it heals not only the heart but our soul as well. We never forget…"

Epilogue

HAPPILY EVER AFTER

Preston

C LOSING MY EYES, I COUNTED to twenty. "Ready or not, here I come, Presley!"

Hearing her little laughter echoing from the trees, I headed that way. I grinned when I saw dark blonde curls bouncing behind a tree. I slowly made my way over to her.

Right before I got there, she jumped out and yelled, "Boo!"

Dropping down to the ground, Presley came running into my arms. "Daddy! I won! I won!"

Laughing, I wrapped her in my arms and lifted her up as I spun her around a few times. Stopping, I gently kissed her forehead and smiled. "How do you figure you won when you jumped out and ran to me? You're supposed to run from me."

Giggling, she buried her face into my chest as I carried her back to the house. "Daddy, I'm sleepy."

I chuckled. "I wonder why. You played with your little cousin Kimmy for about four hours today, sweetheart. You're worn out." Jake and Sandy had left not too long ago with their three-year-old daughter Kimmy to head back home.

Nodding her head, she grabbed onto my shirt while she closed her eyes and let out a sigh. I was instantly taken back to the first time Harmony did the same thing.

Knowing it was their way of telling me they felt safe in my arms, I held my four-year-old daughter closer to me as I carried her into the house and upstairs to her room.

Laying Presley down in bed, I covered her up and kissed her gently on the forehead as I pushed her curls from her face.

"I love you, Presley."

Letting out a soft sigh, she replied, "Love you too, Daddy."

Watching my daughter sleep filled my heart with happiness. Fighting to hold back my tears, I turned and headed out of her room, quietly closing the door. Making my way back downstairs, I headed into our bedroom. Today marked two years we had been living in the house that I built along with my father, uncle, and two brothers. Harmony and I still had the condo on

Comm Ave. in Boston. It was hard to sell the home our daughter was born in and where so many memories were made. So we decided to rent it out to a young couple, who also just had their first child not very long ago. A little girl.

Hearing the water running in the bathroom, I pushed the door open and slowly walked in. Seeing Harmony in the tub, I quickly stripped out of my clothes and climbed in. Harmony sat up and moved so I could slip in behind her.

Inhaling a deep breath, she slowly blew it out. "Is she asleep?"

I chuckled and said, "Yes. Finally. I think the last round of hide-and-seek pushed her past her limit."

Harmony giggled as her hands moved lazily across the bubbles in the water.

"Touch me, Preston."

Pressing a kiss against the back of her head, I moved my hands and cupped her full breasts. With a moan she dropped her head back against my chest. Even after four years of marriage, Harmony's touch still caused crazy sensations to rush through my body. Every time I made love to her, it felt like the first time.

I placed my mouth next to her ear and asked, "How are you feeling?"

"Tired," she whispered.

Moving my hands from her breasts, I slowly moved them down and caressed her beautiful swollen belly. Feeling the baby kick, we both let out a soft laugh. "He's active," I said as I watched an elbow, or maybe a knee, move across Harmony's stomach.

Nodding her head, she said, "He is."

"Have you decided on a name yet?" I asked as I continued to caress her stomach.

Shaking her head, she said, "Nope." Popping her P in the process.

Grinning, I said, "You do know you were due two days ago."

Laughing, she turned her head and looked at me. "Maybe we can just call him Boy."

"Boy? Hey, Boy, come help your mother with chores. Boy, don't eat that dirt pie."

Harmony giggled and shrugged her shoulders. "Okay, so that isn't a good name. I think we both agree on that. If you have any suggestions, I'm all ears."

"Oh okay, now that we're down to the wire, you want my input. I'm sorry, the bet was if it were a girl, I would name her, just like with Presley. If it's a boy, it's on your shoulders to come up with the name."

Letting out a frustrated groan, Harmony jutted out her lower lip as she looked at me. "Pwease, Daddy?"

Rolling my eyes, I laughed as Harmony looked straight ahead. "I do have a name I've always kind of liked."

"I'm all ears, Mr. Ward."

"Are you sure, Mrs. Ward? Once I say the name, the deal is sealed."

Nodding her head, Harmony said, "Understood."

Taking in a deep breath, I blew it out and said, "Fitzwilliam."

Harmony stopped moving her hands and sat perfectly still. Turning to look at me, Harmony's eyes danced with excitement. "It's perfect. We can call him Fitz for short."

"Really?" I asked, surprised she was on board.

Harmony slowly attempted to sit up. I quickly got out of the tub and wrapped a towel around my waist as I helped my very pregnant wife out.

Standing in front of me gloriously naked with her belly carrying our second child, I felt my dick hardening by the second just looking at her.

"Really, really," Harmony said with a chuckle as I wrapped a towel around her. "So, now that we have that settled, will you call your parents and see if they'll come stay with Presley?"

Pulling my head back, I asked, "Why?"

Harmony's eyes lit up as she gave me a smile that about knocked me over. "Because Fitz is on his way."

The End

Thank you for taking the time to read

Searching FOR HARMONY

To find more of my books, visit Amazon.

And sign up for my newsletter *Between the Pages* at
kellyelliottauthor.com/newsletter/
and get release notices, bonus scenes, exclusive
giveaways, and sneak peeks at covers,
excerpts, and more!

About the
AUTHOR

Kelly Elliott is a *New York Times* and *USA Today* bestselling contemporary romance author. Since publishing her first book, *Wanted*, in 2012, Kelly continues to spread her wings while remaining true to her roots and giving readers stories rich with hot protective men, strong women, and beautiful surroundings.

Her bestselling works include, *Wanted*, *Broken*, *Lost Love*, *Never Enough*, and *The Butterfly Effect*, to name just a few. Kelly's amazing readers have dubbed her "The Queen of Small Town", since a large majority of Kelly's books are based in small towns with swoony cowboys and strong heroines.

Kelly lives in central Texas with her husband, Darrin and their two crazy pups, Gunner and Ellie, along with four cats, and a plethora of wildlife. When she's not writing, Kelly enjoys reading, watching the birds at her bird feeders, and spending time with her family. She is down to earth and very in touch with her readers, both on social media and at signings.

To find out more about Kelly and her books, visit her website at kellyelliottauthor.com.